The Covington Heights Crew

LIE

DEANA BIRCH

Lie
ISBN # 978-1-83943-996-4
©Copyright Deana Birch 2021
Cover Art by Louisa Maggio ©Copyright June 2021
Interior text design by Claire Siemaszkiewicz
Totally Bound Publishing

LIE

Dedication

To my own blue-eyed man.

Chapter One

Samantha

The ventilator rose like a stretched-out accordion then folded back down, forcing air into Anton Myers' injured lungs. The *beep, beep, beep* of his heart rate was probably the only thing comforting his mother, who sat next to his hospital bed stroking her thumb over his battered knuckles.

In the few months that I'd gotten to know Sophia Myers, I'd learned that her strength and will far exceeded her tiny frame. Even in the face of tragedy, she was immaculately groomed and flawlessly presentable. She was cold, hard and serious. I admired her.

I stepped closer to the bed. With his eerie eyes closed, Anton's power or anger or whatever it was that motivated him was less evident. He was just a shell of a man with a tube down his throat and an IV in his hand. It was as if his dangerous draw had floated away.

The sterile odor of alcohol lingered in the air from the hand sanitizer that the nurse had used when she'd checked his vitals minutes prior, and it only added to the cold room. Somehow, the orderly environment suited Sophia. Baking cookies and an apron sure didn't.

My phone vibrated and I flipped my wrist to check the text message.

Shit.

Someone had leaked the shooting to the press. It had already been hard enough to smooth over Sophia's questionable past when my boss—the mayor of the city—had decided to marry her. But *this?* His new stepson involved in a gang-related shooting? It was a public relations nightmare.

My phone vibrated again, this time with Mayor Demsey's name.

Sophia glanced at me as if she understood, and before I turned to walk out of the door, I offered her a tight, sympathetic smile. No matter what her past, I wouldn't want her present.

I swiped the screen to answer, but instead of saying hello, I said, "I just saw. I'm leaving the hospital now."

"Who the fuck would have leaked this?" Demsey yelled through the small speaker. His scratchy voice revealed his Long Island accent. The crass demeanor that came out when he was pissed was one of the few things he managed to keep hidden from the public.

His question was logical, but the answer was irrelevant. Lucky for my boss, I'd already played the game of 'worst-case scenario' over and over in my head for the previous twenty-four hours.

"I'll call a presser and get in front of this. We can spin it. I'll say he was robbed. In the meantime, avoid reporters. And don't you dare ass-dial Mitch from *The Times* like you did last week. In fact, put your phone in your drawer once you hang up with me." My heels clicked down the hall of the private hospital at a rhythmic pace. At the nurse's station, an older, handsome man smiled at me and I rolled my eyes once I'd passed him. Unwanted flirty smiles from men always jabbed at a button in me that said because I was pretty, my intelligence was underestimated. That particular gentleman had 'man-splainer' written in bold above his raised eyebrows.

"Sam?" Demsey asked in a softer tone. "Don't forget to call the chief and tell him what you're going to say so we have a consistent message. Jack likes you way more than he does me, so it will be better... Actually, swing by to see him on your way back to the office. He'll appreciate the personal touch."

"On it." The elevator doors rattled open. "Make this easy for me and keep your mouth shut, boss." I swiped my phone off. It wasn't that I didn't like Demsey or his new family, because I did. He'd taken a chance on me as his spokesperson when I hadn't exactly had a long list of celebrity clients banging down the door of my small public relations firm.

Before agreeing to the job, I'd heard about Demsey and his taste for the corrupt, but it didn't bother me. I'd learned over the years that the line between flat-out lying to the public or dressing up facts to make whatever bad thing seem good was pretty damn blurry. My job depended on how I massaged the truth. Being one hundred percent honest was the only thing I was sure I'd never do.

It didn't matter *if* I lied. It was how much.

Outside, I hailed a cab, and we battled the downtown traffic until I was at police headquarters. I flashed my identification badge at security and stepped through the metal detector. On the third floor, I smiled to the uniformed officers as I made my way through their cubicles to the corner office of Police Chief Jack Galaway.

Jack's eyes were closed and he pinched the bridge of his nose with the phone against his ear. I wrapped my knuckles lightly on his door, causing him to look up. His frown switched to an easy grin and he waved me in.

I took the empty chair to the right and sat patiently as he 'mmhmm-ed' his way through the rest of the call. He spun his finger around in the universal sign that indicated he wanted the other person to wrap it up already, and I crossed my hands in my lap.

The walls of his office were lined with plaques and certificates with gold seals. Jack was a family man but specifically kept any sign of his personal life to himself. We'd never really believed in small talk. We were both direct in the interest of time, but I did know that he'd married his high-school sweetheart and he had two sons, both of whom were on the force. He was a good man, as good as he could be while he navigated a system and city that favored the depraved.

"Jesus, Mary and Joseph," he said when he'd hung up. "Why can't my guys keep their dicks in their pants?" Jack frowned and the wrinkles in his clean-shaven face deepened. "You don't look like you have good news either. Spit it out."

"Anton Myers was shot two nights ago." I re-crossed my ankles, and the movement caught his eyes. He liked to tease me about my shoe addiction. I was wearing a new pair of black heels and their red souls matched my red dress. Much like Sophia Myers, I, too, took a lot of care in how I presented myself. I never showed cleavage, my skirts always hit just above my knees and my nails were perfectly groomed and color-free. I wore makeup but it was subtle. My lips only saw red on Christmas or for parties.

Jack leaned back into his massive leather chair and swiveled. "First I've heard of it."

"It was" — I shrugged and scrunched my nose — "cleaned up. But it's about to break in the news. I'm going to do a presser this afternoon and claim he was robbed at gunpoint."

He shook his head. "That's bad for me."

I knew Jack wouldn't like my plan. It would be another unsolved crime and feed fear to the public, but that wouldn't stop me. Plus, I knew the chief of police was a tit-for-tat kind of man.

"It will be good for your budget." I stood and flattened out my dress. "You can refer all press to the mayor's office."

"Gee, thanks."

Jack's desk phone rang, and I headed for the door. "Hey, Sammie?"

I turned around. He had the receiver pressed into his chest under his badge.

"You may want to consider someone like Anton Myers would prefer the truth to your spin. You're about to make one of the most dangerous gang members in our city a victim. He's not going to like that — and neither will his crew."

I gave exactly zero fucks about what Anton Myers would or wouldn't like. I worked for the mayor, not him. Sophia had warned him to lie low. Getting shot by a rival gang? Not exactly my idea of exceeding his mother's expectations. And his crew? There was nothing left of it. Any loyalty they'd had for their leader had been wiped away the second he'd fallen. Sophia had spoken to one of them and forbidden them from returning to their neighborhood, effectively disbanding the entire gang.

"Well, fortunately for me he's mute and in a hospital bed. He doesn't have a choice." But the confidence in my voice wavered just a little. "I'll email Debbie my statement before I go out."

He nodded then barked, "What now?" into the phone. On the way down to the lobby, I mulled over his advice. So what if Anton woke up and was pissed about how I'd handled things? His life as he knew it was over. His mother had assured it. But the chief had a point. I could cut out the 'robbed' part.

Once out of police headquarters, I dialed my assistant. "Hey, Fanny, can you let the press know that I'll be making a statement with limited questions at three o'clock?" I crossed the street with the crowd, the blue-and-white police cars all around us. As I approached city hall, Mitch from *The Times* came into view. His signature checked shirt stood out like a flashing sign that read 'pain in my ass'.

"I've already gotten calls from six reporters." Fanny's tone held a little bit of a question.

"I'm coming up now but stay on the line. Fucking Mitch is downstairs." I held the phone tight to my ear. "Tell me anything. Read me a menu or recite a damn poem if you have to. He won't let me walk by without pestering me."

Fanny let out a small laugh. "So I met this girl at a bar last night..."

Mitch's eyes lit up like the Fourth of July when he spotted me. I quickened my pace and shook my head as I pointed to the phone and said, "Super important call."

Fanny continued, "We totally hit it off. I was laughing and having the time of my life. Then it hit me like a bulldozer. She had long blonde hair, sun-kissed skin and a banging body."

I climbed the stairs of City Hall with Mitch at my heel. "I'm so sorry to hear that."

Mitch spouted questions but I ignored them. At the top of the stairs, I opened the massive door. I just had to get through security then I would be home free.

Fanny continued in my ear. It wasn't the first time we'd faked a phone call. "She looked exactly like you. It freaked me out so hard that I literally stood straight up and walked out."

"I'm at security. I'll call you back." I ended the call and placed my phone in a black plastic basket on the conveyor belt.

"Nice try," Mitch said as he rolled his green eyes. "But my source tells me that Anton Myers was shot in the chest. Can you confirm?"

My job was to talk to the press. The cat was already out of the bag, and there was no putting its fuzzy ass back in. Information was fluid and it had to run both ways. Mitch was only doing his job, as annoying as it was. There were so many other things that he could have been reporting on. But sensationalizing the shooting of the mayor's stepson was click bate and would get him seven more followers on social media. It would make his superiors happy, and if I just threw him a tiny crumb, he would stop.

I stepped toward the metal detector and set my shoulders. "I confirm."

The crooked grin on Mitch's face soured my stomach. "Thank you!" He spun around and left the building with a bit of pep in his step. Being the first one to get confirmation meant everyone else would use his story and say his name all day long.

I grabbed my phone, which was lighting up with notices of the confirmation I'd just given, and went upstairs to my office.

Fanny sat behind her immaculate desk and typed into her laptop. Her dark hair was down and her long bangs kissed the top of her eyebrows.

"Was that true? Did you fall for my doppelganger?" I walked over to our community fridge and grabbed a bottle of water.

"Sam…" She stopped typing and spun around on her chair to face me. "It was literally you. She even had great shoes. I may not recover from this."

I grinned. The lighthearted banter was a refreshing break from my otherwise-stressful day. I stepped into my office and just before shutting the door deadpanned, "I think you have a crush on me."

"Me and Mitch."

"Eww." I shivered, and when she faked offense, I said, "Not you…Mitch. Also, now that I think of it, maybe a little you too. You're like my kid sister. Shame on you and your twisted mind, Fanny." I tapped the door and forced an exhale out of my mouth. "Hold my calls. I have a statement to write."

Three hours later, I stood at the mayor's briefing podium with the statement that Demsey had approved and that I'd emailed to Debbie, the police chief's assistant. I rubbed my lips together, spreading the freshly applied nude gloss even more, and waited for the room to fall silent. Three rows of reporters sat eagerly facing me as the local and national news cameras flanked the back and walls.

Showtime.

I adjusted the microphone and scanned the crowd of familiar faces. "Good afternoon. As I confirmed earlier, the mayor's stepson, Anton Myers, was the victim of a shooting two nights ago. I'm happy to report that after a long touch-and-go surgery, he is resting and in stable condition. The mayor and his wife ask for your understanding for their need for privacy in this difficult time."

The hands flew up for questions and I repeated my motto — reassure and deflect.

There were a few reporters I loathed less than others because I could always count on them to throw me a softball. I found one and called on her. "Stacey."

"Thanks, Samantha. Do the police have any suspects? Do we know what happened?"

"As you know, I can't comment on an ongoing investigation, but I have nothing but respect and confidence for our men and women in uniform."

Mitch waggled his fingers and his eyes bulged. I skipped over him. Where was the guy from the local station who had winked at me the week before? Ah, yes. Middle center. "Steven."

"Anton Myers is a convicted criminal. Was this gang-related?"

My throat tightened and I willed the heat in my chest to cool. "Ongoing investigation, but there's no reason to start rumors about a man who was inches from losing his life." I glared at Steven. He wouldn't be getting called on again anytime soon.

Mitch was practically halfway out of his seat. Experience and poise kept my eyes from rolling.

"Mitch."

"Thanks, Sam."

Sam? Uh, no. It's Samantha in this room, dipshit. We aren't buddies.

He cleared his throat. "A source tells me that Anton was taken to the hospital by two men in suits and a gang member. Can you confirm?"

So his source was someone at the hospital. The director would be getting a massive earful from me...or Fanny. Fanny would actually be fantastic at bitching someone out. Then I could stay nice-ish.

"I don't have those details, but I'll try to find out and get back to you." I closed my binder and addressed the room. "Listen, guys... I know it's been a boring news week and we're all a little hungry right now, but let's not turn a victim of a violent crime into a criminal because he has some misdemeanors on his record from when he was barely eighteen."

Someone scoffed but I wasn't quick enough to catch who.

I narrowed my eyes, scolding them for their lack of empathy. "I'll update you as soon as I can." What I really meant was that I was going to brush this under the rug and try to get them to forget about it as soon as I could. That little nugget from Mitch about the men who'd brought him to the hospital was a nightmare for me *and* the police.

As I stepped away from the podium and exited the room, they all hollered questions at me — questions that weren't that different from the ones ping-ponging in my own head. And with Anton still unconscious, I was walking the tightrope between what I could spin and what other information was out there.

Sophia had said she trusted the men who'd brought him in and that the rival gang had been *"taken care of"*. But it wasn't the first-hand witnesses of the shooting who bothered me. It was the aftermath that had to be pieced together perfectly to sell a believable lie.

Fanny followed me down the corridor and it wasn't until we were in our office that she said, "What the fuck is with the hospital?"

I paced in front of her desk. "Call them and take out all your sexual frustration on them. Fucking leaks."

"On it." She slid into her seat and wedged her phone between her ear and shoulder as she typed on her computer.

As much as listening to her would have been fun and I was sure I'd miss some fantastically creative insults, I needed silence to think. I closed the door to my office, only to have Sophia's number pop up onto the screen of my phone.

"Hey, how is he?" I asked.

"He's awake and…" Her calm tone was ominous. "Cranky. You've officially been summoned. He's waiting — and not patiently either."

Crap.

Chapter Two

Anton

Victim?

I was no fucking victim. I was the head of a crew who had successfully stopped a plot to kill us. I'd expanded my territory to Bradford Manors. My crew had ended up on top, despite my wound. I glared over at my mother again. Her new way of handling shit was a new way of pissing me off. Since when did the Myers family marry politicians? My father had probably put his fist through the concrete wall in his prison cell.

A sharp pain hitched in my chest on my inhale. Getting shot had been a miscalculation on my part. It had made sense that they'd gone for me first. Actually, I was glad I'd been their target. It had given the rest of my crew the perfect moment to take out those Bradford fucks. *Fucking Jimmy.* I should have known he was too eager for his own good. *My* own good.

The nurse who'd removed the tube from my throat came back in and somehow managed to cut the tension in the room. Her sympathetic brown eyes struck me as an oddity. Warmth wasn't something my mother was good at. Neither was I, if I thought about it. She checked the drip, along with my pulse and temperature. All the fussing made me a little nauseated — or maybe it was the drugs they had me on. Either way, I didn't like it or the blurry vision that came along for the bullshit ride.

"Do you think you could eat?" The nurse tilted her head and offered a soft smile.

I snarled then started coughing. With every movement, I felt like I was being shot all over again. Drops of blood peppered the tissue the nurse held to my mouth.

"Slow breaths," she said with a cautious tone. She was annoying. I hated her already.

My mother walked over and tried to rub my shoulder, but I swatted her hand away. *Oh, no, no, no. She can't get all mushy on me. Fuck that.*

Jesus fucking Christ, though. Who'd put a knife inside my chest and was scraping away layers of my lungs? I coughed again for a bit before willing myself to stop. The pain dulled but hovered, not unlike my mother.

Had I cheated death? Probably not. Jimmy wasn't as much of an impressive shot as he'd thought. He should have gone for my head.

Then it hit me… Rafa had shot his fucking girlfriend. I stopped myself from laughing because it would have been more torture than the cough. The nurse offered me a drink of water and it both cooled and stung my throat on the way down. Yeah, that tube had been a bitch, too.

My mother's light gaze followed the movement of the nurse. She was waiting. There was more to tell me, which meant she'd taken matters into her own hands. There might be a bright side, but it would be hers, not mine.

The nurse tucked the white covers around me like I was some kind of invalid. What was it the blonde had said? *A victim. Fuck that.*

"If you need anything, just ring. I'm just down the hall. I'll check with the doctor and try to get you some applesauce."

She had to be kidding. *Baby food?* Maybe I should have stayed asleep with the drugs a while longer. It was getting fucking ridiculous. I frowned and she left my private room, either not seeing my disgruntled look or not caring.

My mother pressed her lips together, the final moment of contemplation before she would speak. After twenty-eight years, I'd gotten pretty good at recognizing when I wouldn't like what she would say next.

Her posture stiffened. "Leo assured me that the money you took before meeting him is in a safe place and that he'll deliver it when you're ready. I've forbidden anyone from going back. As far as you're concerned, Covington Heights is over. Everything else has been…handled."

Maybe my head was still foggy from the drugs, but I was pretty sure she'd just informed me that she'd shut down my crew, shut down my income and basically shut down my entire lifestyle. All because I'd gotten shot? Didn't she know me getting back up would make me stronger? I could take over Jefferson with the right kind of planning. And while I didn't officially have Leo or Jackson back, they still were there for me when I'd needed them. She had no idea. She couldn't take away all I'd worked for.

My body sank into the mattress, somehow heavier than the seconds before she'd spoken. "What the—?" I closed my eyes and shook my head, but it didn't do anything for the dizziness. "What makes you think you can just shut down my whole organization? Because I got shot? I'm not dead, Ma."

She leveled me with her eyes. Yeah, no sympathy behind those baby blues—not that I wanted it. "Let's face it, Anton. We were phasing it out before all this happened. Quite frankly, you should be grateful I'm not screaming at you right now. Do you know how this is going to play out for the election? I haven't worked night and day to get myself in the governor's mansion for it all to come crashing down because of your recklessness."

And there it was. She wasn't concerned about me, but about how the shooting would look among her new influential friends. I'd seen her slow climb in society. At first, she'd been shunned because of my father. But over time, when the crooked people who ran the city had realized that money was money, no matter how dirty, they'd let her in. She'd gotten addicted to mingling with the rich and powerful.

Another horrid truth weaved itself together. There had been such confidence when she'd spoken. Who was going to go against her wishes? *Scooter?* It was one thing to be afraid of me, but we were *all* afraid of her. She'd *handled* things, and any choice or will from my part had been an illusion. An emptiness swirled in my gut and expanded like a slow-motion tornado until it swallowed me whole. I had nothing—no crew, no territory, no livelihood.

Thanks, Ma.

I couldn't look at her. She didn't deserve a taste of the hurt she'd imposed by doing things her own way. It wasn't like I was a child. No, she wouldn't get the luxury of my temper. Someone would, just not her.

A gentle knock came from the door. Samantha Whatever-Her-Name glanced at me before locking her dark brown eyes on my mother. "Am I interrupting?"

"Not at all." My mother waved her in with grace. Her tone had lightened, as if this woman was going to be some kind of relief to the situation. Not that it pained me to look at Samantha... Jesus, she was a level of beautiful that I hadn't thought existed outside of movies. She wore the kind of shoes that needed to be left on during sex. And below that conservative red dress were curves that hugged in all the right kind of places. My mother had declared her off limits the second I had laid eyes on her, but that was before she'd taken away everything I'd busted my ass for.

Game fucking on, Mommy Dearest.

I grinned, and the wicked pleasure of my idea was like cool water in a scorching dessert. *Sorry, Samantha. You just became my new favorite way to piss off my mother.*

She stepped toward the bed with a polite smile. "I'm so happy to see you're awake." Her lie was so slight that someone else without my experience in reading people wouldn't have caught it, but I understood everything. From the moment she'd met me, she'd seen me as an inconvenience to her boss...a nuisance.

"Thanks." My throat was still dry, and I reached for the small plastic cup on the side table, but the tiny butcher inside me stabbed my wound and I sat back with a wince.

"Allow me." Samantha poured some water from the pitcher and handed me the cup. With her so close, I was finally able to really take her in. Her skin was tan, but not orangey fake. It glowed. Her perfume was light but distinct. I had no idea what it was. There was none of the fruit or spice that my mother wore.

"What's that scent?" I asked in a soft voice I didn't even know I had.

"I'm sorry?"

"Your perfume. It's really…nice." I nearly puked in my mouth. It was like speaking a foreign language that made a stomach turn. With any luck, she would think I'd had a life-altering moment. Hell, I'd woken up without a life. Maybe she could be sympathetic. Then again…the lie was in there.

"It's French, with wisteria and jasmine." She stepped back, realizing how close we'd been. "My guilty pleasure."

"Is that the only one?"

Her face fell and eyes tightened. *Shit.* I'd gone too far. To my mother she said, "I thought you said he was cranky?"

"He's a lot of things." My mother fiddled with her black designer purse then looked over her shoulder. "I have a meeting. I'll call you later." After a final rake of her eyes over both of us—it was her usual goodbye— she left.

"Mind if I sit?"

A million dirty responses filled my sick head. Leo had once told me that controlling the body and words were easy. It was the mind that required discipline. He was right. My mind was headed down a very tempting and perverted street with the beautiful woman in front of me.

"I'm not really in the position to object. Eat your heart out." Okay, so I'd slipped in the word position and said 'eat'. I hadn't mastered my words just yet.

Samantha dragged over a chair and its stuttered clank pounded in my head. I closed my eyes. Being weak fucking sucked. As soon as I got out of the hospital, I was going to ask Ricci to kick my ass.

She smoothed her skirt and crossed her ankles. Damn it if those shoes wouldn't look fucking fantastic next to my ears. I licked my lips and she frowned.

She started, "I don't know what your little *nice* act was about, and quite frankly I don't give a fuck, but I have at least one reporter who is dying to break open this story, so I'm going to need you to tell me the actual truth about what happened so I know how to spin it."

All right. Two points to Samantha. She saw through my bullshit. That didn't mean I was going to give up my plan. *In fact, challenge accepted.*

New approach. "Listen… You're fucking gorgeous *and* smart. It's not something I'm used to dealing with."

She raised her eyebrows. They were light brown and perfectly groomed — a natural blonde.

Lord help me.

"Cut the shit, Anton."

"Fine. I'll tell you all my dirty little secrets, but I want something in return."

"I'm shocked." Her sarcastic tone brought a true smile to my face.

But the thing was that I knew she would do it. She was one of those fucking career-minded bitches who put work first. She may have been perfect from head to toe but it had nothing to do with vanity. She wore a public face. I'd seen the same behavior in the woman who'd raised me. The immaculate hair, makeup and wardrobe? It was all for show.

There was only one way to see what was underneath. "A date."

"Screw you."

I shrugged. *Totally on the table as far as I'm concerned.*

Samantha recoiled and I was a tiny bit insulted. There were far worse men out there, for fuck's sake. "I'm not going to be seen with you in public."

"Perfect. Then we can go to your place. Apparently, I live with my parents now so…"

"I don't cook." A little snarl came with her words, but it wasn't a no.

"I don't care." I held her gaze and sent all those dirty thoughts her way.

And she got them. Her mouth dropped open and a blush crept up her neck. "You're serious."

I tried to hide my grin but damn it if it wasn't pulling at my cheeks.

She crossed her arms. "I'm not having sex with you. Jesus."

"Relax… I'm just asking for a meal. It seems I lost all my friends, so I just want something on the books to do. Humor me."

"Sorry, but no. I don't trust you and I have no intention of sharing a meal with you unless there are other people present."

"Then no information for you, sweetheart."

There was a new flush on her skin. It was darker and it came with a little flare to her nostrils. "One, don't call me 'sweetheart' ever again. And two, this is bribery."

I stretched and the movement brought a sharp pain in my side. "I think we both know I'm not above that."

Samantha let out a groan and rubbed her temples. In that moment, her surrender was bittersweet. I'd somehow hoped she's say no. I liked the challenge. "All the fucking truth, Myers. The first rule of spin is that it has to be believable. I need an ounce of truth to sell the lie. If I find out you weren't honest, I'll use my contacts at the police station and take down you and your whole fucking former crew. I don't give a shit who your mother is."

I hadn't seen that coming, but okay, I'd jump on that bus. I held up two fingers. "Scout's honor."

She closed her eyes for a beat. "That is tremendously un-reassuring."

Chapter Three

Samantha

Anton Myers had been out of the hospital for three weeks when he knocked on my door to collect the date debt that I owed him. It had been stupid at the time to say yes, but I'd had a feeling Mitch from *The Times* had a source I didn't know about, and I was nervous that the *real* story would get out. But he hadn't printed anything, just fished around with questions that I'd swatted away like an annoying fly.

Demsey was leading in the polls and the election was right around the corner. I couldn't risk bad press and my chance at a place in his new administration. It was one thing to be on a city level. Moving up to state would mean national exposure.

I opened the door and Anton stood solid with a crooked grin and a bottle of wine. His eyes were the kind of light blue that didn't seem real, and there was a sharpness to them that could have cut diamonds.

"Stole this from my mom's cellar." He tapped the bottle and dropped a shoulder as he passed by me, *forever a criminal*.

I paused and gathered strength before closing the door. It was only going to be an hour of my time, then I would be rid of this asshole for good. I'd had pressers that had lasted longer. *No big deal.*

Anton set the bottle on my kitchen island then turned around. "You wear that on all your dates?"

I'd made a concerted effort to *not* make an effort. Yoga pants, fluffy socks and my Vassar hoodie were sure to send the signal that I didn't want him to like anything about me. I'd also washed off all my makeup and put my hair in a messy bun. "Only the ones I don't want to go on. Hope you like cold Chinese takeout."

Anton crossed his arms and, okay, so maybe he had a chest of steel and ridiculous muscles. That didn't make me attracted to him. He was hotter than the fourteenth level of hell. I would give him that. *Jesus…* Bad-boy sexy had never looked better, but he had a wicked mind, I wasn't going to let myself wander around in that darkness. Well, I could have… It had been awhile since anyone had seen me naked, and Lord knew I needed to blow off some steam, just not with *him*.

"You think that oversized sweatshirt makes you less gorgeous somehow?"

An uncomfortable heat crept up my neck. I didn't like the way he was looking at me, like he could swallow me whole and it would be the best fucking day of my life. *Nope, not falling down his bottomless pit.*

I shook my head. "Don't do that. Don't try to compliment me to get on my good side. We both know you're only here to torment me *and* your mother."

"That's not true. I'm trying to get laid."

"Oh, Jesus Christ." I dropped my head back and headed to my utensil drawer. I found the corkscrew and handed it to Anton. "Open that. Alcohol is the only way to get me through the next hour."

I grabbed two forks then reached for the glasses in the cabinet above my sink. I moved around the island over to the couch and sat in front of the table where I'd set the take-out.

Anton sleeked over, poured the wine then handed me a glass. "Cheers. To our first date."

"May it be the last." I tapped my glass to his and took a big drink. He sipped his own then placed it back on the table. "Here." I handed him the white cardboard box filled with sautéed noodles and a fork. "Enjoy."

Anton ate a few bites before licking his lips and turning to me. "You know what I think?"

"Can't imagine." I pronged a piece of broccoli. "And truthfully, I don't really care."

"See? That. All this effort to not impress me. Makes a man wonder why."

I rolled my eyes. "It's literally *not* to impress you. I don't want you to think you have any chance of reaching goal number two."

"You like me."

I sat back deeper into the couch. "I actually don't."

"Keep telling yourself another one of your lies, Samantha."

I put the half-eaten box back on the table with the fork sticking out. "Another one of my lies?"

Anton shrugged and finished chewing. "It's what you do, right? You lie for a living. No disrespect..."

He was technically right, but it didn't mean I appreciated it. I tried to calm my breathing. I'd let the asshole get under my skin. Damn it, I was practically huffing and puffing like the Big Bad Wolf.

"You gonna finish that?" He pointed to my dinner.

"I've lost my appetite." Maybe if he ate the rest of the food, the date debt would officially be paid and he would get out of my apartment.

As Anton reached over my leg, his arm brushed it. *Shit*. That stupid spark of electricity that confirms when people are attracted to each other shot up my spine. He glanced over to me like he knew. *Smug asshole*. And why was my body betraying my mind so fucking fast? He'd been there what? Ten minutes? Stupid lonely libido.

I stared out of my window and waited in silence as he finished the meal. When the white box was empty and back on the table, he stretched out and winced.

"You still in pain?"

"Nah." He frowned and gave a quick shake to his head. "What movie did you pick out for us?"

I recoiled. "There's no movie."

"Dinner, movie, kiss. That's how people date, right? I admit, I'm a bit rusty."

What the hell? "There's no movie and there sure as shit isn't any kiss. You're insane."

Anton leaned closer to me. "Samantha...sweetheart."

"Don't call me sweetheart. I fucking hate that." And I hated him bullying himself into making this into an actual date. That couldn't happen.

"Samantha," he corrected in a quiet tone. His haunting gaze tugged at me and urged me to admit that a hot man on my couch with zero strings attached was exactly what I needed. I might have even pleaded with God to bring me the same thing that I was resolute on rejecting.

I swallowed over a lump that had formed high in my throat. Jesus Christ, was he going to kiss me? Worse, did I actually want him to? One sexy stare and breathy tone? That was how desperate I was for physical contact? I backed away slightly.

He continued, "You know I can be a real thorn in your side. Make a big mess of shit right before the election."

"Get out." I stood and pointed at the door. He couldn't bribe me for sex. I didn't know how things worked for him, but I needed a little bit of seduction. *Asshole*.

"I'm gonna need that movie first." He smirked and adjusted himself deeper into my sofa.

"You know the chief of police is a personal friend of mine?" Possibly overstated, but worth a try.

"Do it," he dared. "Then I call up some reporters and give my own version of what went down in here."

Oh, he'd worked out his leverage on me. That was for sure. What did I have on him? For whatever reason, I didn't think he would physically hurt me. Maybe that was stupid, but boys with strong mothers like Sophia were usually brought up to respect women.

"Okay, okay. Listen." He held up his hands in surrender. "This started shitty. I'm not trying to force my will on you or some shit like that. We had a deal. I gave you the truth, which I've never fucking done outside of my crew before, and, in exchange, you gave me this date. You could have at least put on some fucking mascara or something — or those fucking shoes. Jesus Christ, your shoes, Samantha." He shook his head and looked away.

Had I hurt his feelings? Did Anton Myers *have* feelings?

I rolled my neck around and fluttered my eyes. "Fine. You can pick the movie."

I tossed him the remote and he caught it at his chest not far from where his wound was.

"I don't want to pick the movie. I want to see what you pick."

I bent my knee and sat on my foot then reached for the remote. "Are you always like this?"

"Like what?"

"Pushing to get your way. Using everything for your advantage. A grown man but a spoiled brat."

"I think you left out devilishly good-looking." He beamed. Jesus, he meant it.

I tapped my finger on my mouth. "Conceited. Pretty sure that's the word you were looking for." I flipped on the flat-screen and decided to take pity on him and not make him sit through a romantic comedy.

I scrolled through the choices and he said, "Wait. Have you seen that series about the old school mafia dudes in Russia? I've been dying to start it."

"I thought you said I was choosing...and a movie. I'm not starting a series with you. I see what you're doing there."

"Are *you* always like this?" Anton's face crinkled up like he'd smelled something sour.

"If you mean 'right', the answer is yes."

He rolled his eyes before sending over a sexy smirk charged with danger and lust. *Shit, I'm toast.*

"Fine. We can watch one episode of your series. Then you go."

He grinned. He'd won. "This date is so romantic."

I snarled and clicked on his show. We sat there for an hour on opposite ends of the couch. The story was dark and enthralling. Anton occasionally let out a '*damn*' or an '*oh shit*' and the fucking episode ended on a cliffhanger as to whether the main character was going to die.

When the end credits rolled, Anton and I both had our mouths open and exchanged a knowing glance. Yes, I wanted him out of my apartment—out of my life, really—but even I wasn't cruel enough to prevent us from seeing what happened next. I let the next episode start and he poured the rest of the wine into our glasses.

An hour later, I turned off the show. It was dark in the apartment, just the streetlights below shining through the windows. I stood up—not giving him a chance to make a move—and headed for the door.

"Sorry. I have an early meeting. Time for you to go." I opened and held it at arm's length.

He walked over while slowly nodding.

"Just one thing," he whispered in my ear and chills raced over my skin.

I closed my eyes. Heaven help me, I wanted him to kiss me. A man hadn't touched me in far too long and I hoped my desperation wasn't showing. *Crap.* What if I'd forgotten how to kiss? What if I was terrible?

The warmth of his breath on my neck was the perfect tease of what was to come. He stayed there, and when he licked his lips, the moisture sent a rush of desire between my legs. The pause before the kiss was a torturous bliss.

"You're missing the best part." He stepped back and winked at me. After all that bravado, all his cocky comments about wanting to kiss me—nothing.

And me admitting to wanting it was not going to happen. He was playing me. I should have seen it a mile away but my lonely hearts club had blinded me.

"Bye." I closed the door before he could say anything. He wanted to toy with me? Fine. I could play his stupid little game. He didn't want me? I doubted it. There had been a spark, a buzz, the tension of attraction. I may have been out of practice at the physical part, but I still knew how to read a room.

Anton was going to try to get me to throw myself at his feet. *Good luck, muscle man.* If he thought for one second in his Neanderthal brain that I didn't know how to make a man want me, he would be wrong…very, very wrong.

Then he'd be sorry.

Chapter Four

Anton

One of my mother's goons followed me down the street in his signature black shiny jacket. There was no point in trying to shake him. It would only end up with both of us suffering her wrath. Chances were she'd find out where I was going anyway. She had snitches all over the damn city.

Maybe it was stupid, walking right back into the snake pit, but I couldn't lie. I missed the snakes. The way people looked at me with respect, fear — it was my own personal addiction. Just breathing the shitty air uptown gave me life.

"You can wait here. I'm not gonna run out of the back," I said to the goon. Maybe I should have asked him his name.

He chewed on a toothpick and nodded before turning so his back faced the storefront as if he were some kind of security. *Hilarious.*

The glass rattled as I opened the door, and I immediately locked my gaze with the owner. It wasn't hard to figure out who Rafa's cousin was. The family resemblance of hazel eyes was a dead giveaway. She nodded to the back of the hair salon and the small glimpse I caught of Jimmy's ex—or whatever she'd been—was the fix of panic I'd been craving for weeks.

That's right, bitch. I'm back and I know what you did.

In the small room, with just one look at my number two man, a rush of calm spread through me.

"Jesus Christ, Goldie. I've never been happier to see your face."

He stood and smiled, and, damn it all to hell if I didn't go in for an epic man hug. *Good thing no one is looking.*

"How you feeling, Boss?"

We sat at a chipped table and I kicked out my legs for a long stretch, careful not to wince when that fucking little butcher inside me scraped my scar.

"A hundred percent," I lied. No point in showing weakness. The truth was that I'd tried to work out a few times and I'd ended up coughing like a seventy-year-old chain smoker. The doctors had told me to give it time, but a full month had gone by and I wasn't exactly known for my patience. "How's that girl you shot?"

"Annoying. But I have some good-ish news for you." Rafa pulled out a piece of paper from his back pocket and slid it toward me. "Full disclosure... She had a pretty impressive side hustle going on. Sorry I didn't realize sooner, but your cut is in this account."

I studied the paper. On the one hand, that was the beauty of Rafael Santos. He fucking made money like nobody's business. On the other, I understood this was a goodbye. I really had no one. Scooter wasn't even returning my texts. Leo and Jackson had gone 'legit' somehow and Rafa was about to disappear.

There was an apology behind his eyes but thank fuck there was no sympathy. It would have made it worse.

"Where you headed?" I asked, and the acceptance relaxed him a bit.

"I don't know." That was a lie. He knew. He just didn't want me to come knocking on his door. *Fair enough*.

"So that's it. You hand me some money and I forget about you? My entire crew?" I tapped the table with my index finger and it was a hell of a lot lighter than the punch I was itching to throw against the wall of his cousin's salon.

"I shot my girlfriend. I could have killed her. That loyalty should mean something." Rafa had never talked back to me in all the years I'd known him, and I didn't like it.

"Your girlfriend is the whole fucking reason I got shot." My tone was flat and it barely kept the boiling blood beneath my skin at bay.

"I didn't come here to argue, but you and I both know that's not true. Yes, she massively fucked up that situation. But, Jimmy? That was all our faults. We were *all* sick of working that fucking bench, selling dope to our former friends and fucking neighbors. We were tired and sloppy. Jimmy happened because we wanted change."

I worked my jaw. He wasn't wrong. The daily cycle and grind of Covington had gotten mundane. The lack of profit from the games had pushed us onto our heels, so when Jimmy had started earning, I'd looked the other way on a few things.

Rafa continued, "I'm fucked up in my head, man. I shot the woman I love on purpose. I need to get the fuck out of this city before it kills me."

We were all fucked up in our heads, but it was a 'chicken and egg' situation. Were we born warped or had the time and circumstances bent us into the criminals we were? Either way, I'd never asked one of my crew to take a stupid oath of loyalty, so it wasn't like Rafa was going back on his word. We didn't have an initiation ceremony or any shit like that. Maybe I should have had one, though.

I smacked the paper. "How much?"

"About two hundred thousand."

Apparently, that was all his loyalty was worth. *Damn.*

"How do I get it? You know I'm fucking hopeless with technology."

"M seems to think that pre-paid credit cards are the safest. But you have to have them mailed to you. Get a P.O. Box under a fake name or use a business...but change it up."

"Sounds like a lot of work."

"Keeps me busy." He offered a sideways smile. "But once you have the credit card, you can take out cash from an ATM. Mix that shit up, Boss. Cameras are fucking everywhere."

I scratched my head. Maybe I'd get my haircut while I was there. The thought of all the fucking hoops I would have to jump through just to get a measly thousand bucks made me light-headed.

Rafa stood and frowned. "I'm sorry you got shot."

I had to give him something. He could have gotten lost and never reached out. Instead, he'd given me some money and faced me like a man. He was loyal to a fault and a fantastic thief.

"Two things. Thank you for shooting your girlfriend. It was the best calculation you could have made. No one thought you would do that, myself included. It probably saved my life and shocked Jimmy just enough so that he aimed at my body and not my head." I quirked a smile I wasn't feeling. "And I'm going to miss you and all that fucking money you made us over the years."

Rafa nodded with a pained look on his face. "I'll go out first. Angela is probably shitting her fucking pants thinking she's next." He glanced at me one last time. It would be the last, I was sure of it. Rafa parted the hanging beads that acted as some kind of dangling door, kissed his cousin on the cheek, handed her a wad of cash and left.

I waited until Juliana's client had left then walked out of the back room and plopped myself down in her chair.

"Just a little off the sides."

"Remember who has the scissors here." Juliana opened and closed her silver sheers and lifted her eyebrows. She threw a cape over me and reached for the electric shaver and a comb. "You're not going to beat the shit out of Angie and throw her in a ditch, are you?"

"Not really my style. My mother taught me not to hit girls."

"Not everybody got that memo."

What had Rafa ever told me about his cousin? *Think.*

I watched Juliana in the mirror as she leaned in to start shaving. A lock of her dark hair fell over her shoulder and revealed a bruise on her neck. *Right.* This was the cousin who liked guys who were physical. I never understood that.

"You still dating that douchebag?" I asked.

"I'm always dating a douchebag. But sorry… I'm not giving you any information about him or Bradford. He's in charge now and he likes it that way. Consider yourself lucky I put family first and I didn't tell him about your little meeting today."

The buzz from the shaver filled the space between us and I let her do her work. Just being around Covington answered a calling inside me that I'd been trying to ignore. I wasn't interested in high-class crime like my mother. There was too much pretention, too many favors and palm greasing. Street crime was easy. Besides, I had a shed full of product to push in my Upstate backyard. Rafa's gesture of money was kind, but I wasn't going to buy two hundred credit cards and go to two hundred different ATMs to withdraw a thousand dollars at a time. I needed to get my cash from Ricci and start back up. But this time, I wouldn't bother with a crew. I'd just be the supply chain.

Juliana finished and I followed her over to the register. I showed her a hundred-dollar bill.

"Tell your boyfriend I have a business proposition for him."

"Keep your money and stay the fuck out of my salon."

I leaned my forearms on the counter, sighed for the sake of drama and tilted my head. "Like you said, not everyone got the memo. Just because I don't like to rough up girls doesn't mean I don't know anyone who will."

She crossed her arms and pretended to be brave. "You threatening me?"

"Nah." I jutted my chin in Angela's direction. "I'm threatening her." I clicked my tongue and stared into her light eyes.

"Fuck you."

"Relax, Juliana. I just want to make him some money." I handed her the bill and she studied it for a long beat before swiping it out of my hand. "Come back next week. I don't want your number in my phone."

I tapped the counter and smiled over to Angela, who was watching me like a hawk. She was lucky to have a friend. I blew her a kiss for good measure and walked out of the salon where the goon was still standing.

"Come on, Grandpa. My ma's got to yell at us for getting a haircut." I called for a car and we rode back downtown to the nicer neighborhood around the park where my mother lived—fucking night and day, all in the same city.

At home, Ma was in her study on a phone call. She motioned for me to sit on the opposite side of her huge mahogany desk.

"Thank you for your generous donation. I look forward to seeing you tonight and introducing you to my husband. I definitely think there's something we can do about that pesky regulation when he's elected governor." She hung up the phone and I remembered she had bought me a new fucking suit and I had to mingle with fucking rich idiots all night. I'd done a lot of shit wrong in my time, but these ass-kissing events were a brutal kind of karma.

She raked her light gaze over me. "Thank you for getting a haircut. Is it odd that you had to go to Rafael's cousin's salon to do so? There are so many other places close by."

"He gave me the money he owed me." I stuck out my bottom lip and shrugged. "He's skipping town and wanted to say goodbye."

"How sentimental of him." Her sarcastic tone meant she was on to me, but I didn't care. Half-truths were all I had. What had Samantha said? The first rule of spin was to make it believable.

"You know what? It got me thinking. I need some fresh air myself. I'm going to go Upstate for a few days. Alone."

My mother folded her hands on the desk. "That's a little convenient, Anton."

"What's your game plan here, Ma? Keep me under your roof forever? I'm a grown-ass man. I need some privacy."

"You're a grown-ass man who got himself shot in the chest."

"I feel like you should have some emotion in your voice when you say that." I winked at her and it worked. She cracked a little smile.

"You know your wellbeing is my top priority."

I was reeling her in. I just had to play the right card. "Ma, I'm going crazy here. I can't have your guys watching my every move, counting the squares of toilet paper I use and reporting back to you. I need some freedom if you want me to play by all your rules."

She frowned. She knew I was right. I loved to rebel, just for the sake of it. It was like when I was a kid. If she asked me to clean my room, I wouldn't do it. But on the weeks that she didn't ask, it was spotless every Saturday. Once she'd realized I was as stubborn as her, the space she'd given me had brought us closer and given her the results she ultimately wanted.

"You hate being alone."

I shrugged. "Maybe it's time I learn how."

She closed her eyes. I'd won. Me going stir-crazy in her house was way more dangerous than cutting me a little slack. Even though it was a mistake on her part, I would have caused more trouble had she said no. Damn, it was good to be Mommy's favorite.

"You're still coming tonight. Be ready at seven."

I hopped up and leaned over her desk to kiss her on the cheek. "Wouldn't miss it for the world."

In my room, I sent a text to Leo, asking to meet the next day and get my cash. I'd been waiting until I really needed it, and since I'd finally figured out a plan to make money without my crew, it was time.

I showered, put on the new suit—there was no fucking way I was wearing a tie—and plastered a great big smile across my face all the way to the fundraiser. I shook all the hands, said all the 'nice to meet yous' and kept my shit as fake as fuck. That was, until Samantha walked in on the arm of some lawyer-looking fuck who was at least ten years older than she was.

And fuck me to pieces if she wasn't stunning. Her blonde hair was styled in one of those ways that looked messy but perfectly in place. There was a slit in the front of her navy-blue gown that showed off her shimmering legs. The lace on the top of the dress was see-through but incredibly classy and her bare arms had the perfect balance of tone without being overly muscled. She was a knock-out, and every pair of eyes in the room hovered a second longer to take in her beauty.

To top it all off, she had on another pair of those fucking hot shoes, which made me wonder if I was developing a fetish. I clenched my teeth and sent daggers to the lawyer dude with every bat of her eyelashes and touching of his forearm. It wasn't that she was overtly flirting with him, but if she had so much as glanced in my direction, I'd missed it.

When she excused herself from her table after dinner, I couldn't handle it anymore. I followed her out of the ballroom to the restroom area where she'd headed. I leaned back against the wall and propped a foot on it behind me. I crossed my arms and waited.

Five minutes. Five full fucking minutes later, she came out and stopped in her tracks.

"Oh, hey," she said way too casually, "I didn't know you'd be here."

I pushed off the wall and stalked over to her. "See? Now that's a lie." I traced her lovely jawline with the crook of my index finger and stopped on her chin, which I tilted up so she couldn't avoid eye contact. "You know every damn person in that room. You wouldn't be doing your job if you didn't. And you knew exactly where I was, so you didn't look in my direction. You're playing a little game, Samantha."

Her gaze raced back and forth, and I could almost feel her pulse doing the same.

She swallowed and rubbed her lips together. The heat between us was undeniable, and I was sure there was a part of her that was begging me to kiss her—but I wouldn't give in so easily. If she was going to fall for me, it was going to have to be hard. I would have to tease out her desire to the point that she wouldn't know which way was up.

"I'm not playing anything with you." The fire in her words lit up every nerve, every cell of my being. She walked away.

Chapter Five

Samantha

A bead of sweat dripped at a snail's pace down from Demsey's temple and created a horrible line where it had wiped away his stage makeup. He was flailing and I wanted to crawl into a small hole and forget about his bad debate forever.

"I can assure you that all my campaign money came from real New Yorkers, not people looking to grease palms and cut deals." His opponent was going to attack Sophia next. I could feel it in my bones. "Take your wife, for example... Where did she get all her money?"

It had been bound to happen. We'd played dirty early on in the campaign, and they had to hit back somehow. Demsey had a uniqueness about him that gave the common man confidence in him and his Irish work ethic but also had a savvy way of working with big business. I was pretty sure we'd still win the election, but this debate wasn't doing us any favors.

"Mayor Demsey, would you care to respond?" The young moderator was from a local television station and also not doing us any favors by the softballs she was throwing to our opponent and the fastballs coming at Demsey.

"Thank you. I don't know what Representative Carver is referring to, but it occurs to me that throwing out accusations without any proof is an act of desperation. My wife's fortune was built with American spirit and New York grit. She's a self-made woman who has brought me a lot of joy and important counsel. Attacking her is an obvious sign of weakness. Now, are campaign finance laws a mess? Yes. But I wasn't the one in the state legislature where we make the laws. I've been busting my butt down here in the city, trying to keep the streets clean and safe. That's why I'm a better choice."

It wasn't solid but it was something. Closing statements were next and I excused myself down the aisle of reporters and spectators in the dark hall to check my makeup before the post-debate interviews would start. As far as the public was concerned, I was the spokesperson for the mayor of the city and therefore worked for them. But, behind the scenes, I was choosing his ties, suggesting talking points and keeping him quiet when need be. Demsey had an inkling to go off the cuff, and sometimes it worked but sometimes it didn't. His debate performance had been a solid 'meh'.

In the bathroom, I applied my subtle gloss, fluffed my hair and let out a big breath. I smoothed down my cream dress and fixed the thin black belt mid-torso. *Spin time.*

I made my way backstage, congratulated my boss and blew a little smoke up his ass before turning around and running directly into Mitch from *The Times*.

"What does Carver know about Sophia Myers?" he asked as his eyes lit up.

"From the sound of it, nothing. As the mayor said, it was an obvious act of desperation." I grinned then froze.

Across the room, in a white button-down shirt that fit him entirely too well and a pair of dark jeans, was Anton. He locked his gaze on me, licked his lips, then looked back to his mother and nodded. *What the hell is he doing there?*

"Something wrong?" Mitch asked, and he suddenly became the most interesting person in the room.

"Not at all. Anything else you wanted to ask?" My polite smile threw him off his game. He'd never been on the receiving end of it before.

"Wanna get a drink?" he tried.

Damn. I wondered how long he'd had that one in his arsenal. But even though I wanted to escape the pull Anton had on me, I wouldn't be bellying up to a bar and sharing my secrets with Mitch anytime soon.

"You know I can't do that. Besides, what would your colleagues say? They'd think you'd gone soft."

"Come on, Sam."

"Hey," Anton said from my right, "who's this?"

Mitch immediately forgot all about me and offered his hand to Anton. "Mitch Greene, I'm a reporter for *The Times*. Anton Myers, right? Care to comment on your shooting?"

"Nope. Samantha, my mother wants to know if you're joining us for dinner. We're leaving now."

Mitch studied Anton then me.

"I'll be right there." *Please walk away now.*

But Anton stayed, and in an act of alpha-male pissing contest, he offered one of those fake smiles to Mitch that was doing its damnedest to lay some kind of claim on me. *Fucking spoiled man-baby brat.*

"Have a nice night, Mitch. You can email me your story if you want a comment before press time."

As we walked toward Sophia and Demsey, I casually leaned over to Anton. "Don't you fucking dare touch me. I don't know what kind of animalistic stupidity runs through your thick head, but that was me doing my job. I talk to reporters."

"He was a douchebag."

I stopped and glanced around the room. People were watching us. I smiled. "What are you, then?"

"An asshole. It's completely different." He lifted a shoulder in a half shrug.

"And yet equally unappealing."

"Liar." The word was a slow dare and it caught me off guard. I hadn't thought he would be at the debate, so I'd left my 'hot asshole' repellent at home. His tiny grin was a silent way of gloating. He had an effect on me and he knew it. *Shit.*

Demsey came up to us and thankfully cut the tension in the air. I turned to him and winced. "Sorry, but I'm not going to make it to dinner. I have a ton of work and think I'm coming down with something. I'm going to go to bed early. I'll see you tomorrow."

Demsey frowned. He liked a big dinner in a fancy restaurant followed by nightcaps at the bar. "That's too bad. Actually, you look flushed. Are you lightheaded?"

"A little, yeah. I'll just grab a car. See you tomorrow."

"What's this?" Sophia joined us, her posture straighter than ever.

"Sammie's feeling sick. Look at her. She's sweating and says she's dizzy." Anton scrunched his face. That shithead knew damn well I wasn't sick. But if it got me out of dinner, so be it.

I thumbed over my shoulder. "I'll just grab a car. I had sushi for lunch so maybe it's just something I ate."

"Why would you eat sushi on a Monday?" Demsey frowned. It was an excellent point — and why I'd eaten a spinach salad instead. Urban legend said never eat fish on Monday because it wasn't fresh. But the inquisition of my boss, his wife and her son was actually making my head spin. Even my palms were sweaty. All that from a simple word? I blinked several times to try to find some footing.

"Anton, see her home. We can't have the press secretary spilling her lunch on the sidewalk after a debate."

Oh no. Not that. Not Sophia actually wanting us to be together. Then again, maybe it would make me less appealing to Anton if he had his mother's approval. "Oh, would you?"

Anton narrowed his eyes slightly then sighed. "I was really looking forward to trying that restaurant."

"This is no time to be selfish." Sophia's tone was impossible to read. Either she was calculated or generally concerned for me.

"When did I become a babysitter?" Anton asked his mother. She responded with a glare so powerful that not even he could refuse it. He snarled, and it was a good show of resistance. "Bring me home a steak."

I grabbed my coat but didn't put it on. I was still hot. Anton placed his hand on my lower back as we walked toward the exit, and since we were in public, I couldn't swat it away like I was dying to do. At the same time, there was a voice in my head trying really hard to deny that I liked it.

Anton opened the back door of the town car, and I slid in and reached for the complimentary water. He gave the driver my address like he lived there himself.

"Are you really sick?" He settled into his seat.

"I honestly don't know."

"Come here." He reached for my head and cradled my jaw, then pressed his cheek into my forehead. "No fever."

I pulled back. Him touching me was getting too familiar. "Your method is incredibly scientific, Dr. Myers. Thanks." I scooted into the corner and pressed into the cool window.

Anton dropped his head and whispered, "When are you going to admit that you are attracted to me?"

Never.

In five minutes?

I took a drink of water and let his question die in the thick air between us. "You have a jealousy issue."

He stared down at my feet. "I'm also developing a shoe or foot fetish. Jesus Christ, Samantha. How did you do that? How do ordinary shoes look more attractive on you?"

His lightness was refreshing. I needed some levity. "I like shoes, and these are not ordinary." I twisted my ankle and showed off my shiny black heels. They were beautiful.

We stopped at a red light. The doors of a theater opened and a crowd poured out into the sidewalk. They were probably headed to late dinners or after-show drinks. Such a unique pleasure of the city.

"Can I ask you something seriously?" His hushed tone almost made him seem vulnerable.

"Sure."

"Do you think I'm not good enough for you?" The accusation carried a ton of confidence.

"You're about to be the stepson of the governor of the great state of New York. If you're not good enough for me, I have some pretty high standards."

"That's a pretty impressive non-answer, Miss Press Secretary."

"What can I say? I'm good at my job." I didn't like the idea of thinking myself better than anyone else. But he'd told me what he'd done before he'd been shot. He was a drug dealer and a criminal. His potential boyfriend resume was dead in the water. Maybe it was shitty of me and maybe it made me a snob or a bitch, but yeah, even if he was hotter than hell and just a little bit charming, he wasn't right for me. I would end up with someone like the boring man I'd taken to the fundraiser. I was in politics. Although…Demsey had married a criminal mastermind.

We pulled up in front of my building and I said, "I'm fine. Seriously. Thanks for the gesture."

"Nah. My ma would be pissed if I didn't walk you all the way to your door. You're not getting rid of me that easy."

I shook my head, thanked the driver and fished out my keys from my bag. Who knew criminals were so fucking chivalrous? At my door, his stupid grin held entirely too much hope.

He looked down at me and tugged his bottom lip with his teeth. "Can I use your bathroom?"

"No."

He stepped closer and his energy buzzed all around me. He was crowding my space and fogging my mind. Jesus, I'd never wanted to be kissed more in my entire life. Need, want, desire... It all pooled inside me, swirling in a perfect mix of temptation. Because that was what he was, dreadfully sinful. Taking a drink of him would be blissful gluttony. I was sure of it.

I spun around, put my key in the lock and my hand was shaking.

"Please?" His breath on my neck made me pause. I swallowed over the whimper that was trying to escape my throat.

Maybe he really had to use the bathroom. He'd taken me home, after all. He hadn't made any kind of move that was aggressive. It was the least I could do, really.

"Down the hall and to the right." I turned the knob and let him pass behind me then relocked the door out of habit. I rushed over to the kitchen sink and ran the tap cold. The cool splash on the back of my neck was a quick relief and gone too fast.

What was my plan? I could just kiss him a little bit then send him on his way. I couldn't have sex with him. That would be misleading, wrong and probably leave me screaming for more every day for the rest of my life. *Shit, that sounds pretty fucking good, actually.*

The water ran in the bathroom. I was running out of time to figure out if I was really going to go through with kissing my boss's stepson. Anton appeared in the hallway, his crystal eyes shining. I hadn't remembered to turn on any lights.

"Well, thanks again." I fiddled with my hands and there was a little crack in my voice. "Hope you enjoy your steak."

He walked over to me, picked me up and sat me on my kitchen counter. My dress was thankfully too tight to really open my legs, so he straddled the left one. His thighs were massive around my pointy knee. I stared at my hands in my lap and picked at a nail.

"What are you so nervous about?"

"If anyone finds out about this…"

"Then what? You said it yourself that I'm the future governor's stepson."

I hated getting my words thrown back at me. "We both know you're not just that."

He leaned in and all that floaty energy from the hallway was back. "That seems to be the part you like."

The whimper finally bubbled out of me.

"Tell me what you really want. Be honest, just this one time." His words hypnotized me and convinced me that I could let go. There was even a chance that once he'd kissed me, he'd lose all interest. Maybe conquering me was the sport and keeping me was never going to be in the cards. And who said one kiss meant anything more than just that? Surely, I deserved to find out how soft his lips were. Hell, maybe *he* was a terrible kisser, and I would be rid of the attraction.

"Tell me," he pleaded into my ear.

I dropped my head back and he ran his nose the length of my jawline then he cupped my left side and drew me nearer.

"You're so fucking gorgeous, Samantha. Stop running all those fucking scenarios in your head and let me kiss you." Anton brushed his soft lips below my ear, and if I had been a stick of butter, I would have melted.

"Okay." I closed my eyes but nothing happened.

"You have to say it. Tell me what you want." He twirled a lock of my hair and looked deep into my eyes.

I wet my lips and look a long blink. "I want you to kiss me — then I want you to leave."

He dipped his chin. "You sure about that?"

I reached up and took both sides of his cheeks then drew his lips to mine. A slow tease unraveled between us and the anarchy of self-indulgence inside me screamed for more. Wicked, hungry lust burned between my legs as he deepened the kiss. I'd been right. Anton had a skill and pull that was undeniable and intense. It was hopeless. I was instantly hooked. He didn't try to cop a feel of my breasts, but I wasn't as in control as he was. I reached for his belt, tugged him closer, then untucked his shirt and ran my fingers up his rippled stomach. I stopped where his scar began and wrapped my arms around his strong back.

I was spellbound, unable to stop. Each peck, suck or twirl of his tongue hooked me deeper into an enchanted haze. He ground into my thigh and squeezed my flesh tight. He was forceful, brash and beyond adept. He knew just when to let up and when to dive back in for more. My mind went blank and only the physical draw to him mattered. I'd never kissed anyone I wasn't supposed to, and I couldn't tell if the extra layer of forbidden was adding to the passion or if it was just him.

After a frustrated moan, he stepped back and smirked. My lips stung in the best way, and he may have even bitten me. I brought my hand up to my mouth and gently stroked over it.

"Bye." He walked to the door, undid the locks and left without looking back. I must have stared at the empty space for an hour before I finally hopped off the counter and flipped the deadbolt.

He'd done exactly what I'd asked, and I'd fucking loved it—not just the kiss, but the respect that went with it.

Chapter Six

Anton

There was something incredibly empowering about kissing a smart, beautiful woman. There was also something frustrating to all hell about leaving her without getting off. But she'd asked for it, and leaving her wanting more wasn't the worst plan.

I checked into the gym where Leo had set up our meeting. My mother's goon was off duty since I'd argued that having an old dude watching me work out was suspicious and I was trying to blend in — not to mention that it was just fucking weird.

Leo was bringing me my cash, and I was looking forward to seeing him. I was lonely. The whole reason I liked having a crew was that I was making brothers I'd never had. Maybe on some level, we all were. In the locker room, I found my old friend. He nodded in my direction. There wouldn't be any public displays of affection or friendship from him. It wasn't that Leo

Ricci was paranoid, but he was cautious. His priorities had shifted and an association with me was no longer desirable. Because, unlike me, he actually had a brother. And I was pretty sure he was working on a wife.

I waited for a middle-aged man to leave. "Too bad I can't kick your ass. I'm dying to fight."

Leo walked over to me and presented me with a small key. "We both know that would never happen. Seven-forty-six. Don't spend it all in one place."

I took the key. "You seen Scoot? He's not returning any of my texts."

"I see my clients and my family. And I'd appreciate if this was the last time I saw you for a while. No offense, but Frankie was pissed at me and Jackson for helping you. Fucker gave me a black eye."

It made sense but still stung a little. We'd been best friends for half of my life. I put the key into the pocket of my training pants. I was actually going to use the gym.

Leo hitched his bag over a shoulder and moved to leave but stopped. His brown eyes filled with regret. "Sorry I wasn't fast enough and you got shot."

I held his gaze and our thoughts mingled like they used to back in Covington. His apology was sincere, and he hoped I would change my life. But to what? I wasn't interested in protecting people like he was. I had no computer skills like Rafa had. All my motivation was selfish, just like it had always been. I nodded my goodbye and acceptance of his rules. He left — and I already missed him.

I lifted weights, checked out some women whose tits bobbed up and down on the treadmill but was bored as sin. How could these people just play by the rules and never want to get ahead in the rat race? Where was their excitement? How did they feed the ugly beast inside themselves? Maybe they were all secret addicts of porn or prescription drugs. Whatever they were, they weren't much entertainment to watch.

After my shower, I changed and took my original bag and the one from the locker into the bathroom stall. I transferred the money and filled Leo's bag with my sweaty clothes. I threw away the lock and key, then left Leo's bag under a bench. It would be just another lost and found never to be claimed. Walking in with one bag and out with two was the sign of a foolish criminal. This wasn't my first money transfer.

"Did you have a nice work-out?" the pretty redhead asked from behind the desk as I left.

"The best." I grinned and she didn't catch my sarcasm.

"Can we interest you in a monthly membership?"

"I'm gonna think about it."

She reached for a brochure and handed it to me with a fluttering of her eyes. "You can email or call me. I'm the manager."

Two months prior, I would have jumped at a change to 'email or call her'. I understood damn well what she meant. Hell, I may have even convinced her to suck me off in the bathroom by their little snack area. But instead, I took the glossy folded paper and thanked her. The power I'd once bathed in hadn't fueled my ego since I'd been shot. The sensation of being just like everyone else pecked at me. I hated it.

I shoved the brochure into my back pocket and walked back to my mother's place. The high of strutting the streets with a bag full of cash was the only thing getting me through the day—that and the fact that I was going to drive Upstate and get a shitload of drugs to sell to Juliana's boyfriend.

At home, I dropped the bag at the door—no one would dare look inside—and walked down the long hall.

My mother was in the kitchen next to a box of food designated for my trip. I kissed her on the cheek. She liked it when I did that.

"You're in a good mood."

"High on life, Ma."

"Mmm-hmm." She narrowed her eyes. "You sure it doesn't have anything to do with Miss Samantha Powers?"

I crossed my arms and leaned against the counter. "What changed your mind about her? You made it very clear a month ago that she was off limits."

"I only want the best for you, dear. You know that. Besides, a month ago she wouldn't have looked twice at you. Timing is everything."

With my eyes closed, my brain was able to connect her dots. When I looked at her again, she was smiling. I'd understood.

"You made her off limits so that I was more interested. Then you waited until I became a better boy to up my chances. God, you are calculated." It wasn't a compliment. I was all part of *her* plan. Samantha was suddenly a lot less attractive. But then again, if I played nice, my mother would keep me on a longer rope. How had I not seen this coming?

"She's the best possible match for you."

A part of me wondered if my mother hadn't married the mayor just to get to Samantha. I wouldn't have put it past her. But the controlling of my life was making me crazy. Thank God, I'd convinced her to give me a little bit of freedom before I went insane with her interference.

I reached for the box and tucked it under my arm. "Well, arrange the marriage already, Ma. I'm sure she'll be picking out a dress next week. Cuz, you know, she's not an independent modern woman. Nope, not at all."

"She's precisely that. That's why she needs a strong man."

I laughed. "You don't actually think you're doing her some kind of favor with me, do you?"

"I don't like that tone. You have an excellent character and are a natural leader. Despite your temper, you would never hit a woman. Don't try to tell me the son I raised isn't worthy of a woman like that." Her scolding glare was heavier than her sharp tone. "Now go enjoy your little camping trip and be home by Friday for dinner."

I'd never needed a fight more. Maybe I would just kill the guy from Bradford with my own hands to work out my frustration. But I tempered my annoyance with her. Blowing up would only lead to one of her goons following me Upstate—not that she wasn't probably already sending someone to spy on me.

"I'm taking your car," I said with a wide smile. She wouldn't deny me her precious Jag now that I'd caught her scheming. Plus, she'd had a very hard time saying 'no' to me since I'd been shot. Maybe I was milking her concern, but damn it if I didn't want to drive her baby on the open road. I could already see a crack in the sour face she was making in protest.

"Fine." She walked me to the entryway and got her keys out of her purse. After an un-characteristic sigh, she said, "I know you don't like when I pull strings because it makes you feel like a puppet. I'm not trying to do that. But you staying in that neighborhood would never lead you to meeting the kind of woman you deserve."

In all fairness, Samantha Powers was pretty fucking fantastic. Beautiful? Check. Intelligent? Check. The kind of challenge I would ultimately need on a daily basis? Double check. Still, it would have been nice if it had been my idea and not my fucking mother's. The problem was that the dark side of me was dying to get out and play. That might not appeal to a woman like Samantha.

My mother watched me from the window as I walked down the street toward the garage where she kept her car. Lord, I would not miss being under her scrutinizing eyes. It was as if she thought I would crumble to pieces if I stubbed my toe.

I drove the speed limit out of the city then hit the gas a little heavier once I got closer to the Catskills. My mother's Jag had been restored to perfection, right down to the details in the leather seats. It was too cold to put the top down, but that didn't stop me from enjoying every moment behind the wheel as the engine purred.

I parked it in front of my A-frame cabin, took in the groceries and told myself to be patient. If my mom had me followed, the last thing I should do was go directly to check on my stash.

The warm lights of my house glowed in the dark forest. I made a fire in the backyard pit and sipped a beer, buying time if anyone was watching. The flames crackled and the smell of the smoke soothed my bruised ego. My mother constantly thought she knew what was best for me. She'd forgotten that I had the same iron will that she did.

Although, she could have picked a worse woman. I wasn't faking my attraction to Samantha. That was one hundred percent raw and natural. Kissing her had woken up a passion in me I didn't know that I had. I'd never kissed a woman like that before — when there'd been some kind of *feeling* that went along with it. I shivered.

But I didn't want a normal life that tied me down. Being bad was too damn satisfying. Why would I change? So my mother could have some sense of accomplishment when it came to me? The damage of my father's influence had already been done. There would be no rehabilitation for me. Just like him, I was incapable of regulating my wild ways. Ma liked to think I was *her* son and refused to see the influence of the other fifty percent of my genetics and teachings.

I sprayed the hose on the fire, went back inside and flipped off all the lights. I sat in the dark, staring out of the bay window until two o'clock in the morning, at which point I went to the wall safe where I kept my keys.

Outside, there was no need for a flashlight. I knew the path by heart. I paused before I opened the padlock, listening for a twig or a breath. When nothing cracked or huffed, I swung the door inward. If my calculations were correct, I had left at least three hundred thousand in methamphetamines in my little shed. I stepped inside and reached for the string of the single bulb. The dread started before I tugged. I hadn't stumbled over boxes or caught the toe of my boot on anything. My mouth went dry and my heart raced. Three hundred fucking thousand dollars — my future. *My life.*

The light only confirmed what I already understood. There were no drugs. I pulled the string and blinked my eyes to adjust to the darkness again. I hiked back to my house, grabbed an ax from the garage and stormed back to the shed. Under the moonlight I chopped the entire fucking thing down. By the time it was in shambles, I was dripping in sweat and the ache in my side and muscles hurt so bad that I was panting.

I steadied myself against a tree to catch my breath. *My fucking mother.*

After a shower, I went to bed, but sleep wouldn't come. My heart was pounding too hard in my ears and all I could think about was what a fool I'd been. She'd had a month to search the house after I'd been shot and she hadn't let me out of her sight.

But how? Absolutely nothing was out of place. I would have noticed. Whoever had taken the drugs hadn't forced anything. Only my crew knew about the shed. Maybe it wasn't impossible that she'd had one of her guys search the property, but the wall safe would have required a picklock — not that she wouldn't know one of those.

Rafa was a thief. He could have done it. He would have been able to move the meth through his elaborate spiderweb of cousins all over the city. But he was loyal and hated selling drugs. It didn't seem right. Leo was out of the question, plus I'd changed the combination on the lock when Jackson had left and had only given Scooter and Rafa the numbers.

By the lack of contact, Scooter was a suspect. But I had a hard time imagining him trying to get back into the life. He'd been itching to get him and Callie out of Covington since her ordeal. Plus, in all the years I'd known him, he'd been the most loyal one on the crew.

I scrubbed my face and groaned. It had to have been my mother. Only she would have had all the resources to pull it off with such finesse. Besides, she'd shown how fucking premeditated her entire life was. If I hadn't known better, I would have thought she'd sent Jimmy to shoot me. Also, she had agreed to me coming up here a little too easily.

So, I would have to take a detour. Big fucking deal. The easy way was for pussies anyway. I just needed to stay calm. I would call my supplier in the morning and arrange a swap using the cash I'd gotten from Leo. Since when had I let a small hiccup stop me from my goal? Meanwhile, I would keep pursuing Samantha. Because...why not?

I rolled to my side, and with a plan and the confidence I had to pull it off, sleep finally came.

Chapter Seven

Samantha

Sophia had invited me to another dinner party, and since it was on Friday night, I had a hard time getting out of it. Also, I wasn't sure I wanted to. Anton hadn't called or stalked me like I thought he might — may have *hoped* he might.

I wanted to see if there was more to the physical attraction or if I'd just been a quick conquest to see if he could get me to surrender. I didn't appreciate being fucked with, and if that were the case, he would get a full-throttle Samantha in his face.

I couldn't tell if I was convincing myself that the kiss had been as intense for him as it had been for me or it had just been that...heavy. The memory of it had distracted me on loop since Monday night, and Fanny had asked me a few times what the hell was wrong with me. I'd even been kind to Mitch in the last press briefing about the subway repairs we'd budgeted for and were massively behind schedule on. Commuters were pissed—and I couldn't blame them.

I wanted to look my best for the dinner, either to rub in his face what he would be missing or to motivate him to keep pursuing me, which seemed like both a terrible and a wonderful idea.

Lingerie always gave me a silent confidence, and I chose my favorite black lacey set, including a garter belt I'd only worn a few times. The dark stockings were plain, but the rest of the undergarments did the heavy lifting on the sex appeal. If he were lucky, maybe he would get to peel them off one by one. I wore a maroon sweater dress that was way too short for work and just long enough not to reveal the tops of my tights.

The heels of my pointy ankle boots could have been lethal weapons, and the leather shone like a black pearl. I wore my hair down and slightly curled. My makeup was more than usual, but a smoky eye had never failed me.

Fanny called me with video as I applied my plum lipstick. I positioned the phone against my mirror in the bathroom and clicked the 'accept' but kept up my finishing touches.

"Hey, let me guess... Someone's pissed because they realized we didn't give them all the numbers."

"Bingo," she said dully. "But holy shit. Give me a spin, girl. I thought you were just going to Demsey's for dinner. Did you cancel and have a date I don't know about?"

I trusted Fanny, truly I did, but I wasn't breathing a word about my Anton crush to anyone—not even if that person would have my back under any circumstance like trust-fund baby and rebel-with-a-cause Fanny. She didn't need to be my assistant. She didn't need to be anyone's anything. But working for the city pissed off her mother, so she did it with a wicked joy.

I showed her my ass. "Just changing it up. I haven't worn this for ages. Too short?"

"You look hot...like *hot*, hot. Why? You hate when creepy old men look at you—" Her mouth dropped open and her eyes went wide. She knew me too well.

"Don't say another word. Tell whoever that it was a problem on our end and we'll get them the right file on Monday."

"Will we?"

Probably not. "We'll deal with that on Monday. Have a good weekend."

"Sammie?" The concern in her voice rattled me, but it wouldn't stop my plan. I had to see where I was with Anton for my own sanity.

I held up a hand to the phone. "Please don't. There's nothing you can say that I haven't already thought of myself." I was playing with fire, but I didn't know how to put out the flame.

"Be safe, please."

"Always."

We hung up and I did a final check of my ass in the mirror. My morning runs in the park when there wasn't a storm had paid off. I didn't look bad.

I called for my car and rode up to Sophia's brownstone. A waiter answered the door and took my coat. I kept my small clutch with phone, lipstick and keys then set my shoulders as I walked into her drawing room. My heart raced as I scanned the crowd, not finding the man I was in search of. Maybe he wasn't around at all. It wasn't like I'd asked my boss about his stepson's whereabouts.

After a round of hellos, I went to the bar. A little wine to relax me would do the trick.

"You're stunning, Miss Powers." Demsey's brother was younger than him and in the construction business. I'd met him three or four times before. He'd magically known how to underbid on projects then accidentally had overages each time. We'd had to get our stories straight and our numbers in sync far too often.

I brushed my hair over my shoulder and turned to him with my wine glass in hand. "I didn't know you were going to be here. What a lovely surprise."

He studied me for a beat. "Always so polite. Always so full of shit."

Ouch. The sharp tone had come out of nowhere. But I maintained my cool. I blinked a few times, like I really cared. "Have I done something to offend you?"

"Yeah. We had that Gramercy project pulled. I was told it *'wouldn't look good'*. I assume that was you."

What? He was telling me something I didn't know, and on a certain level, I was grateful. But it was my job to know everything, and if Demsey had taken a project away from his brother, he should have told me.

"You can choose to believe me or not, but I didn't know anything about that." I set my wine back on the bar.

He rolled his eyes. "Sammie, you lie for a living. I don't believe anything that comes out of your gorgeous mouth." He downed his Scotch and pushed away from the bar. I locked eyes with Demsey across the room, who winked at me as if to assure me that it was all no big deal. He was his own worst enemy sometimes. Not that I disagreed with his decision… I'd been trying to cut down on the number of contracts we threw to his brother for months. I was just mad that I'd had to find out from a different source.

I turned back to the bar and rubbed my finger around the rim of my glass. Maybe I wasn't spending enough time with my boss. I liked Sophia, but her opinion had taken up some space where mine used to hold. If I got closer to her, I wouldn't miss out on the key decisions. Not that his brother's contract was a huge deal, but it was the principle of the thing. I could take it as a small reminder to be on my toes. Yes. Luncheons, brunches, anything I could do to be in Sophia's good graces was going to be better for me.

The hairs in my nape raised as he stepped closer. I didn't need to see his face or hear his voice to know that Anton had walked into the room. All my senses went onto high alert. The buzz around me tickled my skin and numbed my mind. Getting lost in that brick of a body and taking one step closer to Sophia at the same time? Yeah, I was glad I'd worn the shorter dress. With any luck he'd seen me talking to his new uncle. That would have riled him up.

He pulled my hair back with the crook of his finger, but I stayed facing the bar. His little whispery seductions were the fuel that fed my hungry ego.

"That's a little short for you, no?"

"You like?"

He hadn't even really touched me, and I was on fire.

"I'd like to see what's underneath, to be perfectly honest."

I spun around slowly with my wine and looked into his lust-filled eyes. I'd gotten the reaction I'd wanted. He was still into me. So what if I had a little fling with him? It might be good for me. Anton Myers didn't look like he would kiss and tell.

"Maybe you can."

He lifted his eyebrows and pursed his lips. My boldness caught him off guard. "Is that so?"

"It's a maybe. Excuse me. I see someone I need to talk to." I pushed by him but he grabbed my arm. It was a little rough and somehow that didn't bother me.

"I don't like being teased, Samantha. I need clarity."

"Liar." I mimicked how he'd said it to me days prior — slow, breathy and daring.

He scanned over me and I walked away high on my small victory. I spoke with a campaign worker I'd recently met, but Anton's constant scrutiny tore at my attention. When dinner was announced as ready, I hooked my arm into Demsey's and gently tugged him backward.

"Sorry about that, Sammie. I should have warned you about my brother. It slipped my mind."

I wondered how much truth there was to any of his words. It sounded a hell of a lot like he'd pinned it on me. I couldn't have been that far from his thoughts.

"Don't worry about it. I actually wanted to thank you. If you remember, I never liked working with him to begin with."

"See?" Demsey clicked his tongue and pulled his arm out of mine. He waggled a finger. "That's what I like about you...always finding the bright side."

I stood there pondering for a moment, and by the time I got to the dining room, all seats were full except the one to the left of Anton. I didn't know who'd arranged it, but it was no mistake. I slipped in and placed my napkin on my lap.

"This is convenient," I said in a low voice for only Anton to hear.

"I guess you're the only one brave enough to sit next to the prodigal son."

I sent a warm smile to Sophia, who returned it then shifted her gaze to her neighbor.

Anton sat up straight in his chair and slowly rolled his head in my direction. "Care to make a friendly wager?"

"Maybe." My heart raced. Why could he destabilize me so quickly? Worse, why did I welcome it?

"That seems to be your word of the day."

The guests at the end of the table were being served the first course and the clanking of plates gave us some privacy. Nevertheless, he leaned in a little closer.

"I bet you three orgasms that you have killer lingerie on under that dress."

My eyes widened. How could he have guessed that?

He chuckled. "Looks like I win, no matter what."

He was cocky, crude and somehow refreshing. He would have been someone I'd avoided in a bar or the subway, just based on his looks alone. Muscleheads had never been my type. Yes, I liked a fit body but normally went for a trim swimmer's build instead of the thick muscles trying to burst through his light blue button-down shirt. I should have placed my own bet that his mother had picked that out for him.

And sitting next to him was an odd, sweet torture. He was in a good mood and it was contagious. He teased his mother but was respectful to his stepfather. His disposition was light and guests paused in their conversations to pay attention to him. It struck me that he was the kind of person who had 'it' — the ability to draw people in and make them feel special with just a wink or a quirked smile. The model behavior was surely a ploy — for what, I didn't know. But if Sophia thought I was the cause of it, I could earn some of her goodwill and influence. Lining up my career goals with my sex drive had never happened before, but why the hell not?

Dinner ended and I moved to stand, but Anton held me down with his heavy hand on my thigh. I wasn't sure anyone caught the correction, but I stayed where I was, staring at Sophia's barely touched plate. It was probably how she stayed thin.

A group of businessmen huddled at the opposite end of the table and Sophia and Demsey led the rest of the group into the study for nightcaps.

"You have a decision to make, Samantha." There was no flirt, no lightness in his words. They were so matter-of-fact that if his eyes hadn't tightened ever so slightly, I would have taken them as cold.

My pulse pumped fast and strong. His intensity was heady and potent. I shifted my gaze to his hand and back up to his steel eyes.

"A simple yes or no will do. Then you can say your goodbyes and either I follow or I don't."

I'd already convinced myself to go through with it the second I'd sensed his energy by the bar. I wasn't even sure I had a choice. My body was somehow in control of my mind and he seemed to be leading both. It was a powerful call and answer that I had no will to stop and only a thrilling desire to investigate.

"Yes." It was the simplest choice I'd ever made.

"Wait for me outside."

I stood, said goodnight to everyone except Demsey's brother, collected my coat and waited for Anton on the end of the stoop. The cool air blew between my thighs as a reminder of just how warm I was down there. If Anton had sex like he kissed — and in my experience most people did — those three orgasms were seriously on the table. The last time I'd gotten laid, I'd faked it in hopes of getting it over with. It hadn't been bad per se, just predictable — and a little boring.

The door behind me closed and he was next to me within seconds. "Car is three minutes out. Now..." He stepped closer to me and ran his hand up the hem of my dress, over the garter strap and around to my ass where he squeezed the flesh. With his other arm he drew me nearer. "You have one car ride to think of all the sinful things that you want me to do to you. I'll say yes to every single one of them."

My knees wobbled and I was thankful he was holding me up. The alpha male hang-up suddenly made perfect sense. He brushed his sensuous lips over mine before withdrawing his grasp. Anton interlaced our fingers and it seemed so out of character that I almost laughed. The teetering from heat to manners might have been adding to the dizziness in my head.

I studied his profile in the streetlight. With a strong jaw, distinct nose and protruding high cheekbones, he could have been a warrior. No, I was wrong. He could have been a king. And yet, with all that testosterone seeping out of his pores, the act of holding my hand was so gentle, so sexy. I'd been right at dinner. He had that star quality. He made me feel like I was the only woman he'd ever done that with.

What else is he capable of?

Chapter Eight

Anton

She'd dressed up for me, put on sexy lingerie for me and said yes to me. Didn't she know my ego was big enough without the idea of her actually being interested in me? And that shy little smile of anticipation she shot me from the backseat of the town car? Yeah, I was going to have to wipe that out of my memory. It made me all...warm. What the fuck was that?

To be fair, it wasn't like I was suffering in her company. She had this suit of armor she wore in public and a softer, needier side in private. Or maybe I was just imagining she liked me because I'd never met a woman who didn't. One thing was for sure... She wouldn't have agreed to more physical whatever without wanting it for the same lusty reasons I did. We had chemistry. The kiss earlier in the week had only solidified its existence.

But I also couldn't deny that there was a little bit of me wanting to be better in her presence. My mother would probably give me her beloved Jag after my performance at the dinner earlier. I'd been a very good boy, and holy hell, was I ready to be bad again.

Just as my thoughts shifted back to all things blonde in the confined space of the car, we pulled up to her apartment building. The damp night air hit my cheeks, refreshing and invigorating me. I tugged at her soft hand and gave it a squeeze before ushering her into the building. I'd never been the shy type, but I could appreciate that I wasn't in Covington Heights anymore. She was a respected public servant. Smearing her dark lipstick over her face with my mouth and having her neighbors witness it might be the one thing that would send me packing. And I wanted her. I wanted to see her, touch her, be balls-fucking-deep inside her and pull her long, gorgeous hair.

The second I'd seen her at the bar, a craving had built inside me. Her screams, her gasps, her whimpers—I needed them all. She could definitely sense my energy stalking hers. That was for sure why she'd slowly licked her lips and her chest had risen and fallen at a slow pace. She was trying to control it—but neither of us could. The only question that remained was what was on her little list.

In silence, I followed her down the hall to her place. Damn it, I was a lucky son of a bitch. Samantha was a rare breed of woman who had everything—and I was about to devour her. Dear God, let her list be as dirty as mine. Then again, maybe it would be hot to take it super slow.

I shook the ridiculous thought out of my mind. I just needed to get laid. It didn't matter that she was the most beautiful woman ever to agree to it. Samantha was a means to two ends. One, fucking her... I absolutely needed to do that. And two, keeping my mother at bay so I could make some bank. Besides, women like Samantha didn't end up with men like me. Our non-future was a no-brainer. Why was that a little chip in an otherwise perfect cup?

Samantha let out a small sigh then pushed open her door. I closed it behind us while she hung her coat. The thick energy between us crept into her apartment, under my skin and into my bones. I walked over to the island in her kitchen and leaned against it.

A siren hollered by and the flashing red lights lit us up for a brief moment. Samantha twisted her lips then raked her gaze the length of me.

"You clean up pretty nice, Mr. Myers." She was stalling. Maybe she'd lost some of her earlier confidence. Shit was real. I was there. She'd said yes. Verbal compliments hadn't had much of an effect on me for years, so I brushed it off.

In that quiet voice that made her shiver, I asked, "You come up with your list?"

Samantha set her shoulders and walked over to me. She placed one hand directly on my scar. I didn't know if it was on purpose or by chance, but it caught me off guard. Her other hand settled on my thigh.

"It's one thing." She looked over my shoulder then back into my eyes. "Be gentle."

Uh, no thank you and a big, giant 'what the fuck'. I'd already played nice. We were done with that shit.

I searched her face for any sign of a lie and couldn't find it. She had to be kidding. She knew who I was, and it wasn't Prince fucking Charming. But the way she stared into my soul? It was not only a confirmation that she knew what she was asking, but there also was a knowing that I was capable of it. How the fuck had she managed to dig out the tiny part of me that was decent?

"On one condition." I gave her a little yank just to prove that I wasn't all that gentlemanly. My shoulders relaxed at the scent of her perfume and I took an extra deep inhale to enjoy it. I peppered kisses up her neck and ran my hands up her skirt. The skin beneath the lace was like satin. I'd never been so spoiled in all my life.

I pulled the dress up to her waist and she lifted her arms, threaded them through then gave a shake to her long hair. As she took a step back, I chucked the dress into a ball on the floor. What little light there was shimmered off her skin while the lace hid in the shadows.

Her bashful smile had to be fake. There was no way she couldn't have been proud of what she was putting on display. But there she was, vulnerable. How many other men had been fortunate enough to see this? Then again, how many other men could bring it out?

"What's that?" she asked.

I soaked in her sexy image one more time and realized there must not be such a thing as karma, because I sure as shit didn't deserve what was about to happen to me. "I stay till dawn."

"Seems like a fair trade." She twisted her hand in mine and tugged me toward her. I stood and she spun without letting go. Down the hall she led me and into her bedroom, where I stayed at the door and she walked to the bed. A high bed with a light duvet waited in the middle of the room. It took up most of the place with nightstands on each side. Along the opposite wall were drawers and closets that had clearly been custom built. It occurred to me that she must not make enough money to afford the level of lifestyle she maintained. Civil servants didn't live in one-bedrooms with nice things. The shoe habit alone would cost some people their monthly rent. I'd seen the price tags on designer clothing and accessories. *Jesus, maybe she is as crooked as I am.* Oh my God, if she was a criminal, I might be in love.

I kicked off the new boots my mother had insisted I wear to her parties and shoved my hand into the ankles of the scratchy socks that went along with them. Samantha opened a small drawer and placed a shiny box on the table next to the long cylinder lamp.

Gentle. Well, that would be new. But I could try... She deserved respect and I'd promised to do everything she wanted. I started unbuttoning my shirt and walked over to her then took her by the shoulders.

"You sure about all of this?"

"Yeah." She nodded. "I mean, there's a spark, right? Might as well play with a little fire." Her seductive tone drew me in, and I knew at the same time that a woman of her caliber wasn't giving in. She was tempting me.

I hated to be that cliché asshole who was about to have sex then remind a willing and heavenly woman that she wouldn't be getting a relationship out of it, but that was me to a fucking T. Over the years, the disclaimer had come out at particularly dickish times. Once I'd actually said it while I was fucking someone. I should have said it to Samantha then, given her the reminder that fire could burn like a bitch. But she had my head kinda fucked up from how she'd asked me to be gentle.

If I only had until dawn, I was going to make the most of it. I trailed my fingers up her arms but the light contact wasn't nearly enough. Despite her order, I spun her around and pressed my cock into the crease of her ass. The new definition of gentle was going to have to be slow instead. It was all I could manage. I wasn't even sure if I was fully registering that she'd given herself up to a twisted fuck like me.

She dropped her head to the side, providing the perfect access to her neck while I slid one hand under the lace of her bra and dipped the other one directly into her dripping pussy. Fucking hell, she was hot and soft. I groaned into her shoulder and she pressed all her body weight into me. I traced slow, long circles around her clit, and I was sure I was the only thing holding her up. She'd fully surrendered, and for an unfathomable reason, she trusted me.

The devil inside me couldn't let up. I pinched her nipple and her gasp only encouraged my depraved spirit. I pressed into her clit harder, rubbed it faster.

"Let go. They'll be more." I sucked a spot below her ear and she unraveled in my arms. Her breath hitched, then she whimpered and shook. I kissed around her nape, noticing the heat of her skin as I held her still. Her heartbeat thumped into the hand I had on her breast. She slowed her inhales and I wondered briefly if she would ask me to leave. Maybe she'd gotten everything she'd wanted.

And just when I thought she would pull away, she spun around and kissed me hard. She wrapped her arms around my neck and hopped up, crossing her feet over my ass. Once secured, she finished unbuttoning my shirt and I managed to wiggle out of it without dropping her or abandoning the kiss. I knelt to the bed, let her go then whipped off my pants. I motioned for her leg and unzipped her boot then repeated on the other side. I dropped both boots behind me. Maybe if there was a next time, she'd keep the shoes on.

Samantha propped up on her elbows and eyed the shiny box of condoms she'd taken out. I nodded once then ran my fingers up her dark stockings until I found the little clips that were in my way of taking off the soaking lace between her legs. She lifted her ass and I slid off her thong.

She was trimmed, just a light landing strip in the middle, inviting me to taste. How was I going to possibly say no to that? I yanked her knees over my shoulders so that her ass was on the edge of the bed and took one long, blissful lick. Her clit was swollen and I twirled it with my tongue then sucked it hard.

"Fuck…" Samantha dropped all the way onto her back and crossed her wrists before laying them on her forehead. I pushed her legs open wider, and when they dropped off my shoulders, she brought them back in and made her legs into butterfly wings. I cupped her ass, and though I was tempted to stick my fingers and tongue in places she might not have been ready for, I remained focused on her clit and lips. I teased out another orgasm by amplifying the pace then slowing it back down. She rode the wave up then plummeted without release time and time again.

My cock was fucking throbbing, dying for any amount of attention. It had been ignored long enough after another climb without a peak. I stood, dropped my underwear and put on the condom. I caught her watching and a little bit of fear flashed in her dark eyes.

Gentle.

I wiped my mouth with the back of my forearm, kissed up her stomach and sampled each one of her firm breasts. Where did women like her come from? As

I kissed her deeply, I used the tip of my cock to rub against her clit, bringing her back up a wave. She winced a little when I finally pushed in, but I quickly moved my fingers back between her legs and rubbed slowly. She'd shut her eyes tight and clenched her jaw. I slid in and out as slow as I could, but once I was buried in her, the final thrust was so instinctual that I couldn't help myself. Out slow, then in fucking deep as hell. And it wasn't just the sensation of my cock. Her bronzed skin and gorgeous face were stroking my ego and feeding my confidence.

As soon as she started panting, I knew she was close again and I frenzied my pace. Gasping screams came before the rippling massage around my cock and yet I kept on, not giving her a chance to overthink the next orgasm I was sure she was about to have.

Samantha dug her short nails into my biceps as if she were holding on for dear life. Problem was, I would never come in missionary, hot woman or not. And there was no way she'd survive on top or on all fours. She was too tight, too everything. I was teetering on the edge of fucking her raw and I hadn't even moved into second gear. She'd been right to ask me to hold back.

"Flip onto your stomach."

She obeyed and I shoved her legs together with one of my knees. But when I moved my cock to get into the perfect position so she would stop being in so much pain and my balls could rest on the backs of her legs, I brushed against her ass and she shot me a panicked look from over her shoulder.

"Shh..." I teased her pussy with my tip and she relaxed. Jesus, I wasn't a straight-to-the-ass man — not with her anyway. I pushed in slowly so she could see that it was a better position, and as I rocked in and out, her muted pleas went back to desperate groans. The friction from my sack was doing the trick but I couldn't keep my mind off her ass. I wanted to stick a finger inside so fucking bad that it was distracting. I closed my eyes and found a slow and trusted rhythm, which caused her to gulp air whenever I was in my deepest.

I reached up and twisted my own nipple then moaned out a guttural cry of ecstasy. It was one thing to kiss Samantha, but it was another entirely to come inside her—like being a king among men. Never, not once in my sexually active life, had I been so high. It was invigorating and potentially dangerous.

She had a power over me. But what was it—and why? More importantly, *how*? I fell to the side, being careful to take the condom with me, and lay on my back next to her. She shifted her head and folded her arms underneath to look at me. I stared at the ceiling, wondering if I'd been too rough after all, if she would kick me out or maybe even fucking call the police.

She whispered, "Does your staying till dawn matter if we're not doing that again?"

I turned. She was biting her lip and there was an apologetic crinkle around her eyes. Fuck, I'd been too rough. "Depends. Are we not doing that again ever—or just tonight?"

She glanced away, then back. "It had…been a while."

"No shit." I laughed and she smacked me on my arm. "Mind if I shower?"

"No. Is it fucked up that I'm actually considering following you in there?"

"Don't you fuckin' dare." I kissed her on her forehead, headed to the bathroom and locked the door behind me. I didn't trust either of us, especially since

I'd kissed her goddamn forehead twice. What the actual fuck was this sweet side of me? I nearly threw up in the toilet at the thought.

Chapter Nine

Samantha

The fall sun warmed my bedroom, and as I woke, I remembered I wasn't alone. Like in the hospital after his surgery, Anton's intensity was hidden with his eyes closed. He was naked and the duvet only reached up to his navel. Below his left pectoral muscle, the scar was still pink and the skin bunched together in a round, messy spiderweb.

Could a man like him change? Go from making all his own rules to following at least some of them in society? And if he could, would I want some kind of future with him? Initial attractions had a way of fading over time. But what about the draw?

Too many questions... I needed to take it for what it was. *Sex. Hot sex.* His idea of gentle was hilarious, but I'd needed him to understand that a girl like me doesn't get fucked and thrown away afterward. Dipping the toe with a man like Anton Myers was a way better idea than jumping in headfirst. Him showing some restraint, however little it had been, proved to both of us that he respected me.

I padded off to the bathroom and showered. My hair was a rat's nest from the sex but after a bit of brushing and dry shampoo, it was presentable. With the towel tucked into my cleavage, I made myself a vanilla coffee from a capsule and took it into my bedroom. Anton stirred — the smell of roasted beans could do that — and I set the little mug next to the bed.

On the weekends, I always looked forward to being casual, and normally I wouldn't have bothered to match my bra and underwear, but on the off chance that he'd opened his eyes, I chose a cream set and wiggled into them after tossing the towel on a chair in the corner of my room. Next were my stretchy black skinny jeans and an oversized silk blouse.

As I crossed the room to my jewelry box, Anton cleared his throat. He reached across my bed and stole my coffee. As he sipped, he studied me, and the potency of his attention made my heart beat just a little faster.

I had to break the silence. "Hey there, Cinderella. I think you missed your curfew."

"Are you calling me a princess? Is that how you wake up all your lovers? With a massive insult? You could have at least gone for Sleeping Beauty." He took another sip then held the mug at his stomach.

I chose a long gold chain with tassels and draped it over my head.

"How do you afford all this? You can't make that much money working for the mayor."

"What?" *Since when is it okay to ask people about their bank accounts?*

He set the empty mug on the nightstand and stretched. "I'm just saying... You have classy clothes, a nice apartment, those fucking shoes..."

The truth was that I'd grown up privileged. My parents had never married, but my wealthy father had dutifully sent his child support every month and it had paid for me to go to private school and a private liberal arts college. I'd had a lonely home life, but friends like Fanny had taken the place of family over the years. When my father died, I'd inherited everything and lived off his stock portfolio. I'd tried to start my own PR firm but had no credibility or experience — and that had been one of the reasons why I'd taken the job with Demsey.

My mother lived in South Florida with her third husband, and our relationship was cordial but not really warm. I had cousins on my mother's side, but she'd distanced herself from her blue-collar family once she'd gotten a taste for money. Their lack of affection had turned me into the strong woman I was. I didn't hate my parents, but I wasn't going to put out pictures of them smiling at my graduations like they'd had something to do with my success. Yes, I'd been given resources, but the drive was all me.

Not that I was ready to share any of that with him. The daylight had brought back my guard. Plus, those tiny feels from the night before were scaring the shit out of me. "You planning on robbing me?" I regretted the accusation as soon as I'd thrown it out there.

He took a long blink and rolled his neck. "Damn. Okay. I thought we had a good time." Anton swung his feet to the side of the bed and stood naked, not a sign of shame on him. He had tattoos like a warrior, intricate designs that belonged on ancient shields and weapons.

After a scratch of his scar, his gaze darted around the room until he found his boxer briefs and threaded his feet through them.

"I'm sorry." I walked over until I stood in front of him. "I don't know how to do this."

He curled his lips into a small smile. "Do you think I do?" He reached out and tugged twice at a lock of my hair. "I wasn't trying to be nosy. I was trying to" — he dropped his head back and groaned then looked at me again with a pained expression — "get to know you."

A little rumble came from his stomach. I could at least buy him breakfast after the amazing sex. "I'll walk down to the deli and get some breakfast sandwiches, and we can talk before you leave. Deal?"

"I promise I won't steal your diamonds while you're gone." He smirked then cringed. "You may not want to underestimate the amount of food I eat. Otherwise, I'll convince you to give me yours after I promise another three big Os for you."

"You think I'm that easy? That I'd trade my breakfast for another round of *gentle* with you?"

He nodded once. God, confidence on a man was hot. "I do. And I also admit to not knowing what the fuck that word means. Do you have a dictionary? I'll look it up while you're gone."

I let out a little laugh. Damn it, he was charming. "What do you want for breakfast?"

He rubbed his hands together like a kid a Christmas. "Three egg and ham sandwiches on wholewheat English muffins, orange juice and a real coffee — black."

I stared at him. What a spoiled brat. "Are you replenishing or refueling?" I shook my head as I turned around and he smacked my ass.

"Only one way to find out, sunshine."

Thankfully, he couldn't see my eyes widen as I slipped into my black ballerina flats. He'd officially used a pet name, and I couldn't control the *pitter patter* in my heart. I got to the door of my bedroom but stopped when he called for me.

"Last night was okay, right? I didn't, like, disrespect you or do something you didn't want?"

I'd never had a man check in with me after sex in that way. Usually, they said things like, *"That was so good, thanks,"* or *"You came, right?"* His words touched me. They were real. He wasn't as cocky as he came off to be.

I walked back over to him and put my hand on his stomach. "Like you said, your version of gentle is a little skewed, but everything you did makes me want to do it again."

His small smile was almost tender. God help me if it didn't seem borderline sweet. It was an unexpected and confusing side of him. He pulled me close and squeezed my ass. "Good. 'Cuz there are some not-so-gentle things I may need to do to you."

I raised my eyebrows. Was that a promise or a threat?

Another rumble came from his belly.

I pushed away from his magnetic hold, shaking my head. "I'll be right back."

"Can you get a toothbrush?"

That implied a whole slew of assumptions. "Sure," I said, because why the hell not spend my Saturday having sex? I could swing by the drycleaners and do my stupid shit some other time.

I grabbed my keys and saw that my phone was dead, so I plugged it in to charge. My sex haze had made me forgetful. I grabbed my bag and was out of the door and on the streets of the city. The crisp fall air welcomed me and a maintenance man from the building next door sprayed down the sidewalk leading into his building. He cut the stream from the hose as I stopped and said a cheerful, "Good morning."

The deli was busy, and I waited in line for the cooks then placed my order. While they prepared his *three* sandwiches, I grabbed a pre-made juice and a granola mix for me. I found a blue toothbrush and plucked it off the metal loop in the toiletry isle. I was sure I had one of those goofy Saturday morning smiles on my face and me ordering that much food was also probably a dead giveaway that I'd gotten laid the night before.

That stupid fluttering energy where suddenly the birds sang prettier and it was impossible to see the filth and grime in the city tingled around me like a child's fairy tale. Everyone was attractive. The black hairnet on the cook behind the counter was an accessory, not a safety precaution. The dad who snapped at his toddler had probably just gotten terrible news and didn't mean it. The smell of bacon was healthy.

Yeah. A couple of orgasms, a rock-hard body and a little bit of charm had me crushing hard. I was doomed. I just hoped my brain could keep me from picking out China patterns or doodling his name on my press briefs.

"Miss?" The man behind the counter jutted the paper bag in my direction and something told me it wasn't the first time he'd tried to get my attention.

"Sorry." I cringed. "Thanks."

I took the bag and headed for the cashier. My eyes naturally wandered to the headlines. Normally, I would have checked them all online while I sipped my coffee. But my head had been in the clouds for twelve hours, and I wasn't myself.

Mitch from *The Times* had a byline where he whined about Demsey's lack of transparency and the photo next to it was a taped-off subway station in Queens. That was a bit of a dick move, because that particular station had been closed for major cleaning and it had only been for twenty-four hours. *No questions for Mitch on Monday.*

I moved down to *The Scoop*. It was more of a gossip rag than proper informative news. The cover was a dark and grainy photo but the headline stopped my heart. *Stepson and Sammie* and in smaller print, *Mayor's Press Sec in Family Affair.*

No fucking way.

I looked closer at the picture, and sure enough, it was me—and Anton had his hand up my fucking dress. My face was blurry, but the location was very much in front of Sophia Myers' brownstone. *Motherfucking paparazzi.*

The man with the toddler nudged me from behind. "You're up, blondie." Okay, he was just an asshole. I shot him a dirty look and he just rolled his eyes, but I placed my items on the counter and the clerk rang me up.

"Anything else?" she asked.

"Yeah, I'll take this paper." I reach down and showed her the back of *The Scoop*, then tucked it under my arm. My walk back to the apartment was swifter, and the stank of vomit and urine was all around me. Next to the dumpsters in an alley, a homeless man in a tattered brown coat slept on a sheet of cardboard and his dark green stocking hat had fallen off, revealing his thick, greasy gray hair.

I couldn't get inside fast enough and thumb-punched my floor in the elevator several times. I dug out my keys and juggled breakfast as I opened the door. Anton sat on the couch. He'd gotten dressed and his smile fell as he recognized my panic.

"You need to eat and leave." I placed the bag on the counter then flipped through the paper. Jesus, it was a two-page spread of pictures — one of me walking out, the next of me waiting alone then of him behind me, the cover again but crisper, where you could really see the outlines of our faces then finally us getting into the town car.

Anton stood, calm. He walked over to the counter, slowly opened the bag and took out his first sandwich. After he'd swallowed his first bite, he said, "Whatcha got there?"

"The end of my career. God, I'm so fucking stupid. Why would I let you touch me in public? Fuck."

"Hmmm…" He tore off another bit of his sandwich then washed it down with coffee. "That feels like an insult again." Anton moved around the counter and peered over my shoulder. "I know you're smarter than me and went to college and all that shit, so maybe you can explain to me why this is a problem."

He had to be joking. My ass was on the cover of the local gossip paper. My reputation and credibility would be tarnished for life. The anxiety in my chest moved up my throat and it was if I was being strangled from the inside out.

Anton moved back to the bag. Where had the first sandwich gone? "Why is it even news? So you hooked up with a man? Who the fuck cares?"

"Not just a man. *You*." Why didn't he understand the gravity of this? I scrubbed my face and groaned.

He took the plastic lid off his coffee again and sipped. He was entirely too fucking composed. It was annoying.

"Me because I'm your boss' stepson or me because of something else?"

I looked away. He didn't understand — or maybe he did too well.

"You knew who I was from day one. Now somebody finds out we spent a night together and you're ashamed? What does that say about you and your motives?" He crossed his arms and lifted his eyebrows.

"I don't have any motives. You don't see the big picture. This hurts my credibility. If I'm part of the story, I can't control the narrative. It takes the spotlight off Demsey and puts it on me. How do you think Mr. Attention Seeker is going to like that?"

"You say you don't have motives. Fine. Prove it to me. Otherwise, last night was all bullshit and you were just playing me to get closer to your boss. I'll be sure to mention that to my mother." He unwrapped his third sandwich and took a huge bite.

I walked over to my phone. There were thirty missed calls and endless texts asking for comments. I scrolled a bit and stopped at Mitch from *The Times*. He'd seen me earlier in the week when I'd left the debate with Anton after his particularly possessive display.

Hey. Heads up. I have an old friend at The Scoop. *You're going to want to get up early and get in front of their cover. Also, didn't come from me. Good luck.*

Anton finished his coffee and threw away the grease-stained papers and empty cup. He held up the yogurt cup and asked, "You gonna eat this?"

"Eventually."

He frowned and dug in the bag for his new toothbrush then headed down the hall.

I gathered all my courage and prayed I still had a job. I dialed Demsey and he picked up on the third ring.

"Hey, Sammie, Sophia and I were just talking about you two."

Us two? One night and we were a couple?

"I know. I'm sorry. I wasn't trying to keep anything from you. It just sorta happened. The vultures will move on, and they might even forget about it by Monday. I'll take care of it." I bit my lip.

"Well, don't bury it too deep. We think it's great, actually. Anton dating the likes of you? You're Ivy League. This does wonders for his credibility. We're happy for you. Besides, this gives you a good reason to be at all the rallies. It's a win-win, as far as I'm concerned. We're headed out to brunch. I'll see you at the office on Monday." He hung up.

I shot a quick text to Fanny, asking her to kill me with fire and adding a crying emoji then put down my phone.

It was all a little rushed. I didn't even know how I officially felt about Anton. Yes, I liked him. Yes, I'd enjoyed our night. But that didn't mean I was publicly ready to be his girlfriend—or anyone's, for that matter.

I walked over to my couch, plopped down and stared out of the window. I didn't know how much time had passed, but Anton eventually came and sat next to me.

"Hey, this doesn't change what we said before you left. Did I want to announce it to the entire city? Not like this with me groping you on the cover of *The Scoop*. But it's not a sex tape, for fuck's sake."

I let out a long exhale and cut my eyes to him. "Your mother and Demsey are through the moon."

"Can you blame them? I snagged the most eligible woman in the city. They're proud of me."

His attempt to draw me back in might have been working—but then again, he didn't have to face the press for a living. What was he going to do for a job, anyway? Maybe I could convince him to be a fireman or a cop. That would stop the rumors about his past. Though, to his credit, his rap sheet was clean since his eighteenth birthday. I'd checked.

"You wanna get out of the city? I have a cabin in the Catskills. One night with no expectations."

Wow. He really was trying his best to be swoony. I almost missed his arrogant side. But a little break from the grind and stank of the city sounded pretty fucking nice. And he'd proven he could control himself—somewhat. Besides, when I'd left the apartment earlier, I was practically skipping at the chance of more sex with him. Maybe it would lead to nothing, but if my boss was happy about it, and now the entire city knew about it, I might as well give it a go.

"That sounds nice."

"Good. I'll run home and be back in an hour." He stood up and put on his jacket. "If you have any normal shoes, there are some nice hiking trails."

"I have my running shoes."

He grinned. "I knew your ass was firm for a reason."

Chapter Ten

Anton

Two birds and one stone was my kind of plan. My mother was downright giddy that I was taking Samantha away. She had the cook prepare a meal and had gone down to the wine cellar herself to select the perfect bottle. I'd never seen her so ecstatic. It didn't suit her at all.

I called Samantha from the street where I was double-parked in front of her building. I had to admit that being with her was easy. The women I'd slept with in Covington had always wanted something from me. Status and money had made that world go round. Samantha certainly didn't need either one of those. Was it possible she liked me for *me*? That seemed improbable, but why else would she have agreed to a last-minute weekend getaway? If it had just been for the sex, we could have stayed at her place. Jesus, I hoped she wasn't catching some feels for me. Then again, what the fuck did I care?

But a tiny part of me had felt bad for her. She was sophisticated, and half of her ass was on the front cover of the paper. That had to be a level of humiliation that hit hard for someone like her.

Samantha opened the car door and startled me. "Hey, nice ride." She tossed her bag in the back and held a thin silver laptop under her arm. "I know it's kinda rude, but if I work in the car on the way up, I won't feel guilty about not doing it later."

"As long as you kiss me hello, you can do whatever you want." I winked at her. *Damn, I'm winking now? What the fuck, Myers?*

She climbed in and quickly pecked my cheek. Was she afraid someone was looking?

"That's all I get?"

After a long blink, she buckled up and turned to me. "I'm a little overwhelmed by all this. I've gone from being a single professional to a slutty opportunist in twelve hours. According to my boss, I'm dating you now and I don't know—" She let out a little huff. "I always thought I would have some kind of say in that."

Fair enough, she could have her out. "No one's forcing you to go Upstate with me."

"Just drive."

I cranked the engine and eased off the clutch as I pulled into traffic. So we were moving too fast for her. Yeah, well, me fucking too. At least she was honest about it.

I let her have her quiet to cool off. I might not be an expert on gentle, but I could do silence. The only problem was that if we were officially dating in the eyes of my mother, I was going to need to do romantic shit—in public. *Fucking hell.*

About an hour into the drive, she'd taken off her shoes and was sitting cross-legged in the passenger seat, typing away on her computer at an impressive pace. She'd barely stopped since we'd crossed the bridge. I had to admit I kinda liked the fact that she wasn't fawning all over me.

"There's this great pizza place in Poughkeepsie, if you want to stop for lunch."

She stopped typing and looked at me with amazement. "Are you talking about Bella's?"

I glanced over, confused. "How do you know about Bella's?"

"I went to school in Poughkeepsie. Oh my God, I haven't thought about that place in years. One hundred percent yes, I want to stop and get a slice there. My mouth is already watering."

I grinned as I hit the gas and passed a minivan. Maybe this dating thing wouldn't be that hard after all. I tried to think if I knew what college was in Poughkeepsie but drew a blank until we pulled off the highway.

Vassar. She'd worn the sweatshirt when she was trying hard not to be pretty on our first date. Sounded like some high-class bullshit for sure. No wonder why she wasn't jumping on my dick like other chicks.

We pulled into the parking lot of Bella's and got out of the car.

"Oh my God, Anton. Seriously. This might just be making my shitty day somewhat okay." She grinned from ear to ear and through their wooden double doors. No lie, there was a little sting that I was the reason for her shitty day.

We were led to a booth in the back, and when the hostess offered us menus, Samantha waved her hand.

"I know exactly what I'm having." She wiggled her fingers and her eyes lit up. I had to admit it was a side of her I didn't expect to see.

I gestured to refuse the menu as well. "I'm good."

The hostess smiled and tucked the menus under her arm. "Well, I can go ahead and take your order then. The kitchen closes in twenty minutes." She looked at Samantha and raised her eyebrows.

"Napoli, extra crispy, and a glass of the Valpolicella."

I pulled back. She couldn't have. I was officially spooked. The waitress turned to me with the same eager but friendly look. "The same, but a glass of seltzer."

"I'll be right back with the drinks."

As soon as she left the table I crossed my arms. "You eat stinky pizza?"

She smiled and I wondered if I could take any credit for her joy. "I love stinky pizza. I've never met anyone else who wasn't Italian who liked it. Why do you like it?"

I puffed out a breath. "My best friend growing up was Italian. He dared me to try it once and I ended up loving it. Plus, it's a way of eating pizza without feeling bad about the cheese. What about you?"

"My girlfriends and I decided that we would try everything on the menu here." She shrugged. "I liked that the best."

The drinks came and we clinked our glasses. It was possible that I was actually enjoying myself. *Who am I?*

"Damn. This takes me back. Thank you. I needed this." She sipped her wine and looked around the restaurant.

"What were you like, back then?"

She shook her head. "Such a snob. So fucking pretentious. Entitled. What about you?"

"Me? I didn't go to college. I was a social deviant — dice games in back alleys, fights…lots of fights." What I wouldn't do to get into one and let off some of my steam. Then again, the sex had helped. Maybe I was finding a new avenue…

"And yet you never got arrested."

"Oh, I got arrested."

She frowned. "But you have no record."

It was a little unsettling that she knew that, but then again, it was probably part of her job.

"Yeah, Ma wiped that shit clean years ago, right before she sent me off to Covington." The memory of her telling me I had to prove myself before I could take over played out in my head. At the time, I'd been pissed. I was young and cocky and thought I could handle anything. But she'd been right, as she usually was. I'd gone from the easy life of fucking around without consequences to one of the shittiest neighborhoods in the city with no credibility and no real experience. She'd cut me off for an entire year and wouldn't even take my calls. My crew and I had built a good business until we all got tired and sloppy.

The pizzas came and Samantha ordered another glass of wine. When it was halfway gone, her eyelids looked a little heavier and her demeanor was more relaxed. There was a quarter of her pizza left and she sat back and tapped her stomach.

"I can't put anything more in." She shoved the round pizza plate in my direction. "Knock yourself out."

"I'm surprised you got that much down, to be honest. What are you like a buck-o-five?" I took the pizza, folded it in half and bit in. No Napoli would be wasted on my watch.

She bubbled out a laugh. "Have you ever dated a woman before?"

I searched around the table for the right answer. I was pretty sure the honest one was a bad idea.

"I mean... I had regular...err..." Talking about my sex life was not going to be good for me. *Shit.*

"So far you've asked me about my money and my weight. Those are two very serious no-nos in dating. You kinda suck at this." She looked away, confused. "Oh my God. And I went out and bought your breakfast this morning. *I* kinda suck at this."

I swallowed down another bite. I was already more than halfway through the slice. "And yet you're still here. Must mean I do other things well."

"You have confidence. I'll give you that. I'm going to use the restroom before we go. You can spend the free time thinking about another out-of-bounds question." She slid out of the booth and I finished the pizza. I flagged over the waitress and settled the check.

On Samantha's way back, I took her in. Jesus, those jeans fit her like a second skin and I remembered that I knew exactly what she had on underneath, how fucking soft she was. She was right. I didn't know shit about dating a woman like her.

I stood and cracked my neck. "You ready?" I asked when she was in front of me.

"Yeah. Thanks for this." She tapped my chest and smiled softly. "It was perfect."

"Maybe I don't suck at dating after all."

"No. You suck."

We said our thank-yous and goodbyes to the staff and climbed back into the Jag.

After she buckled up, she dropped her head back and groaned. "Why did you let me day drink? And red. I'm too buzzed to work."

"Oh no." I faked shock and started the car. "Now you'll have to talk to me. Tell me stories and shit." I shifted into reverse and backed out of the spot.

"Or I could listen. You could tell me something about you and your previously wayward path."

It was cute that she thought I was done with being a criminal, like I was going to start a youth club, take in dealers and thieves under my reformed wing and teach them how to channel their angst into boxing or delivering food to old people. But I didn't think she wanted to hear about how, after my mother had left me to my own devices, I'd contacted my dad's sister, who'd helped me find a meth cook in Canada, and my drug dealing days had begun. Or how I made my crew fight me every morning to make them tougher. Those were secrets I planned to keep.

So instead of being honest, I got all serious and said, "I'd rather not talk about my past."

"Fair enough." Samantha offered a sympathetic smile. "Let's talk about your future then."

"Oh, God. Are you sure you don't have an email to answer or something?"

"I'm serious. It's pretty exciting when you think about it. You can do anything. I mean, you have resources, and when Demsey wins the election, you'll have plenty of connections."

I'd never considered the possibility that Samantha was naïve, but it was either that or the wine had really gotten the best of her. Or maybe she was just like my mother — trying to make me legit enough to become respectable. Any way I sliced her future pie, it was annoying.

Why did everyone want to fucking change me? I clenched my jaw.

"I have a meeting with a headhunter next week. I'm going to tell him how I succeeded in getting an entire neighborhood strung out on drugs and convinced my best friends to deal for me. Pretty sure the offers are going to pile in." The snark in my tone cut deeper with every word.

Her smile fell and she looked out of the window. But what had she expected?

The formerly welcome silence between us grew thick with tension that I'd been a dick. After five minutes, I couldn't take it anymore.

Softer, I said, "Look. I'm sorry. You don't think I think about shit like that? I lost my entire life. Everyone I thought had my back did...then didn't. I'm twenty-eight years old and have never had a job. Who is going to hire me?"

She finally turned to me. "Why do you think you need to get hired?"

I let her question hang in the air as I merged back onto the highway. Samantha gazed out of the window at the rolling hills. All the points I'd scored with Bella's had disappeared. I'd shown her a small glimpse of who I was, and it wasn't up to her standards. She was probably regretting the trip. *Fuck.*

My sharp tongue was creating a canyon between us. As much as I didn't want to ask the question, I did. "What do you suggest?"

She smiled, and for some stupid fucking reason that was seriously pissing me off, I was relieved.

"Well, it depends on what you want, but real estate is pretty damn easy. You wouldn't believe the idiots the zoning people deal with. Not that you're dumb... Sorry... I didn't mean it like that." She shook her head.

"You know, this morning you called me a princess and now you're insulting my intelligence. You're really starting to chip away at my ego." I winked again, happy that we'd recovered from the small bump.

"That's like saying I stole a snowflake off a Swiss Alp."

"Funny." I flipped the blinker and exited for the little town where I had my cabin. My only problem would be finding an excuse to meet my cook.

Samantha commented on the houses with matching mailboxes and number of hunting supply stores until I drove down the tree-lined road to my place. The leaves had changed to orange, yellow and a deep red. It was an impressive little path.

The crisp, clean air was a welcome reminder of why I liked my little escape out of the city. I'd always picked up the drugs myself and had never once told my crew the identity of my cook. That was the deal I'd struck with her, and I'd honored it.

I led Samantha to the front porch and punched in the security code. Rafa's voice rang in my head that I should change it. Not that it mattered... There was nothing to take anymore.

She went in first and dropped her bag on the couch while she spun around and took it in. I set the box of food and wine on the counter and wondered how I could slip away. I'd turned up the thermostat from my phone before I'd left the city, and while it wasn't cold, the air still had a bite to it. I crossed the room to the fireplace and crumpled up newspaper before stacking the small sticks of kindling on top.

Samantha rubbed her upper arms. *Yeah, a fire will be good.* Plus, it always calmed people's mood. Hell, maybe she would even consider it romantic.

"Your place is beautiful, Anton. Thanks for getting me out of the city."

I hadn't expected the compliment or the sincerity in her voice, but it was nice. I liked making her happy. *Fucking weird.*

"Feel free to look around. You can even snoop in my medicine cabinet. There's nothing really exciting to find."

Her gaze wandered around the A-frame and settled on the stairs to the loft.

"Go for it. There's a sunken tub up there that's pretty spectacular."

She headed for the stairs and I made my way back to the kitchen and slipped my burner phone into my back pocket. I dug through the utility drawer, found the corkscrew and buried it in the bottom of the trash then started to put the food in the fridge.

"Holy shit. This place is heaven." Samantha jogged down the stairs, her blonde hair bouncing on her shoulders. "How often do you come up here?"

"As much as I can. But you know what I just realized?"

She moved over to the fire and added a log then looked up at me.

"I don't have a bottle opener. I don't think I've ever drank wine up here." It was a lie. When we used to spend the night, Leo would insist on a bottle of Italian wine whenever he came.

I continued, "I think I'm out of toilet paper too. I'll just run into town and be right back. Do you mind staying? Now that we've started the fire..."

"Are you kidding?" She curled up on the couch and reached for the fur throw-blanket. "I'm in heaven."

When I got to the main road, I pulled into a church parking lot and dialed my cook. We'd already set the date, so I knew she was in town waiting for me.

"I can be anywhere in fifteen minutes," I said. We didn't bother with hellos or goodbyes.

"Bus station."

I hung up and drove to the station then got my gym bag full of money out of the trunk. There was a row of benches outside and I sat down and placed the bag under the seat then opened a game on my phone that I only ever played when I picked up drugs.

My cook was the most normal looking forty-year-old woman on the planet. Her dark hair was a bobbed mom-do, and her turtleneck sweater was tight and revealed a little muffin top. She wasn't ugly, just not the kind of woman anyone would look at twice. Her messenger bag was black and completely uni-sex and she stored it on the bench between us before she sat down on the other side. From a distance, it would be impossible to know which bag belonged to whom.

When I'd had a crew, whoever was on the job with me would honk and pick me up at that point. But alone, I would have to wait until a bus came and get lost in the crowd. I could only hope that Samantha's wine would make her drowsy and she wouldn't get worried about how long I was gone.

My cook — Jackson used to call her 'Cookie' because we didn't know her real name — answered a call on her phone and said, "Oh shit. I'm at the wrong station. Sorry, honey. I'll be there in twenty minutes. Hold tight." She took the bag with the money and hurried away.

I waited another five minutes but the station was deserted, so I grabbed my drugs and walked back to my car, where I stored the bag under the spare tire in the trunk. The solitude struck me, but what was I going to do? Whine to my mommy that she'd taken away all my friends and toys? *Fuck that.*

I slammed the trunk and did a final look around. Off season, Upstate was really the best time and place to smuggle drugs.

Chapter Eleven

Samantha

A rhythmic and faint tapping repeated over and over woke me from a much-needed nap. Red wine at lunch had always been a bad idea for me. A six-pack of toilet paper sat on the counter and a door was open at the end of the kitchen. The fire was still going — Anton must have added a log — and the fall sun was setting. There was warm lighting all around.

I stretched out on the couch. That morning my life had been catapulted forward, but the sleepy afternoon had taken it back to a more comfortable pace. I stood, my head still a little foggy, and went to the fridge for some water. The tapping was coming from the open door and I walked over. A narrow staircase took me into a perfect mancave of a basement. There was a pool table and a gym in one open space to the left and a spare room and bathroom to the right. A heavy boxing bag hung from the ceiling and Anton's punches into it were the sound I'd been searching for.

He was shirtless, had in wireless headphones and was beating the shit out of the poor bag. The raw power of his muscles was almost as impressive as the choreographed flow of his movements. But something else struck me—his danger. He was the farthest thing from a nice boy from a respectable neighborhood that I could find—but apparently, I was dating.

Anton glanced over at me for a long beat. A shiver ran up my spine. I'd been so wrapped up in his charisma that I'd failed to see the actual threat of a man like him. I played games with politicians and words. Anton's physical intensity could kill someone. It probably already had. His piercing eyes stopped me in my tracks and pinned a claim on my soul. He looked back to the bag and hit it harder, moved even faster.

It was a message—one that should have scared the shit out of me and had me running out of that house and back to the city, but it drew me in instead. What he had was rare. And even if he used me up and spit me out, I knew I would regret it if I didn't try to get closer to him. It would mean giving him what he wanted, which was everything.

Because that was what men in power were like. They were never sated and were eternally thirsty for more. Their drive was relentless. It was also what attracted me to them most. I longed to be the woman who motivated and inspired behind the scenes. I knew I didn't have the spark it took to convince people to follow me, but Anton did. He'd already proven it in Covington. His mother was molding him to be bigger than Demsey—and way, more wicked.

I slowly made my retreat, and upstairs, I dug my phone out of my purse. As I scrolled through the messages, there was one from my mother that read, *That was unexpected.*

Yeah, no shit.

I called Fanny and she answered right away.

"Where are you? God. Finally. Should I bring vodka and ice cream?"

"Hi. No, I'm fine. I decided to go Upstate."

"Alone?" She drew out the word and practically sang it.

I was pretty sure Anton still had his headphones in but I didn't want to take the chance of him hearing my girl talk, so I slipped out of the back door. *Jesus, he has a pool, too?* It was a bachelor's paradise.

"No. I'm with him. Fucking Demsey and Sophia are ready for us to get married. They're probably naming our children as we speak."

"Hmmm. And what do *you* think about it?"

I wasn't quite ready to admit to her what I thought about it. "I think the shittiest paper in the city used my ass for profit."

"Half your ass. And you had on wicked sexy stockings. What I don't get is why there was a pap there anyway. Who the fuck cares about a dinner party?"

I hadn't thought of that. The one time I got felt up in public and there was a dude with a long lens ready to click away? I'd been so caught up in what it meant that I'd failed to search why. *God, I love Fanny.*

She laughed. "You know Mitch is whacking wood right now."

"*Eww.* He sent me a text."

"Gross."

Anton crossed the living room and disappeared up his stairs. So far I'd fallen asleep on his couch, spied on him working out and was chatting on the phone with my bestie. I wasn't exactly rude, but I wasn't sending the right signals. *What are the right signals, anyway?*

I continued, "Actually, Mitch gave me a heads-up and said it wasn't him. I just didn't see the text in time."

Fanny hummed. "Why would you have thought it was him?"

"He saw us after the debate. Anton was all alpha male-y."

The air had changed and there was a damp coolness to it. A chill ran up my spine, reminding me I had no coat and was barefoot.

"Oh, Sammie, I think you may have done the one thing for me to lose respect for you. You're attracted to assholes."

"I know." I sighed. "Blame my daddy issues."

I walked toward the door and wiped the dust from my feet. But she was wrong. I was attracted to power.

"I need to go. I'll see you Monday."

"Love you."

"Same. Thanks for the ear." I went back inside and stored my phone in my bag. The spray from the shower echoed in the A-frame. I climbed the stairs, already unbuttoning my blouse. I tossed all my clothes on a chair and didn't bother knocking on the bathroom door. The shower was huge but Anton's thick body managed to take up all the space.

He spotted me and a crooked, smug grin formed on his face.

I stared him in the eyes. "Do you swear on your mother that you're clean?"

"Why?"

"Because I have an IUD and I think I got dirty outside." I bit my bottom lip, sealing the innuendo tight.

"How dirty?" His calm whisper shot to my center and warmth spread deep inside me.

"*Very* dirty." My tone was like I was telling him a dark secret, but it was just as leveled as his own.

There was a slight narrowing of his eyes before he scanned over my body.

"Then I swear I am clean—and you better get your ass in here."

I stepped into the steam and the hot water splashed my legs. I stood in front of him and my heart thumped so hard that it was pulsating between my ears.

We were moving forward at a speed that was bound to make us crash. But how else would I expect things to play out with a man like him? The second he'd decided to make me his, I was done for. There would be no long walks on the beach or heart-to-hearts where we talked about feelings. We were together and would be until one of us burned to the ground.

He might never love me, but as long as he wanted me, he would never let anyone else near me. That glance he'd given me downstairs had said it all. Even if I'd wanted to run away from him, he would find me. He would convince me to kiss him and I would. His draw was too compelling for me to deny, too intense to ignore. So why bother?

The night before he'd proven he could be trusted, but the fire inside him was bound to escape. And the truth was, I wanted to dance in the flames. I hungered to be burned, engulfed by his power, consumed by his essence. But more, I craved giving in to him physically, showing him he could do as he wished.

I dropped to my knees in front of him and took him into my mouth. I didn't object when he grabbed my hair and thrust deeper into my throat to the point of me almost gagging. No, I wouldn't do that. Instead, I sucked harder on his cock and tugged more on his balls. It was lust in its rawest form, total surrender and total control — and exactly what he needed.

He yanked my head off him and pulled me up. I intuitively knew to brace myself against the wall. He worked my clit and I'd never come so fast in my life. I screamed through the release and he was inside me before the final waves of my orgasm had finished. Mr. 'Gentle' was long fucking gone. Anton pounded into me at a punishing pace. It hurt, but I'd never felt more alive in my life. The palms of my hands burned from the friction of the tile grout and I was sure there would be bruises on my hips from how hard he was grabbing me. He slipped a finger into my ass and swore under his breath. I welcomed the intrusion. The pleasure blended with the knowledge that he was doing what he wanted to me. I'd given in to him, and in that moment, I wondered why I'd ever resisted.

I clamped my eyes shut to stop the room from spinning. The questions pestering my mind about why I was so eager for all of it would need to wait. Reflection and instincts never went hand in hand. Contemplation and speculation could wait. We were answering an impulsive and primitive call inside both of us.

Besides, what would be the point in denying him? I may have wanted his control more than he did. He smacked my ass and I fucking loved it. I whimpered and screamed through his addictive punishment, not caring that he might be ripping me apart.

He grabbed my shoulder and pushed the deepest he'd been then let out a cry suited for battle. I gasped for air and came crashing back to earth. He pulled out and I supported myself against the tiled wall, my chest heaving.

"Shit," he muttered under his breath, "I—"

"Don't apologize. I wanted it." I stepped under the spray and let the warmth cover me. He didn't move, as if he were waiting for me to scold him. But he wouldn't get that from me. I'd made a calculated move. I'd let him show his true colors, and I didn't want him ashamed of them.

After I washed, I passed in front of him and he let out a throaty sigh. He grabbed my wrist before I could step out of the shower. His eyes cut through me, but I held the gaze.

"Why did you let me do that?"

"So that you knew you could."

He stared over my shoulder for a few breaths but didn't release his grip. Then he pulled me into him and wrapped one arm around my waist and the other one up my back. He studied my face, searching deeper for a lie he wouldn't find. My breasts were pushing against his torso and I closed my eyes, afraid he might do it all again—and at the same time, hungry that he would.

He brought his lips to mine, kissed me in such a tender way it was shocking, then said in my ear, "This complicates everything, sunshine." He let me go but didn't look at me while he rinsed off.

I stepped out of the shower and was glad the mirror was fogged up so I couldn't see my reflection. I'd crossed a line, but my instincts had never failed me. If I wanted to play the long game, I needed the real him, not some pretty version his mother liked to put on display. He had to trust me, and that started with proving I could accept his inner demons. But that wasn't why I couldn't look myself in the face. The bitter truth was that I'd lapped up everything he had to give.

He reached for a towel and said, "Take your time. I'll heat up dinner."

I nodded and pressed my lips together. When he was gone, I sat on the toilet with my head in my hands for a long time until I told myself to get up, get dressed and enjoy the evening and following day. Monday was going to be a bitch. I had a meeting with the chief in the morning and a campaign rally at night. I owed myself a little break from thinking about work and Demsey.

The thought of tight jeans sent a chill up my spine and I was grateful for the forgiving fabric of my yoga pants and sports bra. I found a hoodie in Anton's closet and its clean smell was another comfort. I didn't bother with my hair and just wrapped it up in a bun, then headed down to the living room.

Two wine glasses sat on the island of his kitchen, each half full with a burgundy promise of solace. Anton's back was to me and he reached for plates in an overhead cabinet.

I lifted a glass then stopped before taking a sip. "I thought you said you didn't drink wine up here." Someone who'd thought to buy wine glasses was surely someone who'd thought to buy a corkscrew.

"Huh?" He turned around and shrugged. "Oh, right. Actually, you're right. There was a guy on my crew — the stinky pizza one — who'd drink wine here sometimes. But he always opened it with his Swiss Army knife." Anton walked over to the table where the silverware and water glasses were already in place.

I took a drink and wondered why he was lying to me about something so trivial. He'd needed to do something away from me but shopping for a bottle opener and some toilet paper was definitely not it. After what I'd just done for him and the piece of me I'd sacrificed and would never get back, he still didn't trust me. Fair enough… It was all new. But that didn't mean I was going to let him off that easily.

"I don't believe you."

"It's a fucking corkscrew, Samantha. Drop it."

After the day I'd had, I didn't want to pick a fight, so I put on a smile and walked over to the table. "You're suddenly very domestic. I'm not sure this bodes well for your reputation."

"I'm counting on you keeping secrets." His smile was slight, but his gaze said it all. There it was. He was asking for my loyalty.

I sat down and crossed my ankles under the chair then slowly put down my wine glass. "That's my specialty."

He studied me then turned back to the kitchen, the subject officially dropped and ball in my court.

"That was pretty impressive earlier. Who taught you how to fight?" I changed the subject.

Anton brought over a roasted chicken and began to carve it. "Everybody. I had one guy — stinky pizza again — he taught me shit that took it from being physical to making it deliberate. Changed everything for me. White or dark?" He paused his carving.

He was letting me in, perhaps a tiny reward for earlier or dropping the mention of the corkscrew.

"Dark. You sound a little like you miss him. You got feelings inside that massive chest of yours?" I teased as I held out my plate.

"Don't count on it." He served me the chicken and some salad. "It's purely selfish. I hate being alone — 'only child' syndrome. You think I should see a shrink? It's possible I have anger issues, too."

"Hadn't noticed." I waited for his plate to be as full as mine before cutting into the chicken. Dancing around subjects was something I was particularly good at and apparently so was he. But he had something I didn't, an added layer of allure. I understood why he'd been the leader of his crew. Man, woman, animal — we were all drawn to him.

He smiled over at me and it was warm, sincere. There wasn't a trace of a lie in it.

Shit. He'd completely sucked me in.

Chapter Twelve

Anton

The drive back to the city allowed for reflection. Although Samantha was sitting next to me, she was working again and it was almost like being alone. For once, I didn't mind. She'd surrendered to the wild attraction between us, but in doing so had awakened a beast she wouldn't be able to tame. Maybe she understood corruption, but I was capable of far worse.

My phone dinged, and when I saw it was from my mother, I asked Samantha to read it. That would show a little trust and keep her believing that she was somehow a new part of my inner circle. Little did she know that circle was a party of one.

"She's inviting us to dinner. Well, inviting is a generous way to put it. It literally says, *Dinner is at seven. See you and Samantha then.*" Samantha placed my phone back on the leather console between us.

"She's subtle."

"Huh. Kinda reminds me of someone..." She tapped her finger on her cheek. "Can't think of who, though."

Samantha's little teasing was becoming a problem. Hell, everything about her was a fucking problem. I thought she was cute and sexy and gorgeous and smart and fucking everything I could possibly ever want in a woman. It was driving me fucking crazy. If I didn't know better, I would have said I was crushing on her—which would have meant that I'd sniffed glue or something. I did *not* get crushes.

Then again, I didn't take chicks I fucked on long walks in the woods, either. But I'd done that earlier in the day. And if I were brutally honest with myself, I would have to admit to enjoying it. I blamed getting shot. A brush with death had turned me soft. *Fucking hell.*

"Jesus. Lighten up. I was just kidding," she said, shaking her head, then went back to typing.

"What?"

She sent me a side-eye with her eyebrows raised. "You have a serious resting bitch face. One little jab and you frown like I just stole all your candy."

"I was thinking about something else. Sorry." *Sorry? Jesus Christ.* I was going to need a break from this woman to get my shit together. Problem was, I wasn't sure I would know how to do that.

The taste I'd had of her made me greedy for more. And sharing was out of the fucking question—which led me to an entirely different problem. In Covington, I hadn't needed to tell girls that they were only for me. My crew—with the exception of fucking Leo and my sick competitive streak—would have never dreamed of approaching a girl who I was with. And those girls did anything to be in that position. Me and my crew were the only glimpse of nice some of them had ever seen.

The real world? I had no fucking clue.

What if Samantha met someone else? Like a billionaire banker-fuck who had a house in the Hamptons and drank martinis. What would I do?

Kill him. I would probably kill him. I nodded. I could do that.

A lack of typing made me glance over at Samantha. She was staring at me with a furrowed forehead and skeptical gaze.

"I do *not* want to know what's going on inside your head."

For fuck's sake, she was going to make me fucking say it. "You know this is..." What was the fucking word? "Exclusive, right?" I could have thrown up in my own lap.

She laughed and it wasn't fake, the little shit. "Oh my God." She covered her mouth, and her eyes were watering. "That's what pissed you off? That you're afraid I'd date someone else at the same time as you?" She laughed again and I frowned. This was the farthest thing from funny. "You made it pretty clear when you saw me talking to Mitch that you are the possessive, jealous type. Don't worry. I kinda like it."

"I don't like that guy."

She laughed again. "You don't like anyone. You barely like me and we're *exclusive*." Samantha air quoted the last word and I gave her a dirty look before turning my attention back to driving.

I hated that she was right. But more, and that was the killer, I hated that she didn't think I liked her very much. After letting me do wonderfully filthy things to her and accepting the side of me she somehow knew was bound to come out, then sticking around for more, she deserved a bit of truth.

"I like you enough, sunshine."

God bless her, she didn't gloat. She just smiled and went back to typing. We pulled into the covered garage where my mother kept her cars and I handed over the keys to the valet. When Samantha reached for her bag, I told her to leave it and that I'd drive her home after. It would be a good excuse to get my drugs — and my mother would approve of the chivalry.

When we hit the sidewalk, I took her hand and thanked God that Ricci wasn't around to make fun of me. I told myself it wasn't a romantic gesture, and that it was half pride of showing I was with a woman of Samantha's caliber and half 'back the fuck up, she's with me'.

She paused when we got to the stoop at my mother's brownstone and stared at the place we'd been snapped with my hands very much on her delectable little ass.

"Hey." I gently tugged her toward me. "Don't let it get to you. So some people saw that you wear sexy underwear and kiss the guy you're dating. Big fucking deal."

She narrowed her dark eyes. They really were pretty, especially in those moments when her sincerity glimmered inside. She pinched her lips into a tight smile. "You would suck at my job."

No shit. I would suck at any job. "Ready to face an overbearing woman and a politically incorrect politician?"

"Always."

We climbed the steps and I let us in. I gave Samantha a little smack on her ass as she passed by. My mother and Demsey were in the living room. He was nursing a

Scotch and she had a smile plastered all over her face. Messaged received... She wanted us to be together. *Yeah, I got it.*

"There you two are," my mother said in a voice I hadn't heard in ages. It had a hint of pride in it. "I hope he didn't leave you alone and go for a run or hike to brood in the woods. He does that sometimes."

Samantha crossed the room and sat next to my mother. "Hardly. He didn't let me out of his sight. I'm already trying to figure out how to convince him to let me sleep alone tonight. He's just a tad overprotective." She added the gesture with her index finger and thumb.

The lie was flawless. It pointed to what some might consider a weakness in my possessiveness, and at the same time, shut down my mother's fishing expedition as to if I'd left the house without Samantha. She'd covered for me, but the whole me-not-sleeping with-her that night was laughable.

One of the help came to tell us that dinner was ready, and we made our way into the smaller dining room that we used as a family. I hadn't grown up in the brownstone. My mother had purchased it just before kicking me out and sending me to Covington. I would have to talk to her about getting my own place if she ever loosened the grip of the leash she was keeping me on. She'd said it was because she couldn't bear the thought of losing me, but I knew it was because she had a master plan. I seriously doubted she'd even shared it with her new husband. He was just a clueless pawn in her gradual chess game of life.

Demsey sat opposite me and the women were on both our sides. He shook out his linen napkin and draped it onto his lap. "So, you're both coming to the rally tomorrow. Yes?"

"Wouldn't miss it." Samantha smiled and took a drink of her water. Could her boss not see that she sugarcoated everything for him? *Is she doing the same thing to me?* I flashed through the weekend and questioned her every move. Why had she let me have sex with her like that? What if she was just using me to make her boss happy and get a better job or something?

We were served a soup that made me want to laugh. When my mother had taken over my father's business fifteen years prior, I'd lived on canned pasta and chips. Homemade dinners didn't work with her busy schedule. Now we had several forks, knives and spoons. She was a long way from a female bookie and single mom. But I had to hand it to her... She'd worked for it.

The day my father had been arrested, she'd filed for divorce. He couldn't beat the shit out of her from prison. She made a very public display of distancing herself from him, but in private, she'd rummaged through his crew and found men who were loyal but didn't have the ambition to be in charge. She'd paid them better than my father ever had and started paying off policemen and judges. It was years before she asked any of them for her first favor. She'd given them time to fill up their lifestyles with toys and habits she was supporting, and it only took a little convincing for them to betray their duties. The fear of losing their plush lives was too great.

Meanwhile, I had grown into an angry teenager and she'd had a hard time keeping me in line. She had always been working, and I was always fucking around. Somehow, I'd managed to finish high school, but college was very clearly not for me. I did a little bit of physical intimidation for her, but she thought it would be best if I had to learn everything on my own like she had.

The soup came and went, and Samantha was prodding my mother to see if she needed anyone to go with her to some brunch with some rich fucks at some point the following weekend. About halfway through the dinner, I realized my mother hadn't eaten much and was doing a better job of moving food around instead of putting it in her mouth. When she noticed I was watching, she took a tiny bite and smiled back to me like, 'See? Nothing to worry about'.

When I frowned, she patted me on the forearm and leaned in. "I had a late lunch."

It was a lie, but why? She suddenly struck me as frail and skinny, something she'd never been. Had all the years of stress and greed caught up to her? Would they catch up to me someday?

The plates were cleared, and Samantha said, "I really need to get home and get organized for tomorrow." She offered a small smile to my mother and her boss, then a bigger one to me. I didn't like that it made me feel better about the twinge of worry I had for my mother.

"I'll drive you." I gave a final glance to my mother then ushered Samantha out as Demsey barked for someone to get him a Scotch.

The streetlights glowed and the air was cool and moist. A storm was coming. Samantha's pace was slow, and she had her hands tucked into the pockets of her long cardigan.

"So…" She closed one eye and peeked over to me. "Since you're new to this dating thing, I thought it might be a good idea to kinda give you some tips about me."

I groaned. We were talking about this shit? What was I? Some kind of normal adult? *Fucking hell.*

She ignored my feeble protest and went on as she walked, "I work insane hours. I'm basically on call twenty-four seven. There are going to be times when I'm too busy to talk to you. You can't take that personal and get pissy."

Why wouldn't she want to take my calls? I opened my mouth to object, and she held up a finger.

"If you want this to be something, you have to let me breathe." She stopped and looked up at me with those pretty eyes — ones that were free of bullshit. "Don't get me wrong... I like your intensity, your passion, but you're a lot to take in. And this is moving at hyper-speed. So just, please, don't come barging into my office because you saw me take Mitch's question at a press conference. It will make me resent you. And even though you think you've laid some claim to me —"

I scoffed.

"Anton." She took my hand and brushed her nails over my ear. "I see you. I know what you were. I want to try this. But I'm terrified we will crash and burn."

It stung. But it wasn't like I'd given her any evidence to the contrary. Had I dated before? No. Had I been in the real world that wasn't Covington lately? Nope. Had a woman like her ever looked twice in my direction? Probably not more than for a fantasy. She was trying to help.

I frowned. "So I'm *not* spending the night?"

"Not tonight, but soon. I mean," she said while turning to continue down the street, "I'm pretty sure you've ruined me in the best possible way for other men. So what choice do I have?"

There was that sugarcoating again — feeding my ego while telling me something I didn't want to hear.

We got to the parking garage and Samantha's phone rang while we were waiting for the car to be brought around. She walked back to the sidewalk for privacy that I didn't want to give her.

The car came and I pulled out to the street where she got in, made an apologetic face and said into her phone, "How deep?"

She dropped her head back into the seat and closed her eyes as she listened.

I merged into traffic and drove across town like a fucking chauffeur. She hadn't looked at me once since we'd gotten into the car. When we arrived in front of her building, I was pissed and I understood exactly what she'd warned me about on the sidewalk.

"Hey, let me call you back in ten. I just got home and need to get organized." She turned to me. "Sorry. Water main broke and the financial district is turning into a lake. I'll see you tomorrow, right? For the rally."

"Can I ask you a question?"

She reached over the seat and heaved her bag into the front. "Yeah. Sure." She dug through her bag.

"Hey."

"Sorry, what?" She pulled out her keys and looked at me with raised eyebrows.

"Forget it." I shook my head.

She closed her eyes for a long breath. "This is exactly what I was warning you about. You can't think about this as me ignoring you. It's me doing my job. There are already two train lines down due to construction. That will make the morning commute a fucking nightmare, and although it's an accident, if we don't handle it perfectly, your stepfather's chances of being governor get smaller."

The novelty of a woman choosing anything over me was not cute or refreshing. It sucked. But far worse was that I'd let it get to me. She was right. We needed air. Samantha was taking up entirely too much real estate in my head.

"Go, then." Dammit, my tone was ice cold.

She scoffed. "Listen... Do you think I want to deal with this?"

I worked my jaw and stared forward.

"Okay." Her voice had gone calm. She reached for the door handle. "You take your time and be pissy. I'll see you tomorrow." She leaned over and kissed my cheek. "Thank you for a wonderful weekend."

There was no dramatic door slam, flipping off or huffing away. She'd made it very clear that she was the adult in the room. I would need to muzzle my selfish temper to keep her on my side.

I drove home and was happy the house was mostly dark when I walked in. In my room, I found a tattered soccer ball my mom had moved from our old place and let out a bit of the air before slicing open one of the patches and transferring my drugs inside.

Chapter Thirteen

Samantha

Gray suits were for gray days. Under the tight blazer, I wore a thin burgundy crew neck and skipped the jewelry. The security guards at the precinct gave me a doubletake and I returned it with a challenging tip of my chin. *Yeah, fuck off. You saw my ass. I have bigger problems.*

Though, I'd never been more grateful for the rusty pipes of the city. Not only was it way more important than the pictures of me and Anton, but it would also give me a proper excuse to scold reporters if they brought up my personal life.

I marched over to the elevator bay and, with my snarl, dared anyone to bring up the gossip rag's Saturday morning headline. I'd straightened my hair and parted it down the middle, and when it fell in front of my face, I tucked it behind my ear. I had nothing to hide.

On the chief's floor, there was a catcall or two, but all chatter ceased when he popped his head out the door and leveled his eyes over the sea of desks. He waved me in, and I sat in my normal chair to the right.

"Wouldn't want to be you today, Sammie."

"Shitty pipes are my new best friend." I let out a quick exhale through my mouth.

"I bet. Whatcha got for me?"

"Dan Forbes on the City Council is pushing for a later retirement age."

Jack's face soured like he'd sucked a lemon. Every now and again a local do-gooder would get some political momentum and try to throw a tire iron in our well-oiled machine of bribes and favors. I didn't like it any more than he did. My boss had his hand in so many cookie jars that I sometimes had to sit him down and remind him the consequences of throwing his brother a construction job, for example.

"You need to make that go away."

"I know. Just throw it back to me. I'll messy it up with hope then remind them that these people are risking their lives for us. They'll call bullshit, but don't worry. I'll handle it. Trust me, the last thing the mayor needs is to be on your shit list."

Jack raised his bushy eyebrows in a 'ain't that the truth' expression then frowned. "I gotta tell you something."

Whatever it was, it wasn't going to be good. Jack had that stern look on his face. "The boys uptown say that without your new boyfriend patrolling his streets, shit's gone a little wild. Seemed they actually left him alone because there was some order to it. The rival gangs were kept in check."

"And now?" My tone was flat, I didn't need him to coddle me.

"Shit's a three-ring circus. Rapes are up, abductions are up and overdoses are skyrocketing. Civilians are calling in crimes more than ever because they have nowhere else to turn."

"Okay…"

Jack leaned back in his chair and the springs squeaked below him. "When criminals get cocky, they tend to get sloppy. From what I understand, the new guy in charge isn't as smart as Myers and might still seek to retaliate for losing some of his crew in that shooting you so conveniently covered up."

"So you're saying he's in danger?" I played through the ways Anton could be taken out. Unless the new guy uptown had a sniper, I wasn't sure the odds were in his favor.

Jack's face went blank. "I'm saying *you're* in danger. The entire city just saw who his girlfriend is. And while criminals don't read the papers, their girlfriends buy up that gossip shit. Someone will have definitely showed the new guy if Myers was on the cover."

I looked away, not wanting Jack to pick up on my racing heart or throbbing head.

"Do you want a shadow? It could be a plainclothes."

I considered it. No one could get into my office without going through security and having a fixed appointment. Press conferences were secure. Rallies? Total fucking nightmares. Commutes to downtown? Might as well have a target on my head.

"Maybe just an unmarked ride to and from work while you monitor the situation?" I scrunched my face into a painful smile. Jack wouldn't have bothered telling me unless there had been a viable threat.

"It's probably nothing, but I thought you should know." A lie followed by a truth. How very Samantha of him.

I briefed him on the water main and said a somber goodbye. On the steps of police headquarters Mitch was waiting and I didn't even have the energy to fake-call Fanny.

I didn't bother with a hello and I was oddly comforted by his presence. "There's a presser this afternoon. I'll answer questions then."

"Can I walk with you?" He zipped up his sweater, his checkered shirt collar still poking out at the neck.

Any other day and I might have said something snarky. But he'd sent me a text and warned me about the headline, so I had to cut him a little slack. "Sure."

"Did you think it was a little weird that there was a pap outside at the exact moment you left that party?"

We got to the crosswalk and I punched the button. Sometimes I took a car to and from headquarters to City Hall, but I needed the air. Plus, I wasn't sure I'd take the short trip again anytime soon.

"I did. Yes. I mean, only a few people knew about us dating. And who gives a fuck? Am I right?"

"I'd say you're exactly right. That spread benefitted one person and one person only." Mitch had small eyes. They were kinda rat-like and dark. Sometimes during pressers, I could sense them trying to penetrate my skin. I avoided looking into them to confirm that I thought the same thing. Anton had come off way better than I did.

Once we crossed the street, he stopped walking. "I'll leave you with this. My friend from *The Scoop* confirmed that the photographer was tipped off."

"But we both already knew that, didn't we?" I tapped him twice on the shoulder and walked the rest of the way back to City Hall. I couldn't stop my gaze from fluttering over the people in the street, wondering if one of them would be stupid enough to try to kill me in broad daylight.

Fanny and I ordered our lunch in, and we sat in my office to eat it. I pronged the chicken in my Caesar salad and said, "I need to get through this day then go home and turn off my phone."

She finished the bite of her massive sandwich. I honestly didn't know where she put her food. She was the skinniest bitch I'd ever met, and she ate like a lumberjack.

"What about the rally?"

"Aren't you always saying I don't self-care or some shit like that?"

"Self-care is real, girl."

I let out a little laugh. I loved her little lectures. "Oh, yeah? What do you do when you feel like you've completely lost control of your life?"

"Cookie-dough ice cream and bad horror flicks. The characters are so stupid. It feels amazing to yell at them. That won't work for you, though. You'd stress about eating ice cream then have nightmares about the movies." She shook her head, disappointed.

Her idea of self-care was hilarious, but she was right. It would never work for me.

"Maybe I could get a massage or do some yoga." That must work for some people.

My desk phone rang, and Fanny grabbed it. "Samantha Power's office."

She shook her head that I didn't need to take it and I finished my salad.

Deana Birch

"All good for rush hour." She hung up. It was good news for commuters and shitty news for me. My distraction had been handled.

"Call the press. Let's get this over with."

I tossed the rest of my lunch in the trash then re-applied my makeup and set my shoulders back. My time for whining was over. I had to pull up my big-girl panties and go do my job.

The reporters who covered politics and the city were not the same ones who spread gossip, and for that, I was thankful. For the most part, they were respectful and kept to the questions of the day. Much to everyone's surprise, I called on Mitch first and much to my delight, he tossed me a softball.

No one brought up my ass or my new boyfriend, and it wasn't until I was walking back to my office that I realized what calling on Mitch first might mean to said new boyfriend. But then again, why would Anton be sitting at home watching my press conference? He probably spent his days putting stray cats in trees or doing endless crunches to keep his abs rippled.

Either way, I didn't have the energy to fake a smile and deal with the press again at the rally. The media there would be less forgiving than the ones I dealt with on a daily basis. And the whole safety thing Jack had warned me about? That was eating at me.

And, so, at the end of my day, I clicked open the email Debbie had sent me and dialed the number of the unmarked car. I arranged for him to be downstairs fifteen minutes later then finished the follow-ups I'd promised earlier. For the first time ever, I walked out of my office without my laptop.

I grabbed my coat and Fanny studied me. "Is there something you're not telling me?"

My mind had gone a bit fuzzy, but in a bad way. There were so many things I wanted to share with Fanny — that I was afraid Anton's past was going to haunt my dreams, that despite it, I knew I'd let him into my apartment when I didn't show up for the rally or answer his calls, that I'd probably bitten off way, way more than I could chew in an attempt to grab a bit of power. The list could have gone on.

Instead, I said, "I'll be fine," and headed out of the door. The tinted windows of the SUV gave it away, and when the driver spotted me, he hopped out and checked the street. As soon as I was safe inside, I closed my eyes and leaned against the door.

An ache pulsated behind my temples. I reached into my phone and turned it off. Some quiet alone time was just what I needed. Demsey would be pissed, but I needed to get my fear under control or I would be useless. *Just a few hours*, I told myself.

"Need me to walk you in?" The officer's words startled me. We were already in front of my building.

Anton was leaned against the brick wall, staring at his phone and holding a bag of take-out. In his dark hoodie and track pants, he looked like heaven.

"I'm good. Thanks for the ride." I got out of the SUV and the door slam brought up Anton's eyes. He clocked me then the car. I walked over, slipped my hand up his sweatshirt and leaned into him. I relaxed my shoulders for the first time all day and put my head on his chest.

"We're not going to that fucking rally." He kissed my forehead, and if I hadn't been busy swooning, I might have admitted to loving him just a little bit in that moment. He'd given me exactly what I needed.

He tucked his phone into his back pocket and followed me up to my apartment. I'd never skipped school and I was a bit of an over-achiever, but I imagined the feeling was similar.

"Do you mind if I change?" I hung my bag on a hook next to the door and shed my coat.

He ignored my question and set the food on the counter. "You want wine?"

"I want all the wine," I said as I passed by on the way to my bedroom. There was something calming about his energy. The normal intensity was there, but he was presenting it in an entirely different way.

I changed into pajama shorts and my college sweatshirt—the same one I'd worn on our first 'date'. I tied my hair up in a messy bun then washed off all my makeup.

When I got back out to the living room, he'd dished out the food onto two plates and cued up the series we'd started watching. There were two glasses of wine on the coffee table next to the plates and he was sitting on the couch. I decided not to read anything into it and not over-analyze how reassuring his presence was.

We ate as we watched and let the next episode start without any debate. But when that one finished, the longing for another type of satisfaction smoldered inside me. I clicked off the television.

The apartment was dark, the perfect ambiance for what came next. I climbed into his lap and he tucked a stray lock of hair behind my ear. For the first time, I saw the beauty in his eyes. Yes, they held many other things, but they really were stunning. I wondered how many women had complimented him on them over the years and decided it wouldn't be very original to do the same.

"I'm ready for bed." I kissed down his neck and his stubble scratched my cheek. Longing spread from my core and throbbed under my skin.

"Is that so?"

"Mmm-hmm." I stood behind him, removed my sweatshirt and tossed it next to him. I held his gaze as I dropped the shorts and my underwear as slow as I could. I finished with my bra and savored how his eyes raked over me.

Anton licked his lips and lava must have been running through my veins because every cell in my being was on fire. I lifted a shoulder in a move that was way less casual that I felt and said, "See you in there," then walked back to the bedroom and lay down on the bed.

With my legs bent and wide open, I squeezed a nipple and let the other hand drop between my thighs. I was dripping for him, so ready for whatever he wanted me to do. I dipped my fingers in my need before teasing my clit and closing my eyes, so fucking eager for him to come in and take control.

Around and around I went and I kept my eyes shut, even when he came into the room.

"You thinking about how I make you come?"

"Yes." My answer was more a breath than a word.

The bed dipped and his heavy energy blanketed me, but he didn't give me the touch I was craving.

"I think you'd better finish what you started, sunshine." It wasn't a suggestion. It was an order, a dare not to obey.

With one hand I spread my lips wider and with the other I increased my pace and pressure. The fuse had been lit. It was only a matter of time before I would explode.

"Faster," he growled.

I whined and moaned. I wanted him inside me so damn bad that I considered begging, but he'd told me what to do, and pleasing him was sure to be rewarded. I would have given him anything he wanted just to feel the girth of him when my walls would grip his cock.

He brushed my lips and it was all I could do to hold off. The need for him was overwhelming.

"Please," I begged in a voice I didn't recognize.

I rubbed my clit as hard as I could, as fast as I could. I was so fucking close. He kissed down my neck and twirled a nipple with his tongue. When he clamped down with his teeth, I came fast and hard.

"Don't you dare fucking let up." Anton pushed my hand back between my legs and slid in, filling me. Another wave rumbled through me, this one more intense and echoing deep into my bones. I panted through his thrusts, unable to breath and not even wanting to.

He finally freed me of my self-gratifying torture when he yanked my hand away and pinned both wrists over my head. He met my mouth with his, using an animalist force while he continued his battering pump.

Gold and blue lights twinkled and whirled behind my eyes, and he groaned out a curse. The momentary pause allowed me to gasp for air, and it stung in my chest. I swallowed down his perfect taste.

The sound of our flesh smacking together echoed in the air as he fucked me harder. It wasn't that rough sex was new to me, but his brand involved an intensity and claiming that I'd never imagined would turn me on. After years of being a strong, independent woman, it was refreshing to not have the pressure to make a decision. I was lost in his aggressive world and I never wanted to be found. He was an escape from a reality of stress, fear and pressure.

Anton flipped me onto all fours and thrust into me again. I steadied myself with one hand and reached between my legs to cup his balls. With his fingers digging into my hipbones, he rocked me back and forth so fast that I almost fell.

"Tug."

I did as he said and he let out a growl.

"You're. Fucking. *Mine*." Each word was coupled with a deep thrust. It bound me to his soul, branded me his for life. His cock stiffened inside me and he cried out.

I finally buckled below him and he laid on top of me, still inside. We caught our breath for a second before he pulled out and I swiveled under him so we were face to face. A drip of sweat ran down his nose and landed on my cheek. He caught the movement and studied my face with wonder before kissing me, soft and with care. It was like he was mending any wounds he might have inflicted. I ran my fingers through his damp hair, grateful for a glimpse of his gentle side.

"You're beautiful, that was amazing and I need a fucking shower." He shot me a playful wink before getting up and trekking off to the bathroom.

Later, once we'd both rinsed off and were back in bed, I threaded my fingers through his and pushed my back tighter into his chest. In a quiet voice, I asked, "How did you know?"

"What?"

"Exactly what I needed."

He kissed my back. "I saw your press conference. All those reporters were being nice to you, and I thought, these people work with my sunshine on a daily basis and are showing her a little kindness. Maybe I should, too."

Chapter Fourteen

Anton

Samantha's alarm chimed when the sun was barely peeking through the windows. She moved to get up but I drew her back.

"Where you going?" I nuzzled into her neck. I needed a round two or three or shit, I didn't know — just more. The woman was crawling under my skin and invading my every thought. I'd actually done something unselfish for once and brought her a meal. I'd watched her press conference. There was something stewing in her that was beyond the pictures in the paper and it certainly wasn't the water main. It probably had everything to do with why she'd gotten a police escort home. That SUV screamed undercover. *Stupid fucking cops*. She hadn't said what, but I wanted to know. Whatever it was, I wanted to fix it, and *that*? That made me worry I was losing my edge. I'd given her the night, but there was no way she was going out on the streets without me knowing why she was upset.

She stood but I didn't let go of her forearm. "I run in the mornings when there's no rain. It clears my head." Her tight, small smile wasn't reassuring. I would have pry it out of her.

I brushed down her soft skin and interlaced our fingers. "What's in there that needs clearing?"

No one who knew me would call me a talker, but building a crew and getting people loyal required a lot of reading of body language.

She stared at our hands and her mouth twitched. *Spill it, sunshine.*

I waited while she did her internal debate. It wasn't like I had somewhere to be. Patience was something I'd learned early on. Eagerness may have fed the ego, but endurance built success.

She let out a little huff. "I started my day yesterday with the chief of police. I do all the meetings with him, because he hates Demsey. Anyway, he kinda warned me that I might be in danger. It's probably nothing." She shook her head, dismissing the words.

That was vague as fuck. That was public Samantha talking. That was sugarcoating.

Then I understood. "It's because of me."

She tugged away and I let her go, my arm dropping heavy on the bed. We'd spent so much time talking about what the consequences of the photos would be for her career that we hadn't thought about the bigger picture. I was still straddling two worlds. My chest burned at the thought of someone hurting what I held precious. I finally had something in common with the rest of my former crew. I had someone else to think about.

I got out of bed and got dressed. If she was going running, I was too. She sat on the floor tying her shoes and I passed her as I went to the kitchen. I collected our forgotten dishes from the night before, put them in the sink and turned on her little coffee machine.

When she joined me, I was scrolling through my phone. A normal morning in Covington and Rafa would have texted me three times before I'd gotten out of bed. But post Covington? There wasn't a lot of action in my inboxes. I stored the phone in the pocket of my hoodie.

"Do you eat before you run or after?"

She narrowed her eyes. "After. Why do I have the feeling you think you're coming with me?"

"Because I am."

"You're adorable when you're protective, but like I said, it's probably nothing." She put a pod into the coffee machine and it began the loud hum while it brewed.

I waited for the noise to finish after the second cup. I didn't want her to mistake what I was about to say. The machine gurgled to an end and she reached out a hand to offer me one.

A tilt of my head told her to cut the bullshit. "And yet a cop drove you home." I accepted the cup. "What exactly did your police buddy say to you?"

"This is annoying." She shivered a little and rolled her eyes.

"I couldn't agree more. How about you tell me what and who? Since I know them, I can properly assess what level of scared you should or shouldn't be."

She stared at me for a beat before shifting her eyes to the floor and letting out a small huff. "That's actually a really good point." Samantha sipped her coffee then sat on a bar stool at the island opposite me before she continued, "Apparently, the cops miss you. You ran a tighter ship than what's going on up there now."

Was it wrong to be proud of that? Probably in front of her. *Focus.*

"Details, please." I understood she dealt in generalities for a living, but broad strokes weren't what the situation called for.

"Deaths are up. Rapes are up. Disappearances are up. People who used to turn to you are going to the cops."

I fought a smile. I could have kissed her. She'd given me the nail on the coffin as to why Jefferson Manors needed me. Not that I was interested in running *that* fucking crew. My guys had been hand-picked and groomed to perfection…except Jimmy. *Fucking Jimmy.* I still couldn't believe a multi-colored-haired hacker had seen through him before we had.

"Are you happy?" she asked in a horrified tone.

"No. Sorry. So your buddy thinks they might retaliate by fucking with you?"

"Pretty much." She finished her cup and got up to put it in the sink.

The threat was real. Jefferson Manor's thugs were gun-carrying, girlfriend-beating, drug-dealing pricks. But I'd taken out three of their top tier, and from the sound of things, the new guys in charge were failing miserably to keep a grip on their expanded territory. Hunting me down and fucking with me would send a signal of strength. It would be an easy way to flex their muscle, since they obviously had no idea how to be leaders. Desperation could lead to random, pointless choices.

Her brave face was sweet, and even though my little night in had been an escape, it hadn't been the reassurance she'd needed. My past had gotten her spooked. I owed her more than I was giving.

"Hey," I cooed and brought her arms around me then tipped up her chin. "The chief was right to warn you. Those guys wear blue shirts and look like criminals. If you see one, you'll know it. Crews don't do undercover. But I'm going to take care of it. I'll run with you then drop you back here. Take the escort again this morning, and I'll see you tonight."

She closed her eyes and let out a slow breath. "What if I don't want you to handle it? What if I'm afraid of what that means?" Her cheeks flushed with concern and her bottom lip trembled. That dark brown gaze looked up at me with an emotion I didn't want from her — fear.

Holy shit. She thought I was going to kill someone. And I would if it meant protecting her, my crew and family. But that wasn't part of my plan.

"I tell you what, sunshine. I won't throw the first punch if it comes to that. But I'm pretty sure I know how to fight with my words. Besides, if you think I'm going to let you walk the streets without a sense of security, you're insane."

She smirked up at me and the change in her energy was a relief. "If you think I believe you've ever solved anything with your words, *you're* insane. But fine... You can run with me. Just don't talk. You're not my only problem."

"It's cute you think you have a choice." I winked.

Samantha headed for the door then unbolted her locks. She grabbed a baseball cap and threaded her ponytail through the back. Her black yoga pants and thin athletic jacket were probably the tightest things she ever wore in public. Would it have been so wrong to run behind her and stare at that ass for an hour?

"Come on, then." She smiled and it was a ray of light. Her nickname made perfect sense. Jesus, was I catching some serious feels for her. *What the fuck?*

We jogged over to the park and did an internal loop. She had a solid pace, and I kept my promise of not talking to her while our feet hit the pavement. Honestly, it had done me good. We used to run on the treadmill in Covington, and I'd forgotten how much I liked being outside. The next time I went Upstate, I would take advantage of the clean air and run in the forest. It would do my injured lungs some good.

After a solid hour, my side ached and my scar throbbed. I still wasn't a hundred percent, and I took the pain as a reminder that I needed to get back into my daily habit of training. Maybe I could find a shitty personal trainer at the gym where I was a brand-new member. The chances of sparring with Leo didn't seem very plausible.

I'd wondered if Samantha would walk home after we exited the park, but that would have been a sign of an underachiever. When we got to the door of her building, I wanted to bend over and catch my breath. Instead, I kissed her on her cheek then licked my lips. I didn't mind her salty sweat. I may have even liked it. After all, it came out of her.

"You wanna go to dinner tonight? I can pick you up at work."

She dug out her keys from a zipper pocket in the front of her little jacket. "Oh, I have a choice now?"

No. Not really.

Having someone know about my past and accept me how she had? I didn't think that was going to present itself on the reg. I flipped up my hood then spied her from below its edge. Even after a run, she was stunning. I trailed my gaze the length of her, dirty thoughts inventing themselves with each passing body part.

"Don't look at me with those eerie-ass eyes all sexy-like. I need to go to work."

I grinned and went in for another kiss. "I'll pick you up later. And while I think your police buddy was right to warn you, I don't think they would be stupid enough to do something. I may not have a crew, but I'm still me. It would essentially take a sniper to kill me — and trust me, they don't have that."

"Okay." She fluttered her eyelashes, rolling her eyes. "I'll text you when I'm done for the day." I leaned in again and she pushed me away. "Go home."

A big part of me wanted to throw her over my shoulder and repeat our shower sex but I wasn't in Covington anymore. She wasn't some girl who had nothing better to do than spend a day realizing my twisted desires. Nope, she had other things to do than think of me. I both liked and fucking hated that fact at the same time.

I took a regretful step backward and watched her go in her building. The sweat was starting to make me chilly, so I ran across town to my mother's house. I had breakfast alone and went back to bed after a shower. At noon, I ate again as a party of one, then gathered my shit for the gym. I put the drug-filled soccer ball in my bag and covered it with a change of clothes.

I hadn't gone back to Juliana's. My mother would have heard about it. Instead, once I knew I had my product, I'd sent the gym brochure to her in the mail with a date and time. I'd even stolen the stamp from Satan herself. There was no way to know if the guy from Jefferson would show, but based on what Samantha had told me that morning, I was betting he would. If the new leader was anything like me, his curiosity would get the best of him.

I zipped up my bag, flung it over my shoulder and headed out of my room. The house had been eerily quiet, and I nearly jumped out of my skin when I saw my mother in the downstairs hallway — except it wasn't my mother. Not at first glance, anyway. It was an entirely too-skinny old woman whose hair was pulled back with a thick headband. She wore a silk robe that hung off her like a child in a grown man's T-shirt — and she wore no makeup. I would have had to go back a long fucking way to remember a time when she didn't have her 'face' on.

I stopped in my tracks and willed some air to return to my lungs. "What the fuck is wrong with you?"

She clutched her robe and steadied herself with a hand on the wall. She was equally as shocked as I was. "I didn't think anyone was home. And don't use that language with me."

Really, Ma? I see you in the saddest state of your life and you correct my swearing?

I rolled my eyes, trying to ignore the fact that I was holding a shitload of drugs in front of her. "Okay, let me try again. What is wrong with you?"

"I have the flu. You should probably stay away from me. In fact, maybe you should stay with Samantha again or go Upstate." She gagged before straightening up.

Since I'd been shot, she'd only wanted me close. The pushing me away was suspicious — at best.

"Do you want me to call a doctor?" The bag strained and I dropped my shoulder just a little. It wasn't that it was heavy. It was incriminating. Even in her weakened state, she caught the action.

"Don't be ridiculous." At least she still had a sharp tongue.

"Where's your husband? Come to think of it... Where's all the help?"

"I sent him to a hotel and told them to stay away. No point in getting us all sick. He has a campaign to win and a city to run. He was supposed to tell you last night."

"I didn't go last night."

She pursed her lips, and while she could be annoyed for me skipping the rally, there was something deeper going on. My mother was not one to overreact. She was the steady hand that guided boats out of stormy seas. She was a level of ice that could not melt. She'd been fine two days prior... No, she hadn't been. My chest tightened. She was hiding something.

"How do you know it's the flu?"

"Are you calling me a liar?"

"I'm just—"

"I'll be better in a few days. I need rest. You headed to the gym? That's wonderful. I'm glad you're feeling better." She steadied herself on the stairs and disappeared before I could object.

Staying and taking care of my ill mother would have been the grown-up-man thing to do, but I had a meeting, a bag full of drugs and a healthy habit of breaking the law.

"I'll be back later," I called up the steps.

At the gym, I scanned my brand-spanking-new membership card at the front desk and waited until the men's locker room cleared before I stored my bag and clothes in one locker and the soccer ball in the other. Then I went out into the main gym, hunting for criminals. It was the middle of the day, so I mostly found housewives who watched their phones while gliding on the elliptical machine. I still had over an hour, so I went for the free weights and worked my arms and chest.

The minute he walked in, I was on high alert. His dark, slicked-back hair flipped up at his neck and I could practically smell the crime on him from across the room. But he wasn't stupid... Instead of the Jefferson blue shirt, he wore a black tracksuit and had a gym bag flung over his shoulder.

I finished my reps while he filled out a form. I snickered. Did that hottie behind the desk really think that people like him and me gave out real addresses and telephone numbers?

He glanced in my direction then back to the desk while she went through the various types of membership. Once he'd nodded and smiled in his best fake-friendly way, he followed her pointed finger to the locker room. I stopped at the drinking fountain, took a long sip and wiped my mouth with the back of my hand.

His arms were folded, and he sat on a bench with his legs wide and a thoroughly unimpressed smirk on his face. "You should be dead."

"I'm a lucky fuck. Should we just cut the shit and get to it?"

"Gladly."

Deana Birch

I crossed the room and sat next to him. There weren't a lot of men in the gym, but if they came in, I still wanted to be discreet. "Word on the street is that shit's a little bit out of control up there."

He scoffed. I didn't blame him. No one liked criticism.

"Listen," I said with a hint of sympathy. "I get it. Your crew shrank, my old guys bailed and you have triple the territory. New guys want to impress you, so they sell too much. Junkies die. People get scared. But the money is raining and it's hard to control the greed. Don't think I didn't make that mistake when I started."

His expression didn't change but he knew I was right.

I continued, "Dead junkies don't make very good repeat customers. You may have plenty now because we're not there, but think about a year from now when half of them are gone. That's half your money, bro."

"What is this, self-help advice for dealers?"

"Nah. But if you get shit stable, the cops will leave you alone. Let me guess… Your product is blue."

He shrugged an apology.

"Our shit is pink. Our former customers trust that color. We never gave them too much at once."

He gave a little shake to his head. "You want to be my hook-up?"

"I sure do. And I'm willing to make an investment."

He uncrossed his arms and leaned back. "Is that so?"

The finishing touches on closing deals didn't have anything to do with shaking hands or signing dotted lines. It was relatability.

"I get you, man. You've got a confidence problem from two neighborhoods that have been bred not to trust you. I have the key. I mean, what am I going to do? I have no crew and no desire to rebuild one, just to lose it again. I'm not gonna get a fucking job."

"What are the terms?" He let out a little sigh.

"All my former crew are off limits for revenge—as is anyone close to me or them."

A fake smirk spread across his face. "You afraid I might kill your hot new girlfriend?"

I was delighted he'd asked. It was the perfect opportunity to show him some respect and pretend to be humble. "Yeah. Yeah, I am." I nodded.

"Not gonna lie. I've thought about it."

I curbed my temper. I needed to make this deal for my future. If I was too heavy-handed, it would backfire, and he would do something stupid like pull a knife on me then my instincts would take over and I'd beat him to a pulp.

"Can't blame you. But you've gotta get your shit tight. Give them nicknames like—I don't know—Tony the Tweeker or shit like that. Figure out how much Tony can take. Don't let your crew sell him more. My pink crystals will give you that blanket of ease. I fucking guarantee it."

"And what if I say no?"

He wouldn't. Once my former customers saw their precious pink, a cloud of serenity would wash over them. Then, the pink would be so much better than the blue. They might try the blue again out of desperation, but nothing would make them trust it as much as the pink. Jefferson could try all they wanted to re-color their product, but no one could match Cookie's tint. In the end, the crew of Jefferson would be just as addicted to my drugs as their customers. It might not last forever, but it would work long enough to give me some cash flow.

I dug into my pocket and fished out the key to the locker with the soccer ball. "Free sample. I think you'll find it incredibly generous. And, by the way, it would be a real pity if the cops found out about your surveillance camera scam." I tossed him the key and he caught it at his chest.

"I was wondering when the threat would come." He slipped the key into his pocket and the deal was done. "Fuck," he said with a frown, "I have to actually workout now."

Chapter Fifteen

Samantha

There hadn't been a press briefing, an annoying inconvenience to the day or even a picture of me kissing a dangerous man on the cover of a paper that claimed to be news. But that didn't mean Fanny and I weren't busy. If reporters didn't get what they wanted from Demsey's campaign, they would come fishing in our office.

Fanny had spent her afternoon swatting away rumors that Demsey was cheating on Sophia. Apparently he'd slept in a hotel because she had a bad case of the flu. It would have been her idea. She wouldn't have let him get away with that, and I wanted to call her and ask if she'd ever heard of a guest room. I was pretty sure there were a few of them in her massive brownstone.

But my boss was in a mood, pissy that Anton and I hadn't shown up for his rally and left feeling exposed without his wife. I'd watched the rally in the morning. He'd done fine. He was a seasoned politician, after all. Sophia being ill was a weakness, though. It had been said that there is an ounce of truth in every rumor, and a small sneeze could lead to her on her death bed with the wrong amount of spin.

I was hoping to get the facts from Anton at dinner without being obvious, and when I grabbed my light-gray coat to leave at the end of the day, I was reminded of how protective he'd been that morning. Yes, he was rough, but there wasn't a cold heart at the bottom of his steel chest.

As I waited in the elevator bay, for the first time I honestly wondered if I could have a future with him, if we might actually work together. The bigger question was if I really, truly wanted that. Body was one thing, but heart and soul were something else.

There he stood, at the end of the steps of City Hall with a cheeky grin on his normally stern face. I wondered what he'd worn when he'd been the leader of his crew. because the double-layered Henley, dark tapered jeans and casual boots would lead someone to believe he was just and average guy — if average guys had muscles that stretched out their tight shirts and spewed a level of self-confidence that must have only been reserved for demi-gods.

"Hey," I said. Heat crept up my neck and flushed my cheeks. *Jesus. I'm swooning.*

"Mind if we walk? The restaurant is only about fifteen minutes." He reached for my hand, threaded his fingers through mine and kissed just under my knuckles.

I didn't mind at all. In fact, I'd sat behind my desk most of the day, and with him by my side, the threat I'd learned about the day before seemed impossible. Strolling in the city with its buzz of energy had always been one of my favorite things to do. It was a reminder that I was never alone—and fifteen minutes was nothing for me and my heels.

"What did you do today?" I asked and wondered if it had involved crime.

"Ate, slept, went to the gym."

Pedestrians passed us at a faster pace. Anton and I were annoying them with our tourist cadence. In the streets, the cars were equally eager to complete their commute. The honks of taxis and insults that followed faded into white noise.

"Sounds stressful," I joked.

He rubbed his neck with his free hand. "I don't think we want to compare days. We both know it will end up with you chiseling away at my ego."

His ego could have probably used some refinement, but he made a good point. Why would I want to bring him down?

Even though I was interested in helping Anton carve out a future and supporting him in a quest to be legit on paper, I changed the subject. "So, where are we headed, anyway?"

"Little Italian place. It doesn't look like much, but the food is amazing."

"Sounds perfect." With any luck there would be a back booth and I could casually bring up his mother and why she'd put Demsey in a hotel. At the crosswalk, he kissed my hand again and it struck me how normal of a date we were on—like, super-normal. Maybe he was capable of reform—and maybe he even wanted it.

On a downtown side street, we stood in front of a dimly lit restaurant that had red lettering with the word 'Chezzie's' written on the window.

"I have to warn you. This place has been known to cause food comas." He opened the glass door and held it at arm's length. I couldn't resist giving him a gentle peck on the lips as I passed by and was glad I did when it deepened his smile. He was showing me something he knew about the city and that tender side of himself at the same time.

The restaurant was indeed little. There were a few wooden tables near the front and a row of booths lining the wall opposite a bar that led to the double steel doors of the kitchen. The maximum capacity must have been no more than thirty people. A slow Italian song played overhead, the mandolin and accordion making it quintessential. I was pretty sure I loved the place, and I hadn't even tried a bite of the food.

Three older couples occupied the tables by the windows, their deep, wrinkled faces highlighted by the candles burning between their plates. Of the four booths that lined the wall, two were taken. One held a family of four, the two boys eating spaghetti at an alarming rate while the parents whispered and smiled to each other.

In the last booth, two dark-haired men in black suits were having an animated debate until one locked eyes with me. I had no idea who he was, but the recognition on his face said he knew me.

Before I had a chance to digest who and why, a beautiful middle-aged woman with long, dark hair and a stunned look on her lovely face came at us.

"As I live and breathe... I didn't think I'd see those baby blues again." The woman, obviously Chezzie, cupped Anton's face and tapped it twice. When she let go, he kissed her on the cheek with a grin.

"Chezzie, this is Samantha, Samantha this is—"

I didn't need to follow Anton's gaze to know the man in the back booth had locked into it. The tension in the room rose and my throat tightened, not allowing me to swallow.

"Chezzie." She stepped toward me with a warm smile and we shook hands. "Let me show you to your booth."

I followed her to the one closest to the family and took off my coat.

"I can take that for you." Chezzie folded my coat over her arm, cleared her throat just a little and gave a cautious glance to Anton before walking away.

We slid in and I searched for a menu or a wine list or anything to keep me busy. Demanding an explanation immediately was the wrong move. The energy needed to settle and the hairs in the nape of my neck needed to stop standing at attention.

"Samantha," a deep, unfamiliar voice said, and I shot my gaze up to an attractive but all-too-intimidating man. He cut his dark eyes to Anton. "Bar."

Anton let out a little grumble and frowned but got up. "I'll be right back."

I seriously hoped he hadn't brought me on a date where he was planning some kind of coup in his former neighborhood or doing a fucking drug deal before my eyes. I stared at the empty seat in front of me and begged my toes to stop their nervous twitch in my shoes. Controlling my curiosity proved to be harder than stopping my feet. Anton and the man exchanged hushed but harsh words until they both went silent and stared at each other as if they could read thoughts.

Finally, Anton tilted his head and the man relaxed before holding up a finger and sending a friendly warning. They ended in a man-hug, which made the exchange even more bizarre, but reassured me a little that the situation had been handled. The other man from the booth, who once I got a good look at him was very obviously related to the first one, just a little older, shook his head as he passed by.

As both of them walked by the booth, they narrowed their eyes on me before Chezzie met them at the door and their cautious moods flipped to admiration for the woman. They were out of the door without so much as another glace in our direction.

"Sorry about that. I didn't think they'd be here." Anton slipped back into his seat and the fright of the previous five minutes finally passed my throat, but instead of going down to my stomach where it could have dissipated, it rose up and out in my words.

"Who were they?" I hated that bitchy, naggy tone. Fuck me, I needed to control myself. Maybe the chief's warning had spooked me more than I thought.

"Old friends."

Chezzie came over with a carafe of wine and a bottle of sparkling water. She poured us both without a word then left.

I shook my hand out under the table. I didn't want the nerves showing when I reached for my glass. "You gonna tell me what that was about or just let me think you're back to your old ways and you brought me on a date to rub my nose in it?" My mouth wasn't doing me any favors, but the last forty-eight hours with Anton had been a rollercoaster and I was done with it playing with my safety. That man had known my name and it had come out as more of a threat than a greeting.

Anton worked his jaw. He didn't like being challenged — or maybe he didn't like that my fear meant I didn't think he could keep me safe.

"I'm leaving." I tossed my napkin on the table and grabbed my bag.

"Stinky pizza boy," he said before I was out of the booth. "He's legit now and had asked me not to show up in his life. I didn't think he'd be here, but that was stupid." Anton shook his head. "They're not out to hurt you. Trust me."

"Who was the other guy?" I blinked several times, halfway out of the booth and not believing I was considering staying.

"His brother. Can we drop this? I have something I want to talk to you about."

The power behind his stare was too much and I sat down. He'd been honest. I had to admit that I was just a little bit intrigued and flattered that he had something on his mind and was going to share it with me, but that didn't mean I was smiles and rainbows. He'd brought me to the restaurant, and even if the two brothers weren't out to hurt me, their initials stares hadn't been warm welcomes.

I frowned and waited for him to start, but Chezzie served us a plate of grilled vegetables and olives. My manners kicked in and I softened. I re-placed my napkin on my lap and pronged a pepper.

"There's something wrong with my mother."

That was an understatement.

"Demsey said she had the flu. He was pissed we weren't at the rally."

"I saw her without makeup, Sam. That hasn't happened since I was a kid." There was a slight strain

157

in his voice. He'd never called me Sam before. The nickname held less authority.

Maybe it wasn't just the flu. Maybe that was why Demsey had stayed at a hotel.

Anton continued, "She kicked everyone out of the house. It makes no sense. All of the sudden she wants me gone, after two months of not letting me out of her sight."

"Why would she lie?"

"Because we all lie."

I let his words settle between us. He wasn't wrong. I lied. He'd lied about the corkscrew. What else?

"Has she ever done this before?" I asked.

He shook his head. "I mean, she refused to see me when I went to Covington for like two years. But that was because she was pushing me to be my own man."

"Are you sure?" I took another pepper. The amount of olive oil was perfect. Chezzie was a master.

Anton interlaced his fingers behind his head and leaned back. He wasn't helping with the first starters. The food coma was going to be real.

With narrowed eyes, he asked, "What do you mean? And none of your sugarcoating."

I gestured to ask if I could have the last olive and he nodded. How was I going to put it? I chewed and swallowed. "We all have patterned behavior, right? Tells. Mitch from *The Times* wiggles his fingers when he's going to tell me something he thinks I don't know. Demsey can only handle two Scotches after dinner or he falls asleep in his chair."

"What's mine?"

"You're just eternally pissed off. Why is that, anyway?" The last piece of grilled zucchini taunted me from the plate. "Please eat that."

He grinned and popped it into his mouth. A passing busboy saw the empty plate and cleared it away. Anton took a sip of wine, looked away, then said, "My dad used to beat her. You wouldn't believe the woman she used to be. Him getting locked up probably saved her life—and his." He tapped his finger on the table twice. "She completely changed once he was out of the picture. This weak, helpless woman transformed into the strongest, most resourceful person I could imagine."

He reached out and I took his hand. "She doesn't want you to see her like that again. Makes sense, if you think about it."

"I guess."

"Penne in vodka sauce." Chezzie slid plates in front of us.

I was already full, but there was no way I would refuse. "I don't remember ordering this," I said once she was gone.

"Pace yourself. There's a meat or fish after."

I honestly didn't know how I finished the rest of the meal. A roasted whitefish followed and it fell off the bone so perfectly that I couldn't resist. But when we got outside to go home, there was still a concern in his eyes.

I stepped into his space, placed my hand on his chest and looked up into his beautiful eyes. "Go home. Check on her. Stay there tonight. I'm gonna walk for a bit and digest. Besides, it's kinda sweet the way you care about her. Makes me think you have a heart."

He let out a long breath before pulling me in for a tender kiss. All the swoony whirls buzzed around me. I'd gone on a proper date with Anton Myers, and, despite the initial speedbump of his old friend, I'd loved it.

Anton pressed his forehead into mine and stroked my cheek with his thumb. "You don't mind?"

"I insist. Besides a massive man like you tossing and turning in my bed all night for the wrong reasons won't be any fun at all."

He kissed me again but deeper, as if he needed it to survive. I couldn't believe I was letting him get away with it again in public but was helpless to stop. Maybe *I* needed it to survive. Finally, he broke away.

"Jesus. How is kissing you so good?"

Funny, I was wondering the same thing.

"I'll walk you home." He took my hand and the heat that had been between us settled into a blanketing warmth. As we walked down the street, the realization that I cared for him — about him — slammed into me. The idea of me with any other man was impossible.

Chapter Sixteen

Anton

My mother hadn't eaten for three days — three days that *I'd* known of. Fucking Demsey wasn't returning my calls and I hadn't seen Samantha because I didn't want to leave Ma alone. She was managing small sips of water but was mostly just exhausted. I'd begged her to let me take her to a hospital, pleaded with her to call a doctor to come.

In the end, she'd agreed to a female nurse. She didn't like me helping her in and out of the bathroom and the woman needed a damn shower. The only thing good to have happened was that I'd found Scooter.

He'd reached out via text and we'd set a time and date to meet. I found the nurse reading in my mother's study on the way out of the door and said, "Call me for anything. I mean it." The middle-aged brunette reminded me of Cookie, so I softened my tone. "Please."

She nodded. She was the quiet type and that suited me just fine. I was waiting for Jefferson to get back to me about another batch and would have to go Upstate and leave my mother, which I wasn't happy about.

Sophia Myers had certainly had her moments of being a cold-hearted pain in my ass over the years, but I was proud to be her son. My front-row seat to her rise to power had taught me many things—most importantly, it had taught me to never leave anyone behind. She might have tried to push me away, but I knew she was happy I was there and concerned.

I walked down to Midtown, sometimes doubling back to see if I was being followed. My mother hadn't been talking to her gang of goons, and I wondered if they weren't all sitting around in somebody's basement playing cards and shooting the shit. Either way, I was pretty sure there wasn't one on my back.

In a fast-food restaurant that I hadn't eaten in since I'd started taking my body seriously, Scooter sat in the back corner in blue jeans and a beige hoodie. His hair had grown, and it struck me that it had been months since I'd seen him. The time had created a gaping hole between us. And while seeing my crew out of our normal uniform was odd, it was nice to have a familiar face around.

I stood in line then ordered a bottle of water and fries that I wouldn't eat. Once served, I went over and sat next to him. There would be no hugs or displays of affection. It had been one thing with Leo. He had been my best friend. But Scooter and I had grown apart after we'd gotten his girlfriend back from Bradford Towers. It was possible that he'd held a bit of a grudge when Jimmy had stepped up and earned more. But he'd never said anything, and I thought I was being understanding by letting him skip morning workouts. In retrospect, I should have been tougher.

The chair rattled when I dragged it out from the table next to him. I sat facing the wall, able to make eye contact. "How's Callie?"

"Same. I was waiting for your message." He grinned but his leg was bobbing under the table. It must have been weird seeing me again, knowing we weren't a crew anymore. For fuck's sake, I was wearing a flannel. It had checkers on it. We were living in a parallel universe.

But I didn't understand what he meant. "I sent you hundreds of messages."

"Nah, bro." *Bro?* I wasn't his bro.

"That the pink is back in the stink. Callie's cousin said the junkies have never been so happy. You saw Cookie." He lifted his eyebrows.

How did he know I saw Cookie? "Not sure what you mean there, Scoot."

He leaned closer and spoke in a hushed tone, "After you… I went up to your place and got the goods. I saw how your mother was running shit. She would have someone up there digging around in no time."

"Wait! *You* have my shit?" I probably should have said *our* instead of *my*. But he didn't catch the insult. In fact, he was beaming with pride.

"Was just waiting to see if you'd surface again. Speaking of surface, your new girlfriend has quite the ass on her."

Scooter was talking like the only thing we'd changed was our clothes. But there was no more 'us'. Still, he had all my product, and if he could deliver it to me, it would avoid me going Upstate. I needed to hold him close and be his bossman until I had all my shit back. The less he knew about my real intentions, the better.

"I'm just fucking that snooty bitch to keep busy. Listen... Do you think you could put fifty thousand worth of pink into a soccer ball and meet me at a park on Sunday?"

"You know I can."

I stood and grabbed my water and uneaten fries then tossed them in the trash on my way out of the door. Fucking Scooter had my drugs, not my mother. The loyalty of the crew meant something after all.

Back at home, the nurse was exactly where I'd left her. I went to the kitchen and starting prepping for dinner. Samantha had agreed to come over and I was sure I could woo her with my limited cooking skills. As much as I liked someone waiting on me hand and foot, not having my mother's help around every corner of the house had been an odd relief. Maybe I didn't want people to see her weak, either.

The doorbell rang when I'd finished my prep and put the fish in the oven. Samantha wore her gray coat cinched at the waist and had a designer duffle bag hung in the crook of her elbow. God bless her, she had on red shoes.

"I assumed I'd be spending the night." She swung the bag.

I hadn't realized how much I'd missed her until the thought popped into my head that she could spend her life with me, not just the night. It was out of character for me to be so damn sentimental, but I was pretty sure my mom didn't have the flu—and being alone in life was the last thing I wanted. It was one of the reasons I always made my number two live with me. I liked the idea of being around my closest friends.

"You assumed right. Get your ass in here, sunshine."

She sleeked in and I couldn't stop myself from grabbing her. She dropped the bag to the floor with a light thud. A warm relief spread over me like, well…sunshine. I'd forgotten the physical effect she had on me, how her presence calmed me. I undid the belt of her coat. It was an annoying layer keeping me from the real her. Underneath, she had on a silk polka-dot dress that had large white circles on one side and the other one small. It looked like someone had ripped two pieces apart and mistakenly put them back together. But on her, it totally worked. Her hair was down, and I took a lock and twirled it before letting it run through my fingers. Everything about her was soft, as if she was my complete and total opposite.

"You okay?" she asked as she placed her arms over my shoulders then her hands around my neck.

I looked down into her kind eyes. That woman cared for me. I had no idea if I should be honest and say 'no' or brave and say 'yes'. My courage had never struggled with emotion before. She pressed her lips into mine for a long moment. Instead of running from the intimacy she was presenting, I bathed in it. It filled me, recharged me.

"I missed you more than I'm willing to admit," she said when the kiss was sadly over.

My normal, cocky comments didn't surface. I licked my lips, tasting the aftermath of a mint. "Thanks for coming. I don't like leaving right now." I cleared my throat. It wasn't used to the yielding side of me. "Come on. I promised you a meal." I took her hand and led her to the small dining room.

I'd already opened the wine and set the table. There was nothing to do but serve and eat. Samantha sat and placed the napkin on her lap.

"I thought you said there was no help here."

"There's not. I am a full-grown man. I can do mundane shit."

Her eyes widened. "You did all this? Alone?"

I poured the wine. "How do you do that? How do you always take a shot at my ego? Better question… Why do I not even mind? You're making me soft."

"Then I'm doing it wrong. Damn."

As I walked to the kitchen for the meal, it occurred to me that I liked who I was when she was around. The 'bossman' from earlier? That guy was a fucking asshole. Selling drugs was a punk move. If I wanted a real chance with that woman, I would have to find another line of work. She'd mentioned real estate. Maybe I could raise some initial money by feeding Jefferson the rest of my meth, give Scooter a cut to fall off the planet then invest in some buildings. I'd really liked renovating the third floor of Covington once I'd made some bank and wanted a better place to live but couldn't move out. Doing that again would be easy.

I took the fish out of the oven with a hot mitt and carried it down the hall to the dining room. Samantha had a bemused smile on her face.

"Don't you dare ask me if I made this and take another chunk out of my confidence. Besides, you haven't tasted it yet. It could be terrible." I set the dish down on the hotplate and took off the mitt.

"It looks amazing. Smells pretty good, too. I am thoroughly impressed. I don't even care how it tastes." The gleam in her eyes made me smile. It was just a stupid fucking meal, but still... Impressing her was nice.

I served us both and she waited until I sat before picking up her fork. It wasn't spectacular but I hadn't mixed up sugar and salt or burned the potatoes.

"Who taught you how to do this?" she asked after she'd taken a few bites.

Who else? I pointed my knife to the ceiling. "She taught me everything." Funny how the truth stung a little too much.

"Well, she did a good job, then." Samantha smiled and it occurred to me that my mother had been right. Three months prior, that woman wouldn't have looked twice at a low-life drug lord like I'd been. Getting shot and appearing to have changed my life might have been the best thing that could have happened. Except, I hadn't changed that much.

"Can I ask you a question?" I moved around a roasted potato on my plate.

"Shoot."

I put down my service. "This is real, right? You're not faking a relationship with me to—I don't know—climb the political ladder or anything. You're feeling what I am?"

Her gaze tightened and I wondered if I'd insulted her.

I continued, "I'm only asking because, as you pointed out so well, I haven't really done this before."

"Had feelings?" She rubbed her lips together, trying to hide the little smirk escaping at the corners.

"Basically. Jesus Fucking Christ. Is it like this all the fucking time? Like every relationship you start makes you all fuzzy and loopy?"

"Loopy?"

"See? Even that. Since when do I use words like that?"

Samantha set down her knife and fork over her empty plate. She placed the napkin on top then stood, walked over to the door and closed it. I pushed away from the table, making room for what I somehow knew to be her next move.

Sure enough, she came over and straddled me. "It's not always like this. Only when you're —"

"Lucky as fuck?" I moved my hands up the skirt of her dress and grabbed the meaty flesh of her ass.

She cupped my cheeks and looked so deep into my eyes that I thought she'd invaded my body then soul. Her heart was pounding. The pulse from her wrists thumped into my chin.

"Falling really fucking hard for somebody."

She kissed me, and I spun out of control. It was the most exposed she could have been and there was no question that she was genuine. But the most terrifying part was that I couldn't lie to myself that I knew she was right. I was fucking head over heels for that woman. The proof had been all around me. Yes, we'd moved at the pace of a freight train, but that was the only gear I had and I'd dragged her along with me.

Her grind into my zipper was pleasure and pain, but totally effective in getting me hard as a rock. She'd moved her hands from my cheeks and was unbuttoning her dress. Shit, we were going to fuck right there at the dinner table. *And why the fuck not?*

She stood and slinked out of the dress. Her light pink bra and matching boy shorts were a sharp contrast to her red heels.

"Leave on the shoes." I took off my shirt and opened my pants. I wanted her on top to look into her eyes, to

Lie

know I hadn't invented her confession. But more, I needed her to know that it was mutual. After she was naked, I beckoned her to come hither as I stroked my cock and tilted it up so she could take the perfect seat right on top of it.

She straddled me and her wet pussy welcomed me in. With her hands braced on my shoulders, up and down she went. Pure bliss shot into the base of my brain and overwhelmed my body. It was such a foreign level of joy that I doubted its truth.

She's falling for me.

Samantha kissed up my neck between her gasps. I dropped my head back and the top of the chair poked me. I knew I didn't deserve her after all the shitty things I'd done in life, but I there was no way I would be able to live without her.

I worked her clit as fast as I could and whispered, "Tell me it's real, again. Tell me you're real."

Our eyes locked for a moment until she came hard on my cock. Through gritted teeth, she said, "It's real. We're real."

I grabbed her hips and worked her harder, deeper. The energy that had been spinning and growing at the base of my spine burst out and Samantha covered her mouth to muffle her scream. Three full thrusts later, every muscle on my body flexed as I came inside her.

With her head on my shoulder, we caught our breath. I reached for my shirt and draped it over her back. "The bathroom is down the hall if you want to clean up. But there's a nurse in the study, so you may want this."

She flung her hair over her shoulder and sat up straight as she threaded her arms through the flannel. It was like a robe on her but oddly matched her shoes.

She buttoned it with a shy smile. Jesus, she was stunning. "One thing."

"Anything."

"You're real, too, right?"

I understood. She needed me to say it, too. "A hundred fucking percent, sunshine." It wasn't even a lie.

Her huge smile was everything. She stood slowly and walked to the door.

I'm the luckiest man alive.

Chapter Seventeen

Samantha

There were levels of happiness that I could relate to. New shoes made me giddy. The first sip of coffee in the morning was a warm spread of contentment and reassurance. But waking up in the arms of a man who was connected with me on a level I hadn't known I had? It was an entirely new slice of bliss. I could have stayed in his bed the whole day, wrapped up in him.

Anton was on his back with one armed draped over his head as if he were thinking. He was so peaceful when he slept that it was almost childlike. The cigar-sized scar on his chest had mostly healed, and it was a tiny reminder of a previous life. He'd tried really hard to show me he could be 'normal'.

But how long could a man like him play by the rules? And the deeper I fell with him, the harder it would be to recover if — or more likely when — he went back to his deviant ways. What I needed to explain to him was that there was a way to be both. Demsey was a perfect example. He wasn't a bad man, per se, just not completely good. With his connections and power, his bending or breaking of the law was either swept under the rug or flat-out ignored. If we could just find a way to channel Anton's natural charisma, the system was already set up for him to succeed.

At some point in the middle of the night, there had been a round two. I needed a shower and a coffee to wake me up. I crept out of bed and took my bag into the bathroom. I showered and dressed in my running gear, and with him still snoozing, I went down to hunt for caffeine.

"Good morning, Samantha." Sophia sat at the kitchen counter with a cup of tea on a saucer and *The Times* in her hands. She was the perfect picture of her former self, except her cheeks had hollowed and she was paler than normal. But otherwise, it was all there — a light layer of foundation to even out her skin tone, a not-too-dark shade of lipstick that matched the stain on her dainty cup and a black turtleneck and camel-colored pants. She even had on a clunky gold necklace with a citrine teardrop pendent.

"Good morning. Glad to see you're feeling better. You had him pretty worried."

"That makes me perversely happy, but not as happy as seeing you wake up in my house." Sophia didn't have the kind of eyes that twinkled. Her baby blues penetrated brains and crushed spirits.

I offered a tight smile. I wasn't going to gossip about her son with her. "Do you mind if I make a coffee?"

"Be my guest." She went back to the paper and straightened it with a whip of her wrists. It offered a small shield from her inquisition.

On the counter they had one of those incredibly expensive machines that ground the coffee then brewed it to demand. And as it went through its noisy task of making me one single cup, the smell of the roasted beans promised a crisper view of the world.

I'd done everything I could think of to show him that I would be an open book for him. I'd laid my emotions out on the line and my heart with it. I was desperate to keep myself on the ground and delighted to let him spin me out of control. The intensity of our connection was frightening, exhilarating and addictive.

While it might have been his first relationship, it wasn't mine. I'd had boyfriends in college and had dated a financial hot shot the year before, until I'd found out he had a drug habit and a shitload of debt. But none of my past boyfriends and I had started off with the amount of heat and passion I had with Anton. I wasn't even concerned it would wear off. He burned so hot and so bright that there was an endless supply of his magnetism.

As I sipped on my coffee, I made a second one with the intention of taking it to him in bed and seeing if he wanted to run with me, but he appeared in the doorway, shirtless and scratching his head. Thank God his mother was there, otherwise round three could have happened right there on the counter. He had a way of ruining me with just a gentle glance of checking in.

At the sight of his mother, Anton smiled genuinely and fully. He went over and kissed her on the cheek and damn it if she didn't beam.

"Look at you," he said and stepped between us. "Did you eat something?"

I handed him his cup and he nodded his thanks.

"I had a piece of toast." Her lie would have been better sold if there had been crumbs on the counter or a plate next to her tea. But Anton chose to believe her—probably a desire for it to be true.

"One piece of toast?" Anton complained.

She rolled her eyes. "I have one of those massive luncheons later. I'll fill up there."

"So you're better?" Anton eyed her from over the steams of the coffee.

"Stop fussing. It's unbecoming. What are you two doing today?"

"Well, now that my ma is better, the sky's the limit." Anton downed his coffee and put the cup in the sink. To me, he said, "We running?"

"Yes, please."

Anton headed back to his bedroom and I stayed in the kitchen. Sophia's hold on the tension was admirable, not that I saw her as competition. I drank the rest of my cup and said, "If you need anything, let me know."

I was almost out of the room when her voice stopped me.

"Samantha?"

I spun around expecting some kind of mommy praise about being with her son. Instead, I was met with cold, hard eyes.

"I do need something. I need you with my son at the next rally—holding hands, in public."

I shifted my gaze to the floor. There was nothing pleasant about being under someone's thumb. Sophia Myers was focused on the end game. She didn't care if I liked how we got there or not. Her goal would be reached. Make her son legit. Didn't I want the exact same thing?

"Understood."

In Anton's room, I laced up my shoes on the floor. He sat on the bed pulling on a dark hoodie.

"You know what?" he asked with a lightness in his voice that I'd never heard. Seeing his mother up had done wonders for him. "It just occurred to me that I've never worked out with a girl before you."

I lifted my eyebrows. If he didn't think the sex we were having was a cardio burn, he was sadly mistaken.

"Get your mind out of the gutter. You know what I mean."

I stood and climbed into his lap and tickled the back of his neck with my nails. His hair there was the softest thing I'd ever touched. "Do you think we can stay at my place tonight? Since she's better and all..."

"You don't like the idea of her hearing us fuck?"

My face fell and he caught it.

"Sorry, have sex."

I got out of his lap and he tugged me back.

"You know it's more than that." The sternness in his voice was reassuring, familiar. "And, I'm sleeping wherever you're sleeping."

Letting Sophia's ulterior motives fester inside me and poke at my self-doubts that he wasn't serious about me would only lead to me being insecure in front of him, which was not the way to go.

I smiled down at him. "You're going to let me sleep tonight?"

He stood and tapped me on the ass while he held the door open. "Nope."

The weather was threatening rain, and the air was thick with cool humidity. We ran for a full hour, all the while Anton respecting my 'no talking' rule. We stopped at a juice bar on the way home and sipped out of our clear plastic cups as we strolled through the city.

"What *do* you want to do today?" he asked as he reached for my empty drink then chucked both of them into a bin. His manners had once stuck me as odd, but then I'd remembered who his mother was. She'd probably drilled them into him with constant whacks on his head as a teenager.

"Be normal. Not talk to the press. Not get my ass on the front page of a paper."

"If any ass belongs on the front page, it's this one." He stopped walking and checked me out. "Mmm-mmm. That shit is tight, sunshine." He caught up with me and took my hand. "What would you do if I weren't here? What would be your normal?"

I would have been shopping. After the week I'd had, my self-care retail therapy would be soothing my front-page-ass off. I bit my bottom lip. I'd never met a man who liked to sit in a store while I tried on endless shit.

"I'd be shopping. Cliché, but true. Don't worry, though. I don't expect you to do that. We could go to a movie or the farmer's market. Oh! There's a new photo exhibit at the modern museum. Apparently, the photographer goes to war zones and does insane shots with this super-rare camera, and it looks like a glamorous photo shoot."

He looked at me like I was crazy. Maybe there was too much normal in there for him. Then again, maybe that was exactly what we needed. If we went back to my place and chilled out, we would end up in bed and I would never start to crack his steel shell. I would never give him the exposure to higher values.

It was settled, by me anyway. "Yep. That's exactly what we're doing. If you think about it, it's the perfect compromise — violence and fashion."

"Nope. Not going. You know what we could do? Buy you some new shoes then I can bend you over your counter and — "

We'd arrived in front of his mother's brownstone. I smirked and held out my hand. "I'll make you a deal. You come to the exhibit with me then you can do just that."

He shook my hand then waggled his eyebrows. "Have I ever told you I have a passion for warzone photography?"

We showered and changed. Anton packed an overnight bag and a second one for the gym on Monday. Somehow I managed to resist his tempting eyes and wandering hands and got him out of my apartment and over to the modern museum. It was a zoo. Saturday tourists were everywhere but Anton enduring art was totally worth it.

He held my hand loosely as we made our way through the lines. The pictures were stunning, and by the end of the show, Anton admitted to actually liking it. We walked down the avenue in the direction of my place and stopped at a little bistro for lunch.

Without his mother's watchful eye, I'd relaxed. I could be her lapdog in public and pose with her son — I was a professional — but in private, her insistent words had felt like an invasion of my space. The only problem was that she wasn't going anywhere. She had some kind of master plan for her son, and it involved me. I didn't like being a puppet, but I didn't mind my time with Anton. It was an odd blend.

We ordered and Anton weaved his fingers into mine from across the small table and rubbed his thumb into my palm.

"I've been thinking about the future. I liked your idea of real estate," he said with a shy smile. "My mom was right. I need a plan."

It was good and a sign he was leaving the past behind. It was a beginning.

"I actually like remodeling. I did it in Covington. We redid an entire floor."

I squeezed his hand. "If you can make money doing something you love, all the better."

He glanced away in introspection. "I think that's what happened in the end. My guys and I got tired of dealing. We saw what it was doing to the people around us. We got lazy. *I* got lazy."

The confession wasn't just a moment of him opening up. It was a signal that he was letting me in, that we were indeed real.

"You miss them, don't you?"

"It's like walking around in winter without a coat. But I think we're all better off. Besides, I have someone else to warm me up now. Also, I may have overthought your new shoes. I hope you like gold glitter."

I laughed. "Glitter?" Not that I wouldn't wear them.

Anton released my hand and dug out his phone. "Relax. They're not wrap-your-body-around-a-pole glitter." He showed me a picture on his screen of stunning gold sandalettes with a thin ankle strap and a heel that could take out an eye. "I may have done a little research while you were in the shower."

"Those are gorgeous. But I have to admit that I thought you'd go with a red or black."

"Nah... These are bright and shiny...just like my sunshine."

Chapter Eighteen

Anton

Samantha turned from her side to her back and the early morning sun highlighted her profile. Maybe it was weird for me to stare at her while she slept. The last time I'd watched a woman sleeping was Fiona the night after Leo had killed Mac. I'd been so fucking sure she'd choose me over him once he'd taken himself out of the picture. But their connection hadn't failed the test. Hell, they were still together.

I hadn't been lying the previous day at lunch. I wanted to change, but earning money illegally wasn't some kind of switch I could turn off. It was too easy, too thrilling. Knowing the guys walking down the street had to sit at a desk all day and earn jack shit while pushing a few drugs for an hour resulted in the same thing gave me swagger.

But if Samantha found out I was less than legit, would the connection we were building be as strong as what Leo had with Fiona? I'd never met a woman who knew how to give me my power and the desire not to abuse it at the same time. Something told me to hold on to her like a precious gift, that I would never find anyone like her again. She knew how to let me be and push me to be better at the same time. Jesus, she was just like my mother.

Then again, she wasn't. Sophia Myers was cold and calculated. She'd ordered murders and wasn't afraid to witness violence. She'd built a life of crime in the underworld and had successfully transitioned into a respected member of society.

Samantha had begun as legit. She'd gone to that upscale school, and from her taste in clothes alone, she'd come from money. She sure as shit wasn't paying for her apartment on a measly salary from the city. I was pretty sure a life with a drug dealer wasn't in her plans.

But how was I going to stop? Scooter was bringing me part of the stash later in the day, and I would take it to the gym with me every day until that fucker from Jefferson showed up with a bundle of cash in exchange. I'd gotten a lot of good qualities from my mother, but my father's greed ran rabid in my veins.

My selfish gluttony was why I was already thinking about how to lie to Samantha about meeting Scooter. It was buzzing inside my brain, saying that if I just sold off all my product then I could buy a building and renovate it, get legit slowly over time. But as I lay there, next to the best thing to ever happen to me in her expensive sheets with those fucking gold heels on the floor next to us, I knew we would not finish like Leo and Fiona. I would fuck up, and she would hate me.

I scrubbed my face and let out a groan. I needed to be better, do better.

Samantha stretched and opened her eyes but stayed on her back. "You can't possibly be cranky after last night. We literally fulfilled your fantasy."

She'd done it again—given me what I wanted but kept me in check. The more I'd shown her of my real self, the more she'd accepted me. It was mind-boggling. *Might as well keep going…*

"The truth is I'm worried about me fucking this thing up." I frowned. "I think I'm getting rather attached to you."

Her dark eyes twinkled when she turned to me. "The only way you can fuck this up is by lying to me. Otherwise, I dare you to try to get rid of me." She pecked me on the cheek then hopped up and walked naked to the bathroom. The doors stayed open and it hit me that she was the first woman to ever be that free in front of me. It was a small thing. I'd always just assumed girls liked their privacy. But it was also huge, especially considering that I was about to do the one thing she'd just told me would ruin us.

Lie. I was going to lie.

I got up and dressed then shot a text off to Scooter with the address of the children's park around the corner.

"Where you headed?" Samantha crinkled her nose.

"I'm going to get us some brunch. Go back to bed. I'm giving you the morning off." I winked and slipped past her before she could question me any further.

She called out, "Get a lot. I'm starving. Oh! And something sweet." I grabbed her keys from next to the door and left.

There was just one problem with my plan. If I got the food while I waited for Scooter, it would be cold by the time I got back. If I waited for Scooter then got the food, it could take a suspicious amount of time. I prayed he would come by car and counted on the Sunday morning slump in traffic to let him be speedy.

Thirty minutes later Scooter pulled up in a former Covington SUV and handed me a soccer ball. By its weight, I knew he'd filled it with meth. He'd done a pretty stellar job of sewing it back up. I couldn't even see where he'd opened it.

"I'll call you when I have your cut." I tucked the ball under my arm.

"Just happy to be back in business, bossman." He gave me a two-finger wave that was almost like a salute and was gone. That was one thing I always liked about Scooter. That kid got shit done.

Around the corner, I stood in line at the bakery then ordered enough quiche and apple turnovers to keep us fed for the rest of the day. I prayed for rain. Even though I'd liked the art exhibit, I wasn't planning on upping my culture game on a Sunday.

With a coffee in hand and a bag full of food, I walked back to Samantha's. Funny to think that just fifty blocks up I'd led a completely different life.

When I got to her door, I stopped short of turning the key. What if she was on the couch instead of in the bed? I sat the ball on the floor in the hallway and opened the door. The apartment was empty, so I placed the coffee and food inside then quickly stuffed the ball into my gym bag. As I stood, her footsteps came from the bedroom.

"What took you so long?" She was in her favorite sweatshirt and a pair of paisley pajama shorts. Her hair was up, completely messy but beautiful.

I decided on a half-truth. "I ran into somebody I used to know. It was…awkward."

She laughed. "I can't imagine you feeling awkward in any situation. I'm sorry I missed it. But I'm still starving. I need to be fed immediately."

Her hunger didn't catch the lie. I kissed her on the cheek and placed our breakfast on the center island of her kitchen. She set out plates and I divided the food in equal parts. She dug in and groaned her way through the meal.

Right as we finished, my phone vibrated in my pocket.

"Hey, Ma. How you feeling?"

Samantha cleaned off the counter and did the dishes. Her little ass was barely covered by those shorts and I wondered how much time I would have to give her to digest before I ripped those things right off her. She glanced over her shoulder and rolled her eyes. My stare must have burned her skin.

"I'm feeling like my son doesn't know how to date a woman. Have you even asked her out to dinner?" The bite in her tone would have normally been followed by a swat on my head.

"I have, thank you very much. While you had the flu and wouldn't see people, I even cooked for her. So simmer down, Sophia."

"Don't call me by my first name. You know I hate that."

"I'm pretty sure I'm doing just fine."

She sighed. It was over-the-top and miserably dramatic. "Well, I'm pretty sure I know my son. And something tells me you're going to mess this up."

My mother's sixth sense when it came to me was beyond eerie. One time when I was fourteen, I'd taken a gun from her closet and was going to show it off to some of my friends. She'd blocked the front door and said I would have to shoot her before she let me leave the house. But three days after, she had one of her goons drive me Upstate and he taught me how to use a rifle and a pistol.

"Everything is under control, Ma." I gritted my teeth. I fucking hated it when she got under my skin and was right as to why.

"Is that why a certain pink product has magically reappeared in your old neighborhood?"

Fuck. I should have known she'd be on the lookout for that. I walked over to the opposite side of the apartment and lowered my voice.

"Not mine. Not gonna lie, I looked Upstate, but someone got to it first. I assumed it was you."

"It wasn't. My people didn't find anything. Be at the rally tomorrow night with your girlfriend." She hung up and I closed my eyes. I broke out in a small sweat. She'd pressed then twisted all my buttons. I wasn't smart enough to know how to date a woman like Samantha. I was doing shit behind her back and some-fucking-how my mother had accused me of exactly what I was doing.

Samantha stood in the kitchen with her hands on the counter and lips pursed. "What was that about?"

"My mother being my mother." I let out a breath.

Her gaze scrutinized my every fiber. A disgusted frown crossed her face. "You don't think I know that tactic? Say something vague but avoid the real question?"

The getting called out for my shit was getting old quick. I tilted my head to the side, challenging her to keep digging. "You wanna accuse me of dealing again, too?"

Before she could answer, I continued, "Look. I am trying here. My entire life as I knew it is fucking over. My friends aren't lighting up my phone to see if I'm okay. In fact, most of them don't want anything to do with me right now. I don't need her breathing down my neck, telling me to take you out to dinner or I'm going to fuck this whole thing up."

Her frown was gone and she looked away, weighing my words. "Are you?"

"Going to fuck this up? Probably."

She shook her head. "That's not what I meant. Are you dealing drugs again? And before you answer that, you should know that the only right answer is the true one."

She would pounce on any lie I threw out. Jesus, she was better at sniffing them out than my mother. No wonder she was good at her job.

"Remember I said I would take care of any threat to you or my family? I gave the new guy in charge some of my product to encourage him to stay away from you." While not the whole truth, it was a portion of it. My heart raced as I hoped it was enough.

A long, agonizing pause pulsed between us. Holy shit, I was nervous to lose her. The token of truth had to win out. Telling her everything would be the end, I was sure.

"Okay." She nodded once.

Okay? That was it? She was going to accept me for that shit?

"Are you serious?" I didn't recognize the shock in my tone.

Samantha stepped toward me, her eyes narrowed but without anger. "What? You don't think your stepdaddy isn't involved in some murky shit? I do illegal things, too. I got off my self-righteous pedestal a while back. I do think you can do better, dream a little bigger. In fact, I want to help you do that. And just for the record, you haven't mastered the dating experience yet."

With the tension evaporated by her decision, the playfulness between us came back.

I crossed my arms. "That sounds like a challenge. One I gladly accept. Movie and dinner it is, then."

"Wow," she teased. "So original. Look at you." She pawed at me like a stupid cat. "But you're on. I haven't been to the movies forever. Be warned that I like butter with my popcorn."

"You know that shit's unnatural, right? I think it's made from palm oil or some shit."

On her tiptoes, she pecked me quickly on the lips. "Awww, he cares about my arteries." Off she padded to the bedroom and I stared at the empty hall long after she'd disappeared.

I relaxed and her blanket of sunshine spread over me. Whatever it was that we had, it could work. I had a hunger for power, and she had mastered finesse. Together, we could conquer any challenge.

Something clicked inside my head. I'd always wanted to make my mother proud and never really considered our wellbeing. Yes, I'd had to earn certain things along the way. But the threat of my mother abandoning me had never really been there — proven when I'd asked her for help with finding Mac.

But Samantha risked being temporary — and that would never do.

After showing her a little bit of my true self, she was more on board than ever. In fact, she seemed to appreciate my honesty and not give a fuck about the implications. I had to hand it to my mother. Samantha was my perfect match.

Chapter Nineteen

Samantha

"You're all floaty or fleety or some shit today. What is wrong with you?" Fanny had her chin tucked in and she squinted one eye from across the table in the small French restaurant where we ate lunch.

It was unusual for us to eat out, but our day was slow. When we could, we made an effort to not 'desk dine' as she called it. Besides, getting us out of our professional roles reminded us that we were also friends, and a different setting allowed us permission to speak about non-work related subjects.

I had both flat and sparkling water in two different glasses, and we'd had to go back to the office because I'd forgotten my phone. I was all floaty and shit. "Have you ever had sex that was like, 'Oh....*that's* what it's supposed to do to me'?"

She snorted. "Yeah. The first time I kissed a girl. I was like, '*oh yeah*'." She lifted a finger and made a small loop with it. "That's what I was missing."

I shifted the last bit of green-bean salad on my plate. "It's like my boundaries are being pushed but" — I hesitated, searching for the right word — "respected? It's all super intense then he shows me a gentle side. He calls me, 'sunshine'." I practically whined out the last bit, like a 'how can I do anything with that?' plea for her to understand.

Fanny popped in her last fry. "Oh, mama, you've got it bad, *bad* for the bad boy."

After a fake whimper, I scrubbed my face. "I do. And it's not just physical. I actually *like* him."

She shifted a little in her seat. "I would be remiss if I didn't state the obvious speed at which you two are moving. This is very unlike you."

It wasn't a thought that hadn't played over in my head each time he spent the night at my apartment or when I wondered if I hadn't caught a lie because his charisma was blinding me.

I twisted my lips and let out a small huff through my nose. "I'm pretty sure that's the only speed he has."

"I hope you have a parachute."

The waiter came and collected our plates. Fanny left before me, because she had a meeting with some union delegates in Queens, and I sat and sipped a coffee. The night before, Anton had shared more with me, but that was just it — more. I wasn't stupid enough to think it was *all*. A man like him required patience. He wasn't going to just let me in on his every move until he fully, fully trusted me.

But he had been given a test and passed. I'd asked for truth and he'd given me some. Maybe that was all I could expect. The only problem was that I didn't want *some* of him. I wanted *all* of him.

I walked back to the office and without the typical Monday madness, my pace was leisurely. As we reached the beginning of October and with the election five short weeks away, a chill cut through the air. Fall had always been my favorite season. The heat of the summer made the city stink and swelter. The change of climate was always a welcome relief.

Wilted leaves of various colors covered the litter in the streets and helped mask the filth the hotter days had reminded us of. Representing the mayor — and by extension the city itself — filled me with pride and joy. I had my dream job and might just have found *the* man to go along with it.

Yes, it was all fast. But with that speed also came a sense of purity. There was no time for bullshit.

When I got to the steps of City Hall, Mitch stood halfway up, leaning against the handrail. He followed me with his eyes but stayed where he was. I was in a good mood, so I bit and walked up to him.

"Mitch," I said with a tight grin. *No point in being overly friendly.*

"Hey. I'm glad I ran into you alone."

That was an interesting thing to say. He usually ran into me alone. I narrowed my eyes.

He rubbed the stubble on his cheek and twisted his face like he was fighting a sneeze. "You know how I said a friend of mine at *The Scoop* said he was tipped off?"

"Yes."

"He says it was Sophia Myers."

A small sympathy crinkled around his eyes, but I didn't want it. I wasn't weak.

"Does that surprise you?"

"A little," he admitted. "Not you?"

It was sweet, his dopey way of thinking we were friends somehow, thinking he knew more than I did, thinking I was a victim. "Off the record?"

"Sure."

"Nope. See you tonight?" I took a step back and paused for his answer before climbing the rest of the stone steps.

"You know me. My beat is Demsey."

Same as mine. Mitch stayed against the railing as I went in the doors. After security, I went up to my office where an intern was manning the phones for Fanny. I closed my door and tackled my emails in peace for the rest of the afternoon.

At five-thirty, I joined Demsey downstairs and we drove to the rally together. Security met us in a garage, and I let them walk my boss away where his campaign team was waiting to brief him.

Standing alone against a far wall was Anton, dressed like a proper respectable stepson. He wore a shiny navy-blue suit and the light shirt underneath made his eyes pop more than usual. The tight fit hugged his muscles and I wondered if he would be pissed if I asked him to thin out just a little to become less intimidating to the public – packaging mattered. Not that I didn't like it. It just didn't work in our favor.

I walked over to him and interlaced our fingers. He lifted our arms, and the movement drew me closer. The magnetic energy swarmed around us and I went in for a tender kiss on his soft lips. He wrapped an arm around my waist and nothing had ever felt so right. He was home, security and promised a bond that could not be broken. We held the embrace for a long breath until I realized people were watching us.

"Hi," I said as I looked up into his pretty eyes.

"Hi, yourself. I missed you today." He twirled a lock of my hair then gave it a little tug. The sweet side of him was the one that was drawing me in more and more. It had been an unexpected yet very much welcomed discovery.

"You know we don't have to do anything until the end of this thing. That's when the photo ops are—when it's over." Part of my job was watching Demsey speak, and choosing Anton over work was easier than it should have been. I could have stayed in his arms and recharged for an hour instead of listening to the bullshit my boss was going to spew to a crowd of people who already loved him—not that he wasn't known for shooting off the cuff and giving me plenty to clean up the following day.

"Nah," Anton said with a slow shake of his head. "I want to see what he does up there, and I'm pretty sure you do to. Come on."

We held hands and walked to the side of the stage where the campaign team buzzed around Demsey. Noticeably absent was one tiny, powerful woman.

"I thought your mom was coming with you."

"She said she overdid it this weekend by going to a long brunch. That flu knocked her on her ass. I told her to stay home and promised to be a good boy and smile for the cameras."

Without Sophia there, Demsey would need someone else to ground him. I let go of Anton's hand and waited until they were seconds away from introducing the mayor. I stepped in front of him and straightened his tie then dusted off his lapel.

A flash of worry spread across his normally jovial face.

"Stick to the script and we'll take you out for a steak after. I'll even stay for the Scotch and make Anton smoke a cigar. These people already love you. Remind them why."

He glanced to the crowd then back to me. "She's sick."

The words hung between us. It wasn't the time or place to address them.

I nodded once. "We'll deal with it. The election is only a month away. Home stretch. Remember... You know how to win."

Demsey took in a deep breath and plastered a fake smile across his face. I tapped his shoulder then waited next to him with my arm looped into his. The admission about Sophia had been heavy and implied a hell of a lot more than the flu or a common cold. I'd suspected as much and all signs pointed to cancer. Anton couldn't see it out of fear of losing her or seeing her as unable to conquer anything that got in Sophia Myers' way.

One thing I knew for sure was that it wasn't my place to tell Anton, but I did need to know the extent of what was coming at us.

The announcer called his name and Demsey turned to me. I let go of his arm and said in a steady tone, "Just do your thing. Easy."

He winked. He could do showtime better than most and went out with a huge smile on his face and his arms lifted, receiving all the cheers from the crowd. Anton stepped behind me, put his arms around my waist and used my right shoulder as a resting place for his chin.

In his forty-five-minute stump speech, Demsey hit every talking point with an adroitness very few were capable of. He drew in the crowd with personal stories of people he knew how to help with his plans and made pipedream promises seem like ant hills instead of the bureaucratic mountains they would most definitely be. All in all, he nailed it. He may have never been better.

The campaign team, Anton and I joined him on stage at the end — all clapping to a classic rock song about the working man. We waved to people in the audience that we didn't know and, after congratulating Demsey on hitting it out of the park, I found my way back to Anton's side and took his hand in mine.

We locked our gaze, knowing we had to give the press their nibble of our personal life. I nodded slowly, giving him permission to publicly solidify our relationship.

Anton lifted my hand to his mouth and kissed the back of it. It wasn't my imagination that flashes from the press corps sped up, but I didn't care. We walked off stage in a group, Anton's arm around Demsey's shoulder and my hand still clutched with his.

Backstage, Demsey shook hands with people who had special access and listened to their stories with interest, not rushing any of them.

Anton watched it all by my side until he finally asked, "What did you say to him, anyway?"

I shrugged. "It's not what I said. It's that I was there."

He studied me with curiosity.

Yes, I could do the same thing for you.

Anton blinked several times before a stranger came up to him and asked him about his mother. He handled it well, and I fished my phone out of my bag to see what the press was saying about the rally.

Out of the corner of my eye, I caught Mitch hanging back with a confused look on his face. I stored the phone and walked over.

"He nailed that. His numbers are going to shoot up." Mitch's checkered shirt collar stuck out of a navy zipped-up sweater. He was kinda an adorable nerd when I thought about it.

"Yeah, he was good." My job would be easy the next day.

"Care to comment on the absence of his wife?"

"Recovering from the flu." My tone was bored then I teased, "Leave that old woman alone, Mitch. The last thing she wants to do is miss one of these things. But infecting voters isn't a good look." I scolded him with a playful, dirty look.

Mitch showed me the screen of his phone. It was the website of *The Scoop* with a big picture of Demsey then scrolled down to smaller photo of Anton and me the exact moment he'd kissed the back of my hand.

"You two have officially become the 'it' couple. Hope you're ready for all that comes with."

I pursed my lips. "Mitch, you sound jealous. Shame on you." I stepped away, not wanting to admit to the reality of what he'd said. The city's socialites were just as much celebrities as the actors and musicians. *Was* I ready for that?

The backstage crowd started to thin, and I found Demsey talking to a young boy about science. I waited for a break and excused myself to the father then son.

"I'm so sorry. My 'time police' have come to take me away. Thank you so much for coming out." Demsey shook both their hands and I led him back over to

Anton then the three of us climbed into a black SUV and were driven to a restaurant where we were met with a donor from the area for dinner.

High on his performance, Demsey carried the dinner conversation with ease well into dessert. Anton checked his watch several times. He didn't know just how long these things could last. A captive rich audience of one was Demsey's favorite.

I leaned over to my boyfriend, "Hey, why don't you go and check on your mom? I know that it's eating at you. I'll bring him home in a couple of hours then climb into bed with you. I'll skip my run and we can have breakfast together."

His cheeks flushed with relief and he gave me a little kiss. "That's exactly what I need. Plus, I haven't told you that I met with a real estate broker and am going to look at a few buildings tomorrow. I wanted to get your take on the neighborhoods."

I couldn't contain my wide smile. He was doing it. He was taking the steps in the right direction.

Anton left and Demsey went on for two more hours. With the amount of Scotch he'd had, my opportunity for the truth would be a small window before he fell asleep in the car. Plus, he was always easier to get information from if he was drunk.

Once we got on the highway, I dove straight in. "I need to know what we're dealing with. Tell me everything that's going on with Sophia. I know she probably swore you to secrecy, but if I don't know the truth, I can't spin it in your favor. I swear I won't tell him."

Demsey frowned but it was for show. He'd already broken his vow to his wife by what he'd said earlier. He knew he had to tell me. I was his best chance of overcoming it.

"It's stomach cancer. She'd been in remission for years but now it's back and it's fucking everywhere." He shook his head. It had never occurred to me that he actually cared about Sophia, but the stark look on his face proved he did.

"What about chemo?"

He shook his head somberly. "That's what put her in bed all last week. I'm not sure she's going to keep it up. She doesn't see the point and is horrified of losing her hair with the public eye on her. Last time, she suffered in private. She wasn't on the radar, so to speak."

"Okay." I tapped his hand. "Thank you for telling me. Let's stick with the flu for now."

All the pieces fell perfectly in place. She'd sent Anton to Covington because she was ill. He hadn't known about it. That was why it had been so easy for him to believe she just had the flu.

Demsey snored next to me for the hour it took to get us back to the city. I nudged him awake and said good night to him at the top of the stairs before heading in the opposite direction to Anton's room.

I undressed and slipped into bed.

"Hey, sunshine," he whispered and nudged me to get on top of him.

"Hey, yourself." I rocked my hips and brushed over his cock then brought a finger to my lips. "Shhhh...we have to be quiet."

I kept gliding until he was hard then pushed down so he was inside of me. I never stopped looking at him and he never urged me to heighten the intensity or pace. Back and forth I went, making love to him as he watched intently.

When he was ready to come, instead of digging his fingers into me he said, "Slow. Really fucking slow."

It was only then that he closed his eyes and strained below me. His entire body went stiff as a board as he huffed through his orgasm then relaxed as he caught his breath. I kept him inside me and nuzzled down on his chest where his heart thumped below my ear.

We fell asleep like that, both of us knowing everything was different, that everything was real.

Chapter Twenty

Anton

Samantha was curled into a small ball with her warm ass pushing into my side. It was early, too early to get up, too early to wake her from her peaceful sleep. It had been so deliberate and effective the way she'd stood in for my mother the night before at the rally then dinner. She had a way of giving men confidence when they needed it most.

And when she'd crawled into bed with me, we hadn't fucked. We hadn't just had some kind of normal-ish sex. She'd made fucking love to me. And I'd loved it—*me*. Our connection, our bond, just kept getting stronger. The smart, sexy, beautiful woman sleeping to my right had chosen to be there.

Her instincts were a thing of beauty. She'd known Demsey had needed something, then had known I wanted to leave. I was in awe of how easy she made it all look. She never forced her hand to be the center of attention…and a woman like her could. There was a certain grace about her that a person wouldn't see unless they really studied her. I had no idea what love was, but I was pretty fucking sure if I didn't love her already, I was on the road to it. One thing I did know was that I didn't want to live a life without her in it.

For the first time in years, I felt vulnerable. What would I do without her? What if she found out how dark my soul was? But, then again, the glimpses I'd shown her she'd been okay with. I would have to let go of my fears and enjoy the freefall. What did Leo used to say? *'Fear is bullshit. Fear only exists because we allow it to fuck with us.'*

She stirred a little and I flipped to my side and kissed her bare shoulder then threaded my arm up her chest. She was soft, yet strong, cunning and elegant. Fuck, she was everything — and she was mine.

I would be better for her. Hell, I wanted to be someone she was proud of. I would just sell off the rest of the stash Scooter had then let him take over. I would get out of crime. It would make both Samantha and my mother happy. I'd miss the deviant side of myself, but if it meant I could wake up with her next to me, so be it.

There was a building I was going to see that would be perfect. It was on the edge of an up-and-coming neighborhood and was a total shithole disaster, but it could be flipped. If Demsey's idiot brother could make money in real estate, so the fuck could I.

I nuzzled into her a little tighter. I didn't consider myself a changed man, more like a *changing* man. But eventually, I knew I could be everything she wanted. I had to be.

My mind raced for the next hour until the alarm on my phone finally woke her. She rolled onto her back and stretched.

Her eyes fluttered open. "Oh my God, I slept so well."

"Don't move. I have you all to myself for one hour and I'm going to make the most of it." I kissed her forehead then swiveled to the side of the bed and pulled on a pair of sweatpants.

The shower was running down the hall in Demsey and my mother's room and a cleaner was already dusting in the hallway. I made two coffees, scrambled some eggs, buttered four slices of wholewheat toast and left the mess while I piled everything on a tray and took it back up to my room.

Samantha was seated against the headboard of my bed in the shirt I'd worn the night before and scrolling through her phone.

I grinned. "Oh, I like you in that."

She dropped her phone and fisted the collar before bringing it up to her nose and inhaling. "It smells like you. I might just steal it."

I walked the tray over to the bed and placed it between us and handed her a coffee.

"Oh, yeah? What do I smell like?"

She looked me dead in the eyes. "Power." A wry grin appeared before she glanced away and sipped her cup.

That was when I knew. I wasn't falling in love with her at all. I was fucking *in* love with her. She understood everything about me. But what the fuck was I supposed to do about it? Tell her? I didn't think I had the ability.

"So…you had some buildings to show me?" she said after taking a bite of the eggs.

I wanted her honest opinion, so I didn't say which one I was most excited about. Instead, I let her scroll through the email the broker had sent me while I ate.

"This one." She showed me the picture of the one I liked. "We're going to flip the public housing a block east into condos. By the time you get it renovated, the announcement will come out. It's perfect."

I beamed, because that was what it was like to be around my sunshine.

Samantha's phone vibrated to her right. "Crap. Sorry. I should get home and shower. I've been summoned by the chief this afternoon and need to get some stuff done this morning. Thanks for this." She finished her coffee and popped out of bed then got dressed quickly.

"Dinner later?" I asked with a foolish hopefulness I'd never experienced.

She slipped on her heels, they were taupe and classy yet somehow still sexy as hell. "I'll text you later after I see how my day goes. We'll be on an upswing from last night, which could mean anything. But I'd love to."

She came over and kissed me on my cheek, making the entire morning too fucking domestic. With a little twinkle in her eye, she swiped up my shirt she'd been wearing.

"I'm still taking this."

She could have anything she wanted from me. A shirt was a small price to pay for her happiness.

I tugged at her arm. I didn't want her to leave without showing her sign of my feelings. I whispered, "I like what happened last night."

She smiled. It was small and tender. "I know. And don't worry... I still like the other way, too. See you later."

She closed the door behind her without giving me a final glance. She'd somehow managed to put me at ease yet again.

I showered and called the broker who was eager to show me the building that afternoon. I would have to balance it with going to the gym, so I would be walking around either with a bag full of drugs or money. Cash was the safer bet, so I called Juliana's salon and asked her to solidify my meeting with her boyfriend.

The only problem was the tiny twinge of guilt eating at me that I was going behind Samantha's back. Guilt was as new as love, so I had no idea what to do with it but ignore it. I reminded myself that I was *changing*, not changed. I'd get there one day.

Demsey was gone when I got to the kitchen, but my mother was sitting at the counter. She was dressed in her version of comfortable clothes—a black silk loungewear set with a long light blue scarf. But she wore makeup, so for me she was on the mend.

"Morning, Ma. You get some rest?"

"Yes. I heard Samantha stayed. That's very pleasing."

I rolled my eyes. "You know I always pictured ending up with someone you hated. This whole approval side of you? I have no idea what to do with that."

"Nonsense. I would have made any woman's life a living hell if I didn't think she was good enough for you. Besides, since when did you ever think of ending up with someone?" She scoffed and went back to her paper.

Since Samantha.

I liked being in my mother's good graces, and I was sure that me doing things right would bring her some joy. And that might just give her some energy for to her beat whatever it was that didn't want to let go of her. If she stopped worrying about me, she could focus on herself for once. So after making myself a second coffee, I said, "I'm going to look at building downtown. Samantha thinks real estate could be a good way for me to go. Apparently, they're about ready to change the zoning."

She flapped down the paper and perked up. Yeah, I thought she'd like that. A warm grin spread across her normally cool face. "That's very good news. I like it. Also, since I seem to be singing your praises this morning, I won't forget to mention what a good job you both did last night at the rally. I looked at the pictures online this morning. Quite the buzz."

Hell must have frozen over because if I was counting correctly, my mother had given me three compliments in the space of ten minutes. I'd never imagined talking about my personal life with my mother, but I'd also never been in the situation to do so.

"She has something. You know?" I said in wonder. "Like this instinct or ability to read people then motivate them to be their best. I have no idea if she even knows she's doing it. You should have seen her last night with Demsey. He was nervous without you there, so she went up to him and well, you saw his speech. He was fantastic."

"That's why she's perfect for you."

I hated when my mother was right, but I had to give it to her. She'd found the one woman on the planet who was my match.

"Do you want to have lunch together?" The question to my mother surprised even me. This getting along shit was fucking bizarre.

"I have plans...but thank you. You know, I was thinking... With you out in the public, those Ricci brothers may be more open to seeing you again. I know you miss Leo. Why not reach out?" She folded the paper and slid off the bar stool. Her wrists were the thinnest I'd ever seen. They looked like they could snap at any moment and her hands would dangle without any support.

"Are you sure you just had the flu? Did you even see a doctor?"

"Look at you...all mother hen. Call Leo. It will do you some good." She shooed me out of the kitchen with one hand while she stabilized herself on the counter with the other. A change of subject and encouraging me to meet up with a murderer? That woman did not have the fucking flu. I would ask Samantha if she knew anything about it when I saw her. Maybe I would even threaten Demsey.

I walked down the hall and grabbed my gym bag. What I wouldn't do was pressure my mother. She would tell me or she wouldn't. It didn't matter. I would find out the truth my own way.

On the street, I called Ricci and he picked up on the first ring.

He laughed instead of saying hello. "Let me guess. You need to hit someone and you're under the impression it will be me."

After years of friendship, I knew one thing to be clear and certain about the Ricci brothers. They were competitive fucks.

"Well, I figure your brother is getting old and we both know Jackson moves at the pace of an ogre."

"I'm putting you on speaker. The guys deserve to hear your trash talk first-hand. Get this, Frankie. Myers thinks you're dusty."

Frankie laughed in the background. "Cocky as ever. Let me ask you this, former bossman. When's the last time you trained seriously? Cuz me and the boys? We do that shit every morning. If anyone is going to get their ass handed to them, it's you."

I grinned from ear to ear—not because he was probably right, but because they were actually considering letting me join them.

Jackson's deep voice chimed in, "I don't know, man. The mayor's son probably needs to pose for some more pictures with his new girlfriend. Where will he ever find the time in his busy schedule?"

He's talking shit now? Oh, I definitely needed to take his giant ass down.

"Yeah," Leo said. "His face isn't going to look so pretty once we get done with him."

Taking their verbal jabs was to be expected. I wasn't their boss anymore. I would have to prove myself to be their friend again. It would be hard for me to think of Jackson as my equal, but I owed them my life. I could let them have their fun. It would be worth the small bruises to my ego just to be around them again.

"Time and place. Name it."

There was a pause on the other end. If it was just up to Leo, I would have gotten a yes. But Frankie was the big brother and me stepping into their world required his blessing.

"We'll text you," Frankie said before the line went dead.

Chapter Twenty-One

Samantha

After lunch, I headed to the chief's office and went through security with just my phone in hand. When I got upstairs and tapped on his door, Jack frowned and said, "Close it behind you."

My palms got sweaty and my heart raced. Jack's tone only meant bad news. A thousand thoughts flipped through my mind. What the fuck had Demsey done? And we'd just gone up in the morning polls from the buzz of the night before.

I walked over and sat in a chair facing the chief. Whatever it was, I could handle it. I did damage control for a living. I folded my hands in my lap and crossed my legs at the ankle. I sat up straight, ready for whatever he was going to throw my way.

"Let me just start by saying that it gives me absolutely no pleasure to play you this. I like you, Sammie. And while this is bad, there is a solution."

"Okay…"

"Does the name Scott Tucker mean anything to you?" Jack crossed his arms and narrowed an eye.

"No, but I assume it should." I kept my voice level even though my throat was tightening.

"Scooter?" he tried.

"Drawing a blank here, chief."

Jack swiveled his computer screen to me. An audio recording and its graph-like lines took up the bottom of the screen.

"He's the second voice you'll hear. I think you'll recognize the first."

Fuck. What had Demsey said to this Scooter person? And a recording? That meant more than just the chief had heard this. It was going to be a mess to clean, whatever it was up—not to mention Sophia had cancer and if he'd told me, he very well may have let it slip to someone else.

Jack hesitated before tapping the space bar with this index finger. "I'm sorry, Sammie."

"How's Callie?"

Anton's voice was unmistakable, and a thousand pounds landed on my shoulders. It had nothing to do with Demsey. It was my fucking boyfriend. I cradled my chin with my hands and my pulse thumped into my thumbs. This could not be happening. And yet, it got worse.

"Same. I was waiting for your message."
"I sent you hundreds of messages."
"Nah, bro. That the pink is back in the stink. Callie's cousin said the junkies have never been so happy. You saw Cookie."
"Not sure what you mean there, Scoot."

"After you… I went up to your place and got the goods. I saw how your mother was running shit. She would have someone up there digging around in no time."

"Wait! You have my shit?"

"Was just waiting to see if you'd surface again. Speaking of surface, your new girlfriend has quite the ass on her."

"I'm just fucking that snooty bitch to keep busy. Listen… Do you think you could put fifty thousand worth of pink into a soccer ball and meet me at a park on Sunday?"

"You know I can."

Snooty bitch? That's how he refers to me behind my back? What a fool I'd been, afraid that my attraction to him was blurring my ability to catch his lies and I was right.

They unraveled one by one. Sunday he'd *"ran into an old friend"*. He'd lied about dealing again, actually been fucking offended by the accusation, using the excuse he was doing it to protect me. And those were just the ones confirmed in the recording.

They had him in his own incriminating words. It would ruin him, his mother and Demsey in one fell, disastrous swoop—not to mention that I would be pegged as dating a drug dealer. That would do wonders for my reputation and career.

But Jack had said there was a solution.

"So…that's really bad." I let out a huff, not sure I could spin my way out of cold, hard facts.

"Guess who the handling officer is?"

My heart stopped. *Not fucking her.* Demsey's opponent's wife was on the force—in narcotics.

Jack nodded as I understood.

"Well, that's fucking worse."

"Is it?" Jack shrugged and sat back in his chair with his hands laced behind his neck.

What did he mean? This recording was like a giant wrecking ball to everything I held dear—not to mention that my heart had just been ripped out. I'd asked Anton for one fucking condition. No lies. And so far, I had proof of two. But would I be able to just write Anton off? I hated the idea of being weak and accepting bad behavior, but I couldn't deny the pull he had on me.

I needed to focus on Jack. There was a way out of this. He went on, "Turns out Valerie Carver wants to be first lady of the state more than a cop. I told her she wasn't equipped to go up against you in public."

"I can't spin that. It's him." I shook my head.

"It's not a home run, Sammie. There's nothing about Demsey on here. Don't underestimate your ability to play the sympathy card with whatever is going on with his wife. Besides, you have quite a bit of shit on me. I'm not going to let this get out. You're a vengeful woman. You think I'd take that risk?"

Holy. Shit. My eyes widened. He was ready to bury this. But at what cost?

He blinked and frowned. "You just have to decide where your loyalty is. Your boss or your boyfriend."

I suddenly understood. "If I ruin Demsey, she'll forget about this Scooter guy." It was a risk. I would have to throw out some pretty big, stinky fish on Demsey. It would have to be dramatic, and it might just cost me everything. But what choice did I have? If I let the recording surface, Anton's future was at stake. My reputation would be in the toilet and Demsey might lose anyway. But, if I left my job before the election and buried the crime, I might have an ounce of credibility left. And if Anton could forgive me for what I was pretty sure I was about to do, I might have a future with him. Plus, I was willing to wager that Sophia would choose her son every time over her husband. There would be no wrath from her.

It was going to be ugly, but once it was over, I could explain it all to Anton and he would see. Besides, there had to be some kind of consequence for lying to me. Come to think of it, that "*snooty bitch*" comment stung. *Fucker.* But I would save his reputation—not just because he had potential to be an incredibly powerful man but because, despite what I'd just heard, I was pretty sure I loved him.

Jack smacked his lips. "You should probably resign."

"I'll do that now." I stood and swept the wrinkles out of my navy-blue dress. "Tell Valerie Carver she'll make an excellent first lady."

I set my shoulders back, nodded my goodbye to Jack and walked out of his office. My plan would work. I had all the tools at my disposal. I knew all Demsey's weaknesses, starting with his wife.

Outside headquarters, I dialed Mitch from *The Times*.

"Hey there, Sammie. This is a surprise. You usually send all my calls to your voicemail."

"You can quote a source close to the campaign as confirming that Sophia Myers has stage four stomach cancer."

There was a long pause until he said, "Hell hath no fury."

I walked back to my office, and once inside, I said to Fanny, "I'm about to resign and you should, too. This ship is about ready to sink to the bottom of the East River."

Chapter Twenty-Two

Anton

A group of reporters flocked in front of my mother's house, which wasn't ideal considering there was a ridiculous amount of cash in the gym bag I was carrying down the street. Something was wrong. Good news never got that much attention.

I hung back and dialed Samantha, but she didn't answer. Maybe she was busy dealing with whatever shitstorm was likely unfolding. I pulled up the browser on my phone and did a quick search for Demsey.

On the front page of *The Times*, I got my answer. *'Demsey's Wife Dying of Cancer'*. My mind raced. How had Samantha let them publish this? Fucking worse, was it true? A tightness clamped my chest, and I knew it was.

Fucking flu. How had I been so blind? *Because I wanted to be*. I was so caught up in getting my life back that I didn't want to admit I'd seen hers drifting away. I hitched the bag over my shoulder and looked down at the ground until I had to maneuver my way through the crowd at the bottom of the steps.

"Any comment on your mother's health?"

"How do you think this will affect the election?"

"Is this why your mother wasn't at the rally?"

"Why did your girlfriend resign?"

The last question made me stop in my tracks, but I wouldn't give them the satisfaction of my ignorance. I pushed through until I was safe inside and I dropped my bag in the entryway.

Demsey and my mother were in her office and she hadn't changed from her casual clothes I'd seen her in that morning. She'd obviously lied about having plans for lunch, and the look on her face was enough to confirm the reports of cancer.

"Where the fuck is Samantha? Why isn't she dealing with this?" I didn't know which one of them to look at, so my gaze raced between them.

Demsey scoffed. "Why isn't she dealing with this? She's the reason for it. Do you think it's a coincidence that she resigned an hour before the story broke? She and her assistant. Fucking backstabbing bitch."

Wait. *She did this?*

The blow of my mother being ill was one thing, but then to know that Samantha didn't tell me *and* she leaked it to the press? That was a level of betrayal I could not get over.

I was sure I was spinning. That morning I'd almost told her I loved her. But putting my mother's personal life on the front page? I wasn't sure I'd ever forgive her that sin, no matter her reasoning…if she even had any. Maybe she was the most skilled liar to ever exist. Maybe I was a two-hundred-pound fool.

Hot hate spread through my veins then I looked at my frail mother and realized it didn't matter. She was dying. I was losing the one person who truly loved me. Yes, I was angry that she'd kept it from me. But what else was she going to do? She didn't want my pity. She wanted my success.

Demsey's phone rang and he walked out of the room, swearing at whoever was on the other end. I closed my eyes to rid myself of all my anger. I would deal with Samantha later. My mother needed me. I walked over to her and took her in my arms. I hadn't seen her cry since she'd been with my father, but a lonely tear fell down her thin face.

"I didn't know how to tell you."

I reached out and stroked her cheek. Jesus, she was skin and bones. "So all this—the stupid marriage, the throwing me onto the social scene—it was all to get me on the right path before you go?"

"Basically." She pushed me away. "What I don't understand is why Samantha would leak this. It doesn't make any sense. There had to be a good reason."

"Money, power." Or she was just a backstabbing bitch like Demsey had said.

"No, don't hate her just yet. From one conniving woman to another, I recognize a bold move as a decoy for something else."

Although the odds were that my mother was right— just based on past examples—I couldn't help but be pissed off. If Samantha had a plan, she should have let me in on it.

"I need to go lie down. Come check on me later." My mother rubbed a temple and stepped toward the door.

"Do you want me to bring you something to eat?"

She turned back and her small, honest smile sent a chill up my spine. "I haven't eaten in days, sweetheart."

My heart sank. It was the truest thing she'd ever said to me. She turned and left. My phone vibrated in my pocket and for a split second I hoped it was Samantha. Instead, my codename for Leo flashed with an address and *'six a.m.'*. Sparring with those fuckers in the morning was just the medicine I needed. Maybe they'd seen the news and taken pity on me. I didn't care. I needed a fight and I knew just where to find it.

I ate dinner alone in the kitchen. Demsey had his campaign staff over and they were planning how they could try to use my mother's illness to get a sympathy vote. I couldn't listen. When the fall night turned dark, the reporters went home and I was able to leave via the front door.

I walked. One foot in front of the other brought me clarity. Why would I think my mother was wrong? She'd proven to be right so many times before. Samantha wouldn't have thrown the press their raw meat without a reason.

When I got to her building, I waited an hour before someone came out. It was a woman I'd seen before in the halls and I gave her a fake but warm smile as I ducked a shoulder and entered. I rode the elevator alone and the lights buzzed over my head.

And even though I wanted my mother to be right, a number kept running through my head.

Zero.

That was how much warning Samantha had given me. That was how many times she'd returned my calls since the news had broken. That was how much she trusted me with her plan, if she'd even had one. It also turned out that was how much patience I had for her and her shutting me out. With every ding of the rising floors the conflict grew closer and my muscles tensed more.

I wrapped my knuckles on her door and footsteps on the other side gave her away. "I know you're home.

Fucking open up, Samantha." I didn't yell. There was no need to involve the neighbors, but I was serious as fuck.

The bolts unclicked and she opened a small crack with the chain linked. Her dark eyes apologized but fuck that shit. I deserved more and I would reach out and fucking grab it if I needed to.

I toggled my finger at the chain. "You think that little bit of metal is gonna stop me from getting in?"

"I know you're mad — "

"Open this fucking door, Samantha. *Now*." I hadn't wanted to scare her, and yet I did. I couldn't tell if it was the right move, but after a pained look of disappointment, she closed the door and unhooked the chain.

"You shouldn't be here." She held the door open. Where the fuck else would I have gone? I stepped inside her apartment and was relieved she was alone. Something had been chipping away at my ego the entire night and I'd wondered if she wasn't cheating on me.

A glass of red wine on the counter caught my eye. It was half full, and the bottle next to it had a long drip of burgundy that stained the white label. She had on those pajama shorts that showed half her ass and the fucking hoodie she'd worn on our first date. It was probably insane, but as mad as I was, I didn't have the hate in my heart that I was sure would be there when I saw her. The line between love and loathing was thin at best.

I propped my hands on my hips and stared her down. "When did you find out?"

"Last night. I honestly didn't think it was my place to tell you."

As many times as Ricci had hit me in the gut over the years, it didn't even compare to the blow she'd just landed. She'd known when we'd had sex. My jaw dropped.

"I know you're mad. As fucked up as it is, you should know I'm actually doing this for you. So stay away from me until after the election. Stay away from your buddy Scooter. And get the fuck out of my apartment before I become a proper snooty bitch and call the chief of police."

Whoa. That was a hell of a lot of info to drop. She's mad at me?

She wasn't even denying it was her who leaked it. But...

"What, exactly, are you doing for me?" I narrowed my eyes but she wouldn't meet my gaze.

"It's time for you to go." Samantha flared her nostrils. "Don't try to run with me. Don't call me. Stay away until Demsey loses the election."

"Loses? What the fuck, Samantha? Stop spinning your web and tell me why the fuck you would do this to us."

My mother was dying. Samantha was betraying me at the exact moment I needed her. There was a small part of me who hated to admit how much I wanted her by my side, that I fucking wished that when she'd opened the door, it had all played out differently, that fucking someone would comfort me. My mother was fucking shriveling up before my eyes and had kept her illness a secret. Did no one understand that? And why the fuck was Samantha so pissed off? *I* was the one who she'd fucked over.

In my cloud of anger and self-pity, a match struck. I'd never spoken to her about Scooter. I was fucking sure of it. Had my mother given her a roadmap of my past? And a 'snooty bitch'? That sounded horribly familiar.

I narrowed my eyes, hoping their sharp edge would cut through the bullshit. "How do you know about Scooter?"

"I know about him because you're a fucking liar. I asked one thing of you. *One.*" She wasn't even yelling and the disdain in her regard pinned me in the chest.

I walked over to her counter and leaned against it with my arms crossed. My mind was racing in a thousand different directions. "Explain."

"You got caught. Recorded, nonetheless. Your buddy Scooter turned on you. And when you weren't asking him to put drugs in a ball, I think you mentioned how you were just fucking a 'snooty bitch' to keep busy. I asked you not to lie, and yet you did."

"So you pay me back by leaking my mother's cancer to the press? Before you even tell *me*? You slip into my bed and what? Have pity sex with me then the next day steal my shirt? Jesus Christ, Samantha. Talk about lies."

It was odd, I always imagined that when my wicked ways and karma caught up with me, I'd be hauled off in handcuffs like my father. But this was so much worse. Fuck money and power. I was losing people. First Leo, then Jackson and Rafa. Next up my mother and the woman I thought I was in love with. After all the shitty things I'd done, I couldn't say I didn't deserve it, but the irony that I would be alone when all I ever wanted was someone at my side twisted my stomach and my cold heart.

But one thing was off. "Why aren't the police banging down my door?"

"Like I said, I'm friends with the chief. I had a choice to make, and whether you believe me or not, I chose you. Demsey's done."

"So my recording just goes away? What did you have to give your buddy to make that happen?" There was an accusation in my voice but she ignored it.

"The detective on your case is Carver's wife. I'm giving them the election." She shook her head. "And my career and my reputation. I'm sorry you found out about your mom the way you did. I admit it was partially spiteful."

Her chest rose and fell and that energetic connection we shared hummed between us. She said, "The one thing we never had was time. We raced through this relationship at hyper speed and it crashed, just like we both knew it would. We need to be apart until we can figure out if we can trust each again — or if we want to. After the election, if we can forgive each other, let's talk. But before then, seeing each other sends a mixed message. If Demsey doesn't lose, Carver will take her revenge out on you."

"Are you even sorry for what you did?"

"I did it for you." Tears threatened in her bottom lids and her nose blotched red.

"You could have given me a heads-up."

"I'm sorry about your mom. It was a dick move, but it was the only one I had." She bit her bottom lip, and I couldn't make heads or tails of the situation. Forgiveness was foreign to me.

There was so much to sort through. Emotions and lies were tangled into hopeless knots. I gave her one final look before letting myself out and sliding down the wall next to her door. Her sobs on the other side weren't as satisfying at I'd thought they would be.

Eventually they stopped and I left. I walked through the city like a fucking zombie. When I got home, all the lights were off and I laid awake the entire night, replaying all my mistakes, all my lies. What an arrogant prick I'd been. When six a.m. rolled around, I didn't get up. I hadn't earned the right to get my ass kicked by my former crew. I hadn't earned anything.

Chapter Twenty-Three

Samantha

My bed was too big without him next to me. I'd slept in his shirt again and I was afraid it was losing its power to soothe me. When the chief had played me the recording, my instincts had kicked in and carried me through the rest of the day. But when the initial shock had worn off, the depth of the wound my actions had caused ended up to be more the size of a crater.

I was pretty sure I loved Anton, but I hated him for how deep he'd been able to cut me with a lie. I'd acted abruptly and deserved his backlash. I needed time to heal and sort shit out in my head, but I also needed to make sure Demsey lost the election. That was why I forced myself out of bed, out of the door and through the park for a run. Moving my body was the forward motion that started the gears of my mind.

Step one was to distance myself as much as I could from Demsey. That had been accomplished. Step two would be to sleep with the enemy…or at the very least make it look like I was. There was a charity event Saturday night for the environment and there was no way Demsey or anyone from his team would be caught dead there. One of my friends from college was hosting it with her parents. Getting an invite would be pricey, but it would give me a perfect selection of liberal district attorneys to start 'dating'. Then I would take a page out of Sophia's playbook and call the photographers at *The Scoop* and get myself noticed.

Back at home, I showered and waited for stores to open to find the perfect dress. Without the need to represent the city, I could afford to show a little more skin, and I had seen a short nude lace number with golden beading a few months before that would be perfect. I even already had the shoes to go with it.

By Saturday night, I was more than ready to show the town a new Samantha. My friend Eve had been delighted when I'd called her for a ticket. Her mother was one of those socialites that could play each side of the coin perfectly and saw my inclusion as a win for her inner circle, who mostly loathed Demsey. Plus, there was always a push for a younger crowd. It made the older people feel relevant.

My hair was parted down the middle and fluffy with blown-out curls. My eyes were smoky and my gloss shined. Not one detail was out of place when I walked into the museum lobby. I clutched my small purse and plucked a flute of champagne from the silver tray of a waiter as I assessed the room.

A couple of familiar faces tipped their glasses to me, and when I spotted Eve in a black asymmetrical dress that fit her like a damn glove, I walked right over.

She raked her eyes over me with a smile. "Freedom suits you. I didn't think we'd ever get to see our

Sammie with her hair down again after you took that job with Demsey."

Eve's mother joined and we air-kissed next to our cheeks. "Beautiful as always, Samantha. I was quite happy to hear you were coming. Do tell… What's it like having your behind on the front page of a paper?"

"Mother!" Eve hooked her arm into mine and guided me away. "Don't mind her. She loves to stir the shit pot. Drama at parties is how she and her friends decide if it's been a successful night or not."

It didn't offend me. I'd expected scrutiny from some people. My political flip-flop had been rather hot and cold. We walked across the room to a crowd of younger people, some of whom I recognized from private school.

A dark-haired, tall man with glasses walked toward me. In his tuxedo, it took me a second to realize I knew him — and he was perfect.

Thomas Weber was a clerk in federal court. He must have been a little over thirty but had no signs of salt-and-pepper in his thick hair, which was short on the sides and had a high fade on top. A couple of pictures with him and the press would go bonkers. It would destabilize Demsey, and he would do what he always did when something pissed him off. He would fuck up.

I reached out a hand. "I think I met you last year at one of these things. I'm Sam."

"I know who you are. Pretty sure almost all the city knows who you are." His tone was unimpressed. Okay, it wasn't going to be as easy as a short dress and killer smile. But, he was the most ideal fit. Jesus, we would look like Ken and Barbie together.

And to be fair, he had a right to be skeptical about me. Problem was, I knew just how to reel in a big fish like that in. I turned my back to him and started a conversation with the girl who used to sit behind me in math. What was her name? *Jane? June? Jen?*

The dinner chime rang out and Eve guided me to her table. "I'm so glad you called," she said when we were seated. "Chuck is on the west coast for business and I can't bear these things alone. Oh, you remember my brother Jonathan, right?"

No, I hadn't...but I should have. Jonathan had grown up. *Damn*. With his high cheekbones and sharp jawline, he could have been a model. I had seriously been going to the wrong parties. Liberals were hot.

He leaned in and whispered, "I used to have a massive crush on you until I realized it wasn't a crush. I just wanted to be you. My real crush was on Xander Perkins."

"Oh my God. I haven't thought about him in years. I wonder where he is."

"Rehab."

Eve's eyes lit up at the sound of gossip. "I heard he hocked his mother's tennis bracelet to pay his dealer. So sad."

We were served our food and I was glad for the break in the conversation. A week prior, I'd been dating a drug dealer. What did that say about me? After the main course, I excused myself, wondering if I hadn't made a miscalculation. I was both like the people around me and not. But when I caught Thomas standing and buttoning his jacket, I knew I'd hooked him. Ignoring a man with a massive ego was the best way to get his attention.

I set my shoulders back and slowed my pace toward the restrooms.

"Hey. Sam."

I stopped and Thomas stepped in front of me with a tight smile. "I think we may have gotten off on the wrong foot."

"You mean the insult-a-person-you-don't-know foot? That one?"

He cringed. "Yeah. Sorry. Listen... This is going to sound lame, but I was nervous. I wasn't ready for you to be so... Anyway, can we start again?" He extended his hand. "Hi, I'm Tom and beautiful women turn me into an idiot."

We shook and I said, "Sam."

He shot me a winning smile and said, "Can I buy you a drink?"

"I'm pretty sure they're free."

"See? Idiot."

"Let me just freshen up." I gestured to the ladies' room.

I spent more time that I needed—making him wait was part of the plan—then I walked out without an apology. Dinner plates clanked as the waiters collected the remains of the main course while others trailed behind serving dessert and offering coffee and tea.

Tom led me to the bar, ordered both of us a cognac—apparently I didn't get a say—then asked, "So, why did you resign?"

"Ah. Right for the jugular, huh? I don't even have my drink yet. But fine, I'll bite. It's a sinking ship. I hopped off."

The bartender served us our nightcaps with a small doily for a coaster under each one.

"To new ships." Tom gently clanked my glass. "Just one thing." He narrowed his dark eyes. "What about the stepson?"

The amber liquid coated my throat, masking the lie in my half-truth. "He's a lying piece of shit."

Without skipping a beat, he said, "I heard he was a criminal but got shot and his mother had to come to his rescue."

I set my drink back on the bar and reached for my clutch. "Thanks for the drink." I turned to leave but he grabbed my forearm. I didn't give him the satisfaction of looking down to where he was gripping me. It was the exact kind of thing I hated when men did — prove they were stronger by flexing physical muscle.

Any other man or day, I would have ripped my arm away. He let go slowly and said, "Sorry. It's the lawyer in me, always poking my nose where it doesn't belong."

He'd been rough, apologized — but not for the action — then found an excuse. It was pattern behavior of an abusive man. The real me would have never given him a second look. But I needed a decoy to set off Demsey. So instead of walking away, I played the victim. That was what Tom would want, anyway.

I fluttered my eyelashes and sighed. "It's okay. But it's fresh, you know? I mean between Demsey and his stepson, my reputation is basically ruined."

"I have a feeling you'll be just fine. You know what might help?"

My stomach churned. God, he was going to say 'him'. *Gross.* "Let me guess. A date with a respectable member of society?"

He shrugged and lifted his eyebrows. "Couldn't hurt."

"That's nice. But I don't want your pity." I took another sip of my cognac.

"Jesus. I've really fumbled this whole thing. Sam, would like to go dinner with me next week?"

Cha-ching.

"That sounds really nice, thanks. Can I give you my number?"

He pulled out his phone with a smirk, thinking he'd made his first steps toward conquering me, and I gave him my digits.

The lights lowered and the band began to play jazz standards. Older couples got up and made their way to the dancefloor. It was the 'letting the hair down' moment of the night where the proper manners ended and the devilish ones began to surface. It was also the point when the rich liked to take pictures of themselves in their gowns and tuxedos as proof of how wealthy and generous they were before they were too drunk to look good.

Eve scurried up to the bar with a photographer on her heels. "There you are! Come on. We're going to send this one to the alumni newsletter from school." She waved me to her side, kicked out her hip and pursed her lips like an adorable duck.

"Tom, give us some credibility here." I set my clutch on the bar next to my empty drink and posed next to Eve. Tom slid in behind me, and although my skin was crawling and I would have one jealous and pissed off Anton to deal with at some point, I leaned my body in Tom's direction so that my shoulder brushed his chest. It was subtle, but it was enough for a rumor to start.

The flash lit up the space around us for a brief second while I held my coyest smile. Photo op finished and in the books, I turned to Eve.

"Hey, thanks for this. I'm going to head out before I drink too much and get myself on the cover of a paper again."

She frowned but understood and was off within seconds, flagging another alum down for a picture.

I turned to Tom and hoped the twinkle I was sending with my eyes would hide all the lies beneath. "Look forward to hearing from you."

On the ride home, I called Fanny and told her to get the pictures from the event and get them online as soon as fucking possible. When I hung up, a big part of me wanted to send a message to Anton, telling him not to freak out, that I hadn't moved on in record time. But if I did that, I also risked hearing the hate and hurt in his voice again, and I was pretty sure it would break me. No, it was best to keep our distance. Once the election was over, maybe we could start again.

At home, I unbuckled the golden shoes with regret and hung my dress back in my closet. I washed all the makeup off my face and threaded my arms through his shirt. It would have to be enough to get me through the next lonely month.

Chapter Twenty-Four

Anton

Demsey cursed from my mother's office. I'd given up caring about him or his fucking bid for governor — not that I ever really had. I'd played nice to make my mother happy. In the few days following me finding out the truth about her illness, she'd declined...rapidly. It was almost as if the honesty had been a massive burden that she'd carried too far, and when it was off her shoulders, she'd realized it had broken her.

I'd stopped asking permission and started taking action where she was concerned. I'd hired around-the-clock medical attention, and she had an IV keeping her hydrated. The nurse I liked who came at night and sometimes sat with me in silence had said, "*Keep her comfortable and peaceful. That's all she needs.*" She also said we could start the morphine at any time in small doses and that, to me, signaled the fucking end.

So I'd kicked Demsey's ass out of their room and devoted every moment of my day to my mother. It was like there were two opposite realities playing out under one roof. But something in his tone made me stop on the way to the kitchen.

I paused outside the office door and Demsey's campaign manager said, "It's the ultimate 'fuck you'. A fucking fed. I don't care if he's just a fucking clerk. She's doing this on purpose. Jesus, she's calculated. I almost admire her balls."

I leaned against the wall. There was no doubt in my mind who they were talking about.

"Well, she's not as smart as she thinks she is. I've heard that prick is a little heavy handed, if you know what I mean. Maybe he'll smack her around a little bit, teach her a lesson." Demsey's true nature was never hard to find. Poke the bear a little he'd growl on cue.

The campaign manager scoffed. "She'd figure out how to spin that shit into some big pity party. Fuck."

I walked down the hall to the kitchen and nodded a simple hello to a cleaner then waited for my coffee to brew. On my phone, I searched the local society pages for Samantha, and sure enough, there was a picture of her with another man.

How to kill him? Let me count the fucking ways.

But it was true that she was calculated. It was all for show. That being said, she didn't have to wear the fucking shoes I'd bought her in public with a douchebag. That was a petty slight to me or maybe something to piss me off further. I stored my phone back in my pocket. I would need to find out if she was in some kind of danger with that suited-up prick.

I was still mad at her, but there was no way I would be able to let her be abused by a man. That scene had already played out in my dark life. Plus, just because I didn't know if I could forgive her didn't mean anyone else could have her. It made sense that she was putting even more political distance between herself and her former boss. She was officially on the other side of the election.

The morning nurse came into the kitchen as I was finishing my coffee and offered a cool smile. I remembered where I was and pushed away my annoyance of not being in control.

The nurse washed her hands before saying in a soothing voice, "She's asking for you. Try to convince her to ease the pain."

A long, knowing blink was my only answer before I walked up the stairs and plastered a smile on my worried face.

A shell of my mother waited for me in her bed. The nurse had put a pink scarf around her neck and propped her up to a seated position beneath the massive duvet. Her cheeks were hollowed out more than ever, her skin was pale and the liver spots of a youth without sunscreen peppered her face.

"Hey there, beautiful. You want to try some tea?" I held up the little syringe we'd started using to wet her mouth. She'd been sleeping with it open and the cracked skin around her lips was just one more small sign of how shit had all gone horribly wrong.

She studied the small plastic bit in my hands, hating it as much as I did but needing it nonetheless. My mother blinked once for yes—our new way of communication—and I pulled the stopper back and loaded up a small amount of chamomile tea.

As I approached, she opened her mouth and I slowly squirted the liquid inside. It was a gift she was giving me to see her in such a state. That was what I'd decided anyway. Her last moments would be with the one person she loved above all the others, and I would give her my everything. After all, despite the hard lessons she'd forced me to learn, her entire life had been dedicated to making me better than my father. She deserved my love and respect, and she would get it in spades.

"Should I pick up where we left off?" I set the syringe back on the saucer next to the cup of tea and picked up *The Art of War* from her nightstand.

Again, she blinked, and I started in on Chapter six and read about the dangers of direct conflict. It was timely. Killing Samantha's fake new boyfriend was indeed a risk to winning the war. *Damn it.*

Thirty minutes into the Chapter, she fell asleep. I didn't like the idea of reading it without her, so I put the book where I'd found it and tiptoed out of the room. I went down to my bedroom and dialed Leo. He'd sent me a text after my mother's headline had broken. There was still some residual friendship and fucking hell if I didn't need a shoulder to lean on, even just a little bit.

We arranged to meet at Chezzie's for dinner and I marveled that it would be the first time I'd been out of the house in days. I left my scruff—I didn't have the energy to shave—and wore dark jeans and a sweater that would have made my mother smile. She always beamed when I made an effort.

Leo waited for me in the back booth, the one reserved at all times for family. He had on his new uniform of a black suit and came off all professional. I wondered how many weapons that clever fuck was concealing under his guise of a serious businessman.

"Hey." Leo stood and we clamped hands and did a shoulder bump. "Sorry about your ma."

"Yeah. Thanks. I got Demsey to confess that she had it four years ago when she sent me away. So, I'm just glad I know now."

Leo sat back as his aunt brought us sparkling water and wine. There was something about the stress of not ordering at Chezzie's that made it one of the most nurturing places I'd ever been. Pity she never had children... She would have been a fantastic mother. I gave her a tight smile that she returned.

"Frankie missed you the other morning. He's dying to kick your ass after all these years."

I *tsked*. "I'll add him to my list of problems."

Leo stared at me for a long beat. Yeah, I needed his help with a thing. I wasn't just there to weep into his open arms. I dug out my phone and pulled up the charity picture of Samantha and the fuckhead.

"This guy." I pointed to him and gave the phone to Leo.

"Anton..." Leo lifted his eyebrows then leaned over the table and whispered, "You can't kill him. That would be bad, very fucking bad."

"I know. And it's fucking annoying." I took the phone back and set it next to me facedown. No need to look at the prick dreaming of fondling my girl any longer.

"Listen," Leo started and let out a sympathetic sigh. "I don't know why she's doing this to you—"

I held up a hand. "She's not. She's doing it *for* me." The truth of my statement had sunk in more and more since I'd seen Samantha. I sure as shit didn't like her techniques, but she was the spin and public relations pro, not me. I twitched my lips to the side and said, "Which leads me to my next problem—Scooter. He ratted me out."

The weight of my words sank into Leo like a lead blanket on his chest and shoulders. Yeah, there were *implications*. He finally met my gaze with a disgusted look on his face. He frowned deeper. "And we can't kill him, either."

"I told you. Annoying." But the 'we' part was like a warm bath. He was in it with me for sure.

Chezzie brought over some calamari for us to share and Leo divided it between our small plates. One of the many things I had to give that beautiful woman who had fed me time and time again over the years was that I'd never eaten anything from her that wasn't cooked to perfection. I couldn't believe she didn't have a line of customers down the block. I blew her a kiss when I caught her eye, but she just pursed her lips and walked back into the kitchen.

When I'd finished the squid, I mopped up the oil with a piece of sourdough and it was hard to tell what was better, the food itself or basically licking my plate with bread.

"So, about Scoot," I said when we'd finished. "Samantha made some deal where the case was going to get buried, and as long as Demsey loses the election, I go free."

"How the fuck did she manage that?"

"The chief of police is her buddy." Thoughts had run through my mind about what kind of buddy, but I couldn't imagine her like that. Deep down, I wanted to trust her. All that we'd shared couldn't have been fake. And the calmer I got and the more sobering my mother's state, I was realizing that I might just want to forgive Samantha and start again.

"Impressive." Leo nodded and I had to agree. The more I thought about it, the less I understood why she'd decided to throw everything away for me. That was, unless she loved me.

A massive portion of lasagna landed in front of me.

"Enjoy," Chezzie said like a dare. "Also, I don't do doggy bags, so you both better eat up."

When she was gone, I whispered, "She may be the scariest of all the Riccis."

"Only to you. You should see her with Fi's little sis Violet. They get manicures and go to princess tea parties and shit." He shook his head and it struck me how much he'd matured since I'd last spent time with him. Maybe there was hope for me, too.

So far, all the conversation had been about me. That was typical because I was a selfish spoiled brat, but it wasn't cool, especially if I wanted to get my friend back.

"How is Fiona, anyway?"

"Annoying. Guess that's our word of the day. She won't plan our wedding until she's finished with these classes she's taking. And between you and me, it only makes me love her more. But yeah, she knows how to put my ass in place. And don't even get me started on the little one. I see her bottom lip tremble at the threat of crying and I would literally do anything she wants. I've turned into a pussy-whipped, domesticated wimp of a man. I should actually thank you for having dinner with me. I'm a fucking mess."

But he wasn't, not at all. He beamed from fucking ear to ear. His self-deprecation was only to hide that he was far better off without me.

I grinned and dug into the lasagna. If the cold-blooded killer in front of me could find happiness, why not me?

We shot knowing, painful glances to each other while we forced our last bites. Fucking Chezzie... I was going to bloat up like a balloon and I was pretty sure I was going to get up at the crack of dawn and train with my old crew…who were becoming my friends?

When Chezzie cleared the plates, the glimmer in her eye was a dead giveaway.

The lasagna had been no accident. "How much did Frankie pay you to serve us that?"

Leo's mouth gaped. I was right.

She lifted a shoulder while balancing the plates. "He always was my favorite."

"Hey!" Leo whined. "*I'm* your favorite. You told me that last week."

"I lied." She walked away.

My old friend turned back to me, faking shock. "The worst part is she knows we'll be back."

"So what do you think I should do about Scooter?"

Leo rubbed his stomach and stretched. If he couldn't handle that much food, how would I?

"It pains me to say this but ghost him. I'll make sure Jackson does, too. Cut all ties."

"He's got the rest of the stash from Upstate." Those were my fucking drugs. It would be my money.

"What do you want more? Jail or cash?"

The answer was obvious, but it still made me cranky.

Leo chuckled. "Wipe that bitch look off your face. Scooter is dead to us now."

There was that '*us*' again. Jesus, I'd needed to be a part of something bigger than me. Thank fuck for the bond Leo and I had formed as reckless teenagers.

He continued, "I'll look into that fuckface lawyer, and if it's bad, I'll have Jackson tail Samantha. She's already seen me, so that wouldn't work. In order for Frankie to be on board, you show up tomorrow morning and let him kick your thick ass on the mat. Got it?"

Leo moved to slide out of the bench then said, "You know you're paying, right?"

"I assumed. Listen… Tell Jackson that if shit goes sour to call her 'sunshine'. She'll know it's from me."

He closed his eyes, dropped his head back and laughed. "You call her *sunshine*? Jesus, you're more whipped than me. We are absolutely pathetic. I loathe us." He stood and adjusted his suit. "See you in the morning, sunshine."

Chapter Twenty-Five

Samantha

"I'm so sorry about that." I took a sip of my Sancerre then set the sweaty wine glass back between Tom and myself. "Those guys have been on me since, well...since I made the cover. I honestly don't understand their fascination."

Fanny had called the paparazzi earlier in the day once I knew what restaurant Tom and I would be meeting at. But she'd been clever about her instructions to follow me from my place. It would have been too suspicious if they'd all been waiting at the front door when we went in. Instead, they'd flashed their cameras from outside while I walked in and greeted Tom with a peck on the cheek. *A flawless execution on all our parts.*

But still, I couldn't shake the feeling that I was being watched — not by Tom or journalists, but something deeper. I feared Demsey trying to seek revenge, and Anton's former rivals may have been paid off, but if he was being a good boy, their supply would have been cut off and I could have been a target again. That morning while I ran in the park I must have glanced over my shoulder a hundred times.

Tom sat back in his chair. "Well, you are one of the most eligible women in the city. I mean, that's a pretty amazing feat considering you're unemployed."

"Ouch." I faked a giggle. *Fucker. Way to backhand a compliment.*

"So, any good cases? I heard a rumor that you're up for Assistant DA. Impressive." God, I was going to need all the fucking wine in our bottle to get through the date. He'd already checked out my tits three times and I didn't like the hunger in his eyes. Maybe using him had been a horrible idea.

But it had proven effective. After the pictures from the charity event had gone as viral as they could considering no one outside of the state or city gave a flying fuck about Demsey or me, my former boss had fumbled a question at a press conference. The reporter had asked if he thought my appearance at a liberal event meant I was cooperating with his opponent's campaign. Demsey had replied, "*That ungrateful blonde was obviously a liability. That's why I fired her.*"

Which was a whole bunch of lies that the follow-up questions pounced directly on and he'd gotten his feathers ruffled further, then tried to play the sympathy card about his wife dying. That had also massively backfired because the headlines were about him not being able to do his job while his wife was ill. Which then, Fanny had the brilliant idea to spin even further and planted a story about Sophia being the real brains behind the man, and if she was gone, what was he left with? Also, the blondes in the world hadn't appreciated the implication that the color of hair was linked to intelligence.

Overall, it had been a shit-show of a week for Demsey, but that didn't mean my work was done. There was still about three weeks until the election and he needed to tank. Fanny and I were working on some of the donors we knew and trying to spook them into believing that it would be better to get on the other side of the aisle while they still had some power. Once Demsey was out of the picture, any influence would be lost. But giving the other guy a final push over the edge? Then those promises would need to be kept. It was a tangled ball of thread we were trying to sort out.

Tom was talking about his career, and it was dull and boring and obnoxious. God, I hated men like him who thought knowledge was somehow power. Power was something to be taken, not learned. But his ego worked in my favor. It convinced him that a woman like me could be interested in someone like him. Hell, he probably thought he was doing me some kind of favor by taking me out to dinner and allowing me to bask in his holier-than-thou glory.

I left a few bites of my dinner on my plate, even though I was starving. It played into the role of me trying to be meek and needy. Then I laid on the extra layer.

I folded my napkin on the table. "Sorry... I don't mean to waste. I just am *so* full."

Tom studied me. His nose had been in too many books, so he couldn't detect the lie. "I appreciate a woman who doesn't overindulge. But next time, order less. Then there's no waste." His little raise of his eyebrows was a subtle way to scold me. As if I had any control of the portion size.

Could someone win an award for best faked date? Because, I had no idea who my competition was, but I was fucking taking home the golden statue.

The waitress came to clear. "Can I interest you in dessert?"

Tom wiped his mouth with the linen napkin then tossed it to the empty space where his plate had been. "Just the check."

It was another small act of control and punishment that the real me didn't appreciate. So what if a woman didn't want to eat all her meal? Maybe there were good reasons behind it. Mine were deliberate, but still...

Tom excused himself to the bathroom and as he walked away, I contemplated how much I really needed him over the next few weeks. One more public date would do it, then I could pretend to be sick or something to avoid him. Besides, once Demsey lost and if Anton and I tried to work out our issues, that brick of a man wouldn't tolerate me even speaking to someone else.

A little smile lifted my cheeks and tingled my skin. The days away from Anton hadn't done anything to stifle my feelings about him. If anything, I missed him and was worried about how he was handling his mother's illness. There hadn't been much reporting about her status, and I hated not knowing what he was going through.

"That's a nice little twinkle in your eyes. Shall we get out of here? I paid on my way back."

"Sure. Thanks for dinner. It was lovely." *Gag.*

Tom helped me with my coat and I said thank you and goodnight to the waitress. The photographers were gone, and I was thankful to not have to lay on the sugar. The fake date had been exhausting and I was still hungry. Plus, I was convinced I was missing the man I probably shouldn't love but did, and my guard was going down as I grew weary.

The crisp air woke me up a little and I was just about to say goodnight when Tom put his arm around me and nudged me forward. "Let's walk. I don't live far from here."

Uh…that was bold. Did he really think I was a one-dinner-and-hop-in-bed kinda girl? *Damn*. What level of false signals was I sending out? We walked down a couple of side streets and it occurred to me that for all I knew about the city, I'd never been in that neighborhood. I glanced at the street name and wondered why, if I'd never been on it, it rang a bell in my head.

"You live down here?" I asked with a little more fear in my voice than I hoped for.

Calvery. Calvery. Calvery. I knew that street from somewhere.

"You'll come up for a nightcap, right?" Tom let go of me to fetch his keys, and as they jingled, I remembered.

"…*from Calvery to James. The least populated part of the city.*" *Shit.* I'd read about the neighborhood in a housing report. Developers had wanted the city to promise more public transport access. It was no-man's land.

I stepped back and stumbled on my heels. "I'm pretty tired. I think I'll just call myself a car."

Tom's dark eyes narrowed slightly. "You shouldn't do that from down here. Come up where it's warm."

"It's fine." I shrugged, trying to be casual but hearing the small shake in my own voice. "It normally only takes five minutes." I dug out my phone and punched in the code.

Deana Birch

Tom stepped to me and clamped his long fingers around both my wrists in a tight squeeze. My phone fell to the pavement and I didn't care that it had most likely shattered.

In a low, serious voice, he said, "You don't think I see what you're doing here? I'm not stupid, Sam. But using is a two-way street. So get your ass upstairs and prove to me how far you're ready to go to get your reputation back."

I stared at him, still not willing to admit I was a liar and the whole thing was a sham. "You're scaring me."

He sneered. "Cut the shit."

"I…"

He dipped his chin and lifted an eyebrow. A chill ran up my spine and I opened my mouth to scream. With his keys still in his opposite hand, he cupped my mouth and the jagged metal banged into my lip and the taste of copper hit my tongue. He was going to take this as far as he could. And with location and strength at his serious advantage, I was fucked.

"You okay over there, sunshine?" A voice I'd never heard before came from my left and Tom and both turned to see who it was.

A massive beast of a man, bigger than Tom, stepped toward us with a tight expression as he narrowed in on Tom with long, slow steps.

Sunshine. That was no coincidence.

Three feet away, the man said, "You wanna let go of the lady's wrist, bro? Doesn't look like she appreciates that."

Tom dropped my arms and spat, "Who the fuck do you think you are?"

The man grinned and a streetlight reflected off his bald head. "I'm someone who has nothing to lose

244

looking at someone who has everything to lose, Mr. Federal Clerk."

Tom sized up the huge man and snarled. He turned to me. "This isn't over."

"It is, actually." I stared into his evil eyes. We both knew I wouldn't say anything. My word against his didn't tend to favor me.

"Don't bother calling me when this blows up in your face." He shook his head but went inside the building.

I let out a long shaky breath then picked up my phone from the ground. It had just one long crack across the screen and I started to order a car.

"I kinda have to drive you home." The man cringed. It was adorable on such a beast. "Your boyfriend throws a mean punch."

The stress of Tom was brushed away. I *knew* the use of 'sunshine' had been on purpose. If Anton was looking out for me, maybe some of his anger had settled.

"Can you driving me home include stopping at a diner? I'm starving." And I wanted to ask this savior of a man all kinds of questions about my 'boyfriend'.

"And I don't have a boyfriend," I said, just for spite.

"Mmm-hmm. Someone should tell that to him. This way, please."

He led me to a dark SUV and I almost expected Anton to be inside. Instead, the man opened the passenger door for me and I got in. When he was behind the wheel and buckled up, I asked, "What's your name, anyway?"

"Jackson." He held out his massive hand and I shook it. He had long fingers and one of them was crooked as if it had been broken and never healed.

"Samantha. But it seems you already know that. Thank you, by the way. I knew he was a dick, but I didn't think he'd show his true colors so quickly."

Jackson pulled out of the parking spot and we waited for a red light to turn and take us out of the mostly abandoned neighborhood.

"There's a twenty-four-hour diner not far from my place. I assume you know where I live, too."

He let out a small chuckle. "Yeah."

"How long have you been following me?" It was good to know my instincts were still intact. Someone had been watching me, just in a good way.

"About a week. Soon as the bossm—" He shook his head as he accelerated into traffic. "As soon as your man saw you with that asshole and heard his stepdad say something about him having a rep for hitting girls. Also"—he turned to me for a second with his eyebrows reaching toward his bald head—"your man is seriously pissed off about something that has to do with shoes."

I laughed for the first time in weeks. By the time I was not just dropped off but walked up to my apartment door, I'd learned that while Anton had been a strong leader, he'd also been a compassionate one. Jackson had a son and he'd let him leave the crew no questions asked. He'd provided for people who were loyal to him and demanded a certain amount of professionalism and structure that his former crew appreciated. None of them hated him. They were just over the lifestyle.

"So..." I'd avoided the one question I'd wanted to ask Jackson the entire night but needed my answer before I would let him see me disappear behind my door. "How's Sophia?"

Jackson's face went sullen. "You should call your man and ask him."

I nodded, said a final thank you then went in and locked the door behind me.

Chapter Twenty-Six

Anton

The cautious look on Jackson's face when he walked into Frankie's gym spoke a thousand words. He was the last to arrive, and while I watched him, Leo watched me and Frankie watched us all.

For a week, they'd beaten my ass to prove I was no better than any of them and it'd been fucking amazing. In my solo efforts at the gym or my few runs with Samantha in the park, I'd forgotten how exhilarating it was to actually hit another person with full power.

Jackson dipped a shoulder and dropped his bag onto a bench near the wall.

"Come on, Myers. You're up. Show us how bad you want to hear about your girlfriend." Frankie had a way of motivating that was both cruel and perfect. He danced on his toes in the middle of the circular black mat and motioned for me to get off my ass and join him.

I pushed into my knees and stood. If anything really bad had happened to Samantha, I would have gotten a call. So as I pulled off my hoodie, I knew she was safe and that was all that mattered. The day before, I'd studied every movement of Frankie and Leo sparring. They were about as equal as one could get because Leo knew Frankie's habits.

Neither one of the Ricci brothers thought about their muscles or power when they fought. Their minds raced about in and out of offense and defense non-stop. Their footing and balance had become natural instincts over the years. But one thing I'd noticed in both of them was the ability to use the ground as their power source. Whether it was how they stepped into a punch or the ability to perfectly land a blow to the chest on one leg, they both had mastered the art of rebounding their body weight from their feet up. Leo had spoken about it for years, but it wasn't until I saw both of them doing it that I'd fully understood.

I walked to the center ring and cracked my neck.

"You're too thick. You know that, right? Your muscles are getting in your way. No more protein for you. Hope your slow ass likes to run." Frankie grinned from ear to ear while Leo and Jackson went to the treadmills where they would have a perfect view of us sparring.

I'd always thought I fought better angry, but I was wrong. That morning I had a calm about me. Besides, my ego had been crushed by the amount of times Frankie had put me on my ass in the previous days. But that one week had made a difference. I'd become one of them. Hell, Frankie was probably working out a meal plan for me in his sick head.

"I gotta warn you, old man," I said with a quick tip of my chin. "I'm feeling pretty good today."

He laughed. "Bring it."

As I jogged around the ring with my fists up, I paid attention not to my feet but more of how they landed and how that could project me forward. Frankie approached and I blocked his jabs with my forearms then dropped my shoulder just a tick before imagining the floor steadying my back leg and the force of the earth moving from the ball of my front foot and up that leg as I landed a punch on Frankie's floating rib.

He fell on his ass and both Jackson and Leo let out a long "Ooooo."

I cupped my ear. "What were you saying about slow?"

Leo laughed. "Don't instigate him. You're lighting a match, Myers."

With his hands on his knees, Frankie caught his breath then looked up at me. "That was good. What did you do different?"

I reached out a hand and pulled him up to standing. "The ground. I used the ground."

"Fucking finally. I've only been saying that for ten years." Leo shook his head as he continued running.

"Okay," Frankie said to me only. "Now that you've *finally* understood that, let's break it down for all the punches so you master it."

For the following hour, Frankie walked me through how the subtle shift of balance could make all the difference. He had me stand on one leg for three minutes each, constantly seeking out an area of the foot and what that did to the muscles in my leg.

If it hadn't been for my ailing mother and my responsibility to spend my day with her, I would have begged Frankie to take the day off and feed me more of his intricate knowledge.

"All right." Frankie clapped his hands twice, his signal that we were done. "Jackson, give us the debrief."

"Samantha and the fuck-o had dinner then he force-walked her back to his place."

My heart rate skyrocketed, and my nostrils flared. "What do you mean, 'force-walked'?" I asked, I didn't like the idea of 'force anything' with her.

"You know like..." Jackson put his sweaty arm over Leo's shoulder and hugged it a bit too tight then steered him away in the opposite direction.

"I'm gonna kill him," I murmured under my breath and Frankie rolled his eyes. "Then what?"

Leo chuckled and said, "Simmer down, sunshine."

Jackson continued after a shake of his head. "Fuck-o's place is conveniently located off Calvery. I bet that he chose to live there on purpose. She got on her phone to call a car and he whacked it out of her hands and grabbed her wrists. That's when I stepped in. And, well, what was he gonna do?" Jackson took his moment with a small gloat then turned to me. "I took her out for a burger, and we made fun of you for an hour before I dropped her home, safe and sound." The grin on Jackson's face was him taunting me but I didn't care. She was safe. That was what mattered.

"Do we need some kind of insurance policy on this guy?" Leo asked.

"Come on, Ricci." Jackson's voice was light. "This ain't my first rodeo. I filmed that shit. Uploaded it to our server last night."

A recording of her? "I need to see that."

They all laughed. Why was that funny?

"That ain't happening." Frankie tapped me on the back. What the fuck? "Keep lying low. Let Samantha ruin your stepdaddy. She knows how to do that. Stay out of her way."

"But…"

Frankie leveled me with his eyes. I hated that I had to play by his rules, and yet might just have been happy to do so. "I'll see you tomorrow."

The three of them filtered out and I stuffed my bag. On the way home I got a veggie juice and its thin consistency made me miss the thick protein of my milkshakes. But Frankie was right. I was too thick. I needed to lose some of my bulk. Goodbye steak and eggs, and hello broccoli and sweet potatoes.

Less than three weeks… That was all I had to survive until I could see Samantha again.

At home, after my shower and with my stomach nowhere near satisfied, I crossed the nurse in the hall on my way to my mother's room. Demsey hadn't come home the night before. I assumed he was either drunk or fucking one of his mistresses.

"She was in a lot of pain last night and finally agreed to the morphine. She slept well and is alert. A little loopy, but she's talking."

"Talking?" I blinked several times. She hadn't spoken for days.

The nurse put her hand on my forearm. "I know it seems like a bit of recovery, but it's the drugs."

In other words, don't get my hopes up. *Noted*.

I opened the door, and sure enough, she was seated in bed with a smile on her face. Jesus, she even had on makeup.

"I drank my tea. And the nurse is bringing toast." Her voice was scratchy and small. My eyes watered and I fluttered the thought away that I might have just cried in happiness.

"That's amazing." I went over to the bed and took my seat. "Do you want me to read?"

"Let's talk while I have the energy."

"Whatever you want."

She laughed.

"Didn't think you'd hear me ever say that, huh?"

After a shake of her head, she said, "Please explain why Samantha is dating someone other than you, and if you found out her motives for ruining my husband's campaign."

Right. *That.* I hadn't wanted to admit to her being right about me still dealing, and she'd been too weak to read the papers, so it made sense that the first thing she'd done was get an understanding of the disaster that was her son.

But she deserved the truth. "She struck a deal with the chief of police. He buried an incriminating recording of me in exchange for the election. She's not dating that jackass. It was just to piss off Demsey and make him nervous—which totally worked, by the way."

She narrowed her light eyes. "Where is he, anyway?"

"Didn't come home last night."

"Hmmm."

The nurse came back with a piece of wholewheat toast and I gave up my chair next to the bed and practiced standing on one foot and shifting my body weight to various parts.

"Chew it more than you've ever chewed anything," the nurse said as she watched my mother intently.

It was a slow process, but she managed half of the toast before holding out her hand to stop.

"That's good, Sophia. Very good." The nurse stood with a content smile and left us.

When the door was closed, my mother said, "Jesus. Getting praise for eating fucking toast. And here I thought the low point was her wiping my ass." My mother pointed to her dresser and continued, "Top drawer. There's a compartment above with a small book inside."

Still a little shocked at my mother's language, I went over and opened the drawer then felt a piece of light wood move and slid it over. The book fell into my palm and I transferred it to my other hand while I put the top back in place and closed the drawer.

"That is a complete directory of all his mistresses — well, up until a month ago, anyway. Give it to a journalist. The headline can read something like, '*Myers Dying while Demsey's Gratifying*'."

"Are you serious?"

"If getting you Samantha back means throwing the election, so be it."

I frowned. It wouldn't be that easy. Samantha and I still had trust issues. "I lied to her."

My mother looked at me for a long time before saying, "I lied to you. Do you forgive me?"

"Yes. But it's different. You're my mother."

"Sweetheart, if she's doing all of this for you, she loves you. And if she loves you, she can forgive you. That's when you know it's real."

"She told her buddy at *The Times* about your cancer before me. That fucking stings, Ma."

"How many mistakes have you made in your lifetime?"

"Countless." I hated it when she was right.

I walked over to the bed and kissed her on the cheek. Having her to talk to had never meant more. Probably because not having her for those weeks when she'd refused to take the heavy pain medication and suffered had been a sign of what was inevitably to come.

I tapped the little book in my hand. "I'm gonna handle this. Do you want me to get the papers while I'm out?"

"No. They don't matter anymore."

On the computer in my mother's office, I typed out the women's names and addresses. I didn't want this getting back to her somehow. Also, I had no idea how to get in touch with reporters. Samantha wouldn't take my calls, even if I tried. I didn't know how to begin to find her assistant. Where the fuck was Rafa when I needed him?

But I knew how to be sneaky. I just had to think like my former self. I printed out the paper with the names and folded it before slipping into my back pocket then heading out the door.

Downtown, I bought a burner phone and created an email account through the service provider. On my real phone, I looked up *The Times* on the browser and found an address for that Mitch fuck who had always been hanging on my girl. I emailed him the picture then threw the phone in the next wire trash can I found on the street.

There would be no recovery from cheating on a dying woman. That was some cold shit.

Chapter Twenty-Seven

Samantha

I jogged through the park, the fall wind stinging my face but my muscles happy to move. The uncertainty of my future had been weighing heavy on my mind. Who would hire me after all the scandal with Demsey? But more importantly, what did I want to do? I was young, and I could recover. I had the ability to re-invent. Would I have to move?

Even though it had sickened me to see my picture with Tom in the gossip section, it got me through another week of my lonely life. I wasn't sure what I would do after the election, only that I needed to wait until the coast was clear and Valerie Carver had better things to worry about than a drug dealer in a city in which she no longer lived or worked.

I'd gathered a few documents regarding Demsey's favoring his brother in real estate deals, but nothing was a smoking gun. I would just have to hope that he'd mess up in public again and he'd hammer his own nails into his political coffin. Then I'd throw a little gas on the fire the weekend before the election by showing the corrupt side of him. I prayed it would be enough.

Being unemployed had led to a bit of a phone addiction on my part, so I'd started a new habit of leaving it behind when I ran. I preferred silence to music anyway and it would give me at least one hour in my day when I wasn't obsessing about poll numbers, Valerie Carver changing her mind or Scott Tucker taking his case public instead of letting it be buried in the basement of police headquarters.

Run complete, I stopped for a coffee at my local deli and the front page of *The Times* caught my eye. *As Demsey's wife's condition declines, he seeks validation elsewhere.* Then the by-line, *Powerful men and the women they exploit.*

Oh, snap. And the author was Mitch. But none of it had come from me. I swiped up a copy — stories like that deserved the actual paper — then paid for it and my coffee.

In my apartment, I ignored my vibrating phone and sat at the island while I read. Mitch had managed to take a story about Demsey and his many mistresses and turn it into a thoughtful piece of journalism. He'd used recent cases of men in power as examples of how once on top, even the most well-intentioned men find themselves exploiting women. Someone had given Mitch a list of all Demsey's mistresses, and two of them had gone on the record. When prodded for their motivations for sleeping with a married man, both had admitted to being more attracted to his position and money rather than his personality.

Mitch had also interviewed a psychologist who had a theory that if a woman doesn't feel she has power in society, she will seek it in a man as a supplement. Being a mistress had a certain amount of leverage with its secrecy. The article was a damning account of not just Demsey but powerful men everywhere. I considered calling Mitch and buying him a drink. There would be no recovery from his article. Demsey was finished.

After my shower, I checked my phone and returned Fanny's seven phone calls. We decided on a celebratory lunch and met downtown at one of our favorite Mexican places.

At twelve-thirty, Fanny walked in the door with the paper in hand and a grin plastered across her skinny face. We were seated and she took out the article. She'd highlighted certain bits, then over the florescent yellow had circled certain words.

"I can't for the life of me figure out where this came from. No one has this kind of access to Demsey." She shook her head and re-read the byline for what must have been the hundredth time.

It had sparked my curiosity as well, and I did have a theory. And if I was right, it meant that Sophia Myers might just be feeling better and ready to join forces in tanking her current husband.

"We could always call Mitch and ask." I shrugged.

Fanny fought her smile. "We should probably have a drink first."

"Good thinking. I mean, it's not like we have to go back to work."

Stomachs full and officially buzzed with our third margaritas on their way, I cleared my throat and dialed Mitch.

"Hey, Sammie. I wondered if you'd reach out."

"Mitch... Hey... Super-good article. You should be proud."

Fanny giggled across from me. I shushed her then flapped my hand to try and regain my serious tone.

"Care to comment?"

"Nooooo. No. No. I was just curious as to your source."

He laughed. "You know I don't reveal that. I thought it was you, actually."

"Nope. Why would you think that? I would have just called." I managed to find my composure.

"I'll tell you this, since we're friends."

That almost made me laugh. I wasn't his friend. Maybe he knew that and was fucking with me. The tequila had fogged up my logic.

He continued, "I got an email with a list of names and addresses. It took me a few days to figure out what they meant, but when I saw Demsey's car in front of one of the addresses, I understood.

"Good for you for not turning it into sensation-alism."

"Thanks. He's toast now. That's what you wanted, isn't it?" Mitch was fishing. Even in my saucy state, I could catch that.

I answered honestly. "No." It was what I *needed*.

"How's that new fed boyfriend of yours?" Again with the fishing. He must have heard the alcohol in my voice.

"He's perfect, right?" I rolled my eyes to Fanny, who was hanging on my every word. "Anyway, I should go. Congrats again!" I hung up before he could say thank you.

"So?" Fanny's eyes bugged out.

"Anonymous...which means Sophia Myers. I'd bet our next drink on it."

Fanny flapped her fingers at me. "Gimme your phone."

"Why?" I handed it to her anyway.

"Because you're about to get full-on day-drunk. I don't trust you not to call him. We are two weeks out from this election. Someone catches you with him then you're the bad guy. When the votes are in, you can call him...not before." She slipped my phone into her small bag. It was annoying how well she knew me and that she was right.

Because I was fucking pining for him, especially with the booze making me warm, fuzzy and relaxed.

"But," I whined, "I miss him. He could just slip in and out of my apartment and no one would know. Oh! We could meet at your place! No one would look there."

"One...gross. You think I'm interested in a man in my apartment? Probably leave a pee spot on the toilet or drink out of my milk carton." She shivered.

Our final drinks came, and I said, "What do we do after this anyway? I haven't been day-drunk since college. I can't remember."

"Well, we have two choices. Keep going or try and walk it off then go to bed with an early hangover."

We clinked glasses. "I can't possibly drink any more after this. You'd be holding my hair over the toilet."

"I wouldn't do that. But I would toss you a scrunchie from the hallway."

I sat back deep into my chair and faked offense. "I would hold *your* hair."

"No need. I don't puke. Anyway, if we're not going to see this to a tragic ending, I suggest we go to a movie.

That way, you can't use your phone and we both sober up."

"Deal."

We found a comedy an hour later and proceeded to buy way too many snacks with our drunken munchies. The movie was stupid, but we laughed through it, more than it deserved. It was a successful girls' day out. Forgetting about the world outside did me good, and by the time I'd sobered up a bit, I knew it was too soon to reach out to Anton, even though I'd been aching to.

I wanted to know the status of his mother, how he was handling it and what I could have done to help. But there was something else holding me back. If, indeed, Sophia Myers health was deteriorating, she deserved the undivided attention of her son.

Two days later, *The Scoop* published her petition to the court for divorce from Demsey, and if Mitch's article hadn't sealed the fate of my former boss, Sophia had. Anton must have fessed up to his mother about his dealing and let her in on my plan. Like everything Sophia Myers did, she had the better moves. I probably should have gone to her once I'd struck a deal with the chief, but it no longer mattered. Demsey's approval rating had plummeted and there was no road to the state capital for him.

But it all still left me with an uncertain future. I was fortunate enough to be financially stable for the moment, but the drive in me to be my own woman and support myself wasn't going to go away. The new mayor wouldn't want to look in my direction. Holdovers from one administration to the next were scarce at best. I could go private, but with what client list? I'd mastered the art of spin and behind the scenes deal-making but with my key players out of the game, who would want me to straddle their world of sinister and public?

Chapter Twenty-Eight

Anton

I'd officially kicked Demsey out of my mother's house and gotten a lawyer to file for divorce, but it was a precarious situation. With morphine running through her veins and her still bedridden, she wasn't exactly of 'sound mind'. According to her lawyer, there had been a pre-nuptial agreement, but it had several clauses that Demsey could fight — the easiest being her mental capacity.

The pain medication had helped in the beginning. It had given her lucid days and provided for some last-minute memories for me. But with each day that passed, her condition worsened, and we were headed back down the road to squirting lukewarm tea into her mouth with a syringe.

I was pretty sure Demsey was ruined. The election was only days away, and I still had no word from Samantha. I craved her soft touch and gentle but strong manner. Leo and the guys were helping me forget my circumstances in our morning workouts, but no one was there in the dark hours of the night when I would sit next to my mother's bed and listen to her gasp for air.

Her doctor had come to visit, upped the dose of the morphine and explained to me that the tumor in her trachea was probably going to grow over what little space had been left the last time he'd seen an X-ray.

She'd rallied enough to make sure I was safe, but with every hour that passed, she was letting go.

The nurse came into the room and stepped into the light my mother's bathroom was providing.

"Why don't you take a break? I'll sit with her for a while," she said in a soothing voice. Sometimes I wondered if the nurses weren't there more for me than her.

I'd read an article online about how sometimes people wanted privacy to die. I hated the idea of my mother passing alone but also knew I needed to give her the choice to do it without me there. My selfishness of not wanting her to stop fighting might have been getting in the way of her finally letting go.

I stood and kissed my mother on the cheek. "Let's both give her some peace. She probably hates us hovering over her like this."

Downstairs, I tried to sit on the couch, then her favorite chair. I opened and closed the fridge a hundred times and reminded myself that I couldn't eat anything in it because I was on a vegetarian diet until I lost all my bulk and slimmed down.

Fuck it.

I threw on a coat and told the nurse I was going for some air. But as I walked north and west, I knew exactly where I was headed. It was a Friday night, so more people were out than normal, but the residential streets were abandoned. She would still think it was a risk, but no one was following me. I stood and watched the entrance of her building for ten minutes before I approached.

Maybe she would be mad that I hadn't respected her timeline, but I honestly didn't care. Seeing her — even if she had decided she hated me — was the only thing that would get me through the next days when I was sure to lose my mother. I needed to secure the woman of my future before saying a final goodbye to the one who was my past.

I held my finger over her buzzer with my heart pounding in my chest. I was confident she would talk to me but still knew there was a good chance I would be rejected. Hell, she might not even be home.

The laugh of a young couple made me look up as they exited the building, not giving me a second glance. I slipped inside and rode the elevator up to Samantha's floor.

Again at her door, I hesitated. I was putting it all at risk, but how did she expect me to suffer tragedy without her next to me to hold me up? In fact, it was her fault for making me love her. Had she not been so perfect and known how to satisfy every fiber of my being, I would be knocking on Leo's door instead of hers.

I rapped my knuckles lightly and waited for any signs of life on the other side of the door. The second time, I was a bit louder and more insistent. Footsteps gave her away and the energy pulsing through the door confirmed there was just a plank of wood between us.

My nerves buzzed throughout my body and were drawn to her like a magnet. I placed my palm on her door, desperate for the connection. If I could just see her, I would know where we stood.

"Please," I said, not recognizing the desperation in my own voice.

The clicking of the deadbolt gave me an ounce of hope. But when she opened, the chain kept me from her.

"You shouldn't be here." Her face was pinched in a way I couldn't understand. But she was wearing a man's shirt and I was pretty fucking sure it was mine.

"No one saw me."

She closed her eyes and shook her head then re-opened and looked me up and down. "You're thinner. Why?"

I smiled because she'd noticed. It meant she cared. "Because I'm slow. You're wearing my shirt."

Samantha stepped back. She was busted. "Three days. We can talk in three days."

"You're wearing my shirt." Who knew a sheet of cotton could bring me so much joy?

"Go away." She was doing such a good job of trying to remain stern. It was the cutest thing she'd ever done.

"You know I could just drop a shoulder and be inside. You should save yourself the repair money and just let me in. Because *you're* wearing *my* shirt." I pointed to her then me.

"This isn't your shirt." She bit her lips inward and worked her jaw.

"Liar. You beautiful, adorable liar."

"Go home. Three fucking days. Please. Don't ruin this because you're horny." She started to shut the door, but I blocked it with my hand. My teasing her about the shirt had given her the wrong impression about my intentions.

"You think that's why I came here? For sex? I came here because I fucking need you, Samantha. My mother is dying. I'm alone. I came here for comfort. I came here to feel a little less fucking helpless. And despite what we both did, I'm pretty fucking sure just the sight of you makes it better."

She blinked several times. It was the most honest I'd ever been, maybe with anyone. From her drawn brow, it hadn't been what she'd expected to hear from me.

I kept going, the momentum in my favor. "I'm sorry about the drugs. I know you thought that shit was behind me—"

"You're wrong." She cut me off in a soft, tortured voice. "I thought it was beneath you. And there is nothing more I want than to open this door and let you in. But I won't risk it. Then all this is for nothing."

"No one knows or cares that I'm here."

She sighed and her dark eyes pleaded. "We only have three days. As soon as the election is counted, we can have this conversation." This time she closed the door and relocked it—in my shirt.

I walked home with a small pep in my step. Samantha could have her three days. Fine. If that was what it would take to get her back on board, I could do it.

That was until I opened the door and saw the nurse sitting on the stairs. I knew before she said a word. It wasn't the pained look on her face or the sympathy in her eyes. It was the hollow pit in my heart. It was the emptiness in the house. It was the lonely pinch on my soul.

The woman I'd worshiped from a distance but fought when face to face was no longer. Somehow, I found the couch and sat with the profound knowledge that my life would never be the same.

She'd been my rock, my teacher and the only source of pure love I'd ever known.

The nurse came in and sat with me in silence for a long moment.

Finally, I said, "She waited for me to leave."

"Mmm. I read somewhere that people choose who is present when they are born and when they die. Maybe it's all bullshit, and I don't know much about birth, but I have seen a lot of passings. You would be surprised the amount of people who don't want their loved ones in the room when they take their last breath. It's a very private moment."

A tear I didn't know I was capable of streamed down my cheek and my gut ached.

She continued, "My point is, don't beat yourself up about not being there. And don't take it personally if you believe she didn't want you there."

I sat with her words and rolled them around in my head. There were two ways to go. Either I respected her wishes for once in my fucking life or I questioned her judgment like I had at every turn up until that point.

Her choice stung, but it wasn't about me. I didn't like it, but I understood it.

"What do I do next?" I asked and it hung out there with a double meaning.

The nurse stood. "I'll call the funeral home. She made all the arrangements with me two weeks ago. Can I get you anything?"

I shook my head, but when she left, I poured myself one of my mother's favorite brandies and toasted up to her in her bed. I didn't know what happened when people died, if they stayed around and haunted us or went to a better place or what-the-fuck ever. But I would make my mother proud, just in case she was watching.

Chapter Twenty-Nine

Samantha

At nine o'clock Monday morning I stood behind my front door and leveled my shoulders. Going to Sophia's funeral would be a risk to the carefully executed plan of the prior month, but I wasn't sure Anton would ever forgive me if I didn't show up. More, I didn't think I would forgive myself. His appearance at my front door Friday night had broken my heart. The minute I'd closed the door, I'd regretted it. I could no longer not be there for him.

In a black wool dress and a black princess coat, I resolved that I was doing the right thing by letting emotions triumph logic. If somehow Demsey won the election the next day, we would just have to lawyer up and fight any allegations. Hell, I still had shit I could hold over the chief's head. I just didn't want it to get to that point.

I walked down the avenue on my side of the park. The cathedral for the funeral was only ten blocks from my building, and once it came into view, so did the small group of reporters on its steps.

Mitch spotted me almost immediately. *So much for my plan to sneak in a side door without being detected.* I tucked my small clutch under my armpit. If there was one thing I knew how to do, it was talk to reporters, even if I was a little rusty.

He met me halfway. "Didn't think I'd see you today."

"Sophia Myers was a mentor and a strong pillar of our society. She deserves the respect I intend to pay in honoring her life."

Mitch lifted his bushy eyebrows and tucked in his chin. "On the record?"

"Absolutely."

Cameras flashed as I approached, and I silently berated the reporters for making a small circus out of a woman's final services. But I understood that they were hungry vultures, and the reactionary part of the brain was hard to train.

I stared at my feet as I climbed the steps, my heart racing and mind wondering what I might find inside. I was early. The service wasn't set to start for another fifteen minutes, but the pews were filling up. A lone figure stood over the closed casket at the front of the church.

From the back, he looked even thinner than he had in front of my door three days prior. It was a powerful image, his dark suit and bowed head — a painful peace resonating from him and keeping voices to hushed tones.

My heels echoed up the marble aisle in a slow, deliberate speed. The closer I came to him, the more magnetic the pull. When I reached the first row, I removed the glove from my right hand. The eyes of the congregation were on me, burning into my skin like lasers, all wondering if I was bold enough to step up.

I was. I held my clutch and glove in my left hand, took two steps forward to Anton's side and extended my right arm. It was proof for me, for him and for all those eyes behind us.

Without moving his head, he interlaced our fingers then squeezed for a beat with his eyes closed. I gripped back, sending him my comfort and begging him to forgive me for leaving him alone when he'd needed me most.

We stood there for five more minutes until the priest cleared his throat.

Anton kept his gaze forward and said quietly, "I'll never lie to you again." His vow was laced with the pain I'd caused by shutting him out but also a thread of gratitude that I was there.

When he finally turned to me, his light eyes still held the seed of power they always had. I let it penetrate me and I took shelter in it. Anton released my hand and placed his on the small of my back then guided me to the first pew.

We sat, and if anyone had doubted our display, he put his arm around me to solidify our public coming out for the second time. The shifting of people in their seats rumbled behind us, but we kept our gazes ahead.

The priest began his eulogy and we remained like statues for the next hour inside the cold walls of the church. There was no burial to follow and we remained seated as the crowd filtered out, neither one of us interested in their judgmental eyes or empty words. Anton stared at his mother's casket until the priest came over and offered his final condolences.

As we walked out of the empty church, he said, "You don't have to do this."

I stopped in front of the high doors and placed my hand on his heart. "I want to."

He took a slow inhale and a longer exhale. "I've missed you."

"I'm sorry I wasn't there."

"You're here now. And truthfully, I think I needed to go through it alone. It made me realize I shouldn't take things for granted. I meant what I said... No more lies."

"Okay." The simple word said so much more. It said that we were together, that we were going to really try.

"My friends are getting together at Chezzie's. Will you come?"

I nodded, and once he'd called for a car, I stepped into him and he wrapped his strong arms around me. We stood there in silence, and while I liked to imagine that I was comforting him, he was sending back a sense of security and strength that I'd been aching for.

His phone buzzed in his pocket and he pulled back just a little. "Car's here. You sure you want to walk out there with me?"

"From here on out, we face everything together."

He scrunched his face. We were taking a risk, but it was worth it for both of us. "What if—"

I held up my hand. "The story will be that Demsey didn't come to the funeral, not that I did. He can't win tomorrow after a headline like that."

"Are you sure?"

"I'm sure I'm not leaving your side today. We can sort through the rest after."

The first glimpse of a smile tugged at his lips.

As soon as we opened the door, the cameras flashed, and with our hands held tightly together, we made our way to the waiting car on the street. Once inside, the muffled questions ceased and we both let out a breath of relief. My phone beeped from my little clutch and I turned it off. All of it could wait. Being there for Anton and giving him my full attention was more important.

Downtown at Chezzie's restaurant, there were no reporters, no cameras. She'd prepared a breakfast buffet with fruit, meats, cheeses and three coffee cakes. She greeted us with a sympathetic smile for Anton. I spotted the man Jackson who had helped me with Tom and two women and children I didn't know.

The blonde came over first and hugged Anton. "I'm sorry for your loss," she said with such a genuine smile that it struck me as odd that he had a female friend. Then to me she held out her hand. "I'm Lisa. And this is Junior. J.J. for short."

An adorable little boy shook my hand and said, "Nice to meet you. What's your name?"

I bent down to eye level, "I'm Samantha, but you can call me Sam."

"Okey dokey."

Lisa ushered the little boy away while Jackson hugged Anton then said hello to me.

A beautiful brunette stepped up and rubbed his arm. "Your boy's been worried about you. I never thought I'd say this, but it's good to see you."

Anton let out a small laugh. "He says you're annoying. That makes me perversely happy."

"I'm Fiona, Leo's fiancée. And that little rascal is my sister Violet." She pointed to a smaller version of herself tugging at Chezzie's hand and guiding her into the kitchen. Fiona covered the side of her mouth. "She doesn't know she's not a hundred percent Italian, and we like to keep that lie alive."

Stinky pizza boy, who I understood to be Leo, came up behind Fiona and wrapped his arms around her waist. He formally introduced himself and his brother Frankie, who was basically his twin with a touch of gray around the ears.

I looped my arm into Anton's. Whatever bad blood had been between him and these people had passed, and his quiet recognition of their presence made my heart swell for him.

All the tables had been pushed together to form one long one, and once we were seated, a few older men came in. Anton went over to them and shook their hands. He offered them a place at the end, all together.

Lisa sat next to me and poured me some water before serving herself. "You must be some kind of superwoman. I never thought I'd see the day when that man settled down."

"How long have you known him?" I was pretty sure they were all part of his former crew. I just never expected that to include women.

"Ever since he came to the neighborhood. I went to him and offered to watch everybody's kids, and he thought it was a great idea. He gave me an apartment and a salary. I owe him a lot. Plus, when Jackson got the opportunity to leave and work for Frankie, he just let us go. I always knew there was kindness behind those eerie-ass eyes."

"Oh, God. Lisa, what are you telling her?" Anton slid into the seat next to me.

I smiled. "That you're — wait for it — *nice.*"

Anton shivered. "Oh, for fuck's sake."

"Who are those men?" I leaned into Anton and was so glad I hadn't missed the opportunity to see him with his friends.

"Those guys were my mom's original crew. The four of them worked for my father but switched loyalty when he went to prison. I think they all were secretly in love with her."

I sent them a friendly smile and they returned it.

After the plates were cleared and people started filing out, Anton turned to me and there was a softness in his eyes I'd never seen. "Do you want to go Upstate with me? I could use a change of scenery."

"Yeah, yeah, I do." I brushed his cheek and he pushed it into my palm. The small gesture filled me with warmth. He wanted to lean on me, wasn't afraid to show me he needed me.

"I'm sorry I didn't let you in on Friday. Actually, I'm sorry for everything. I hate that I didn't find a way to be there for you."

His eyes fluttered but remained closed. "I know. I also know that I'm not an easy man. You were right. We were bound to crash and burn at the rate we were going."

It stuck me how tired he looked, how much the last month had cost him. And I'd made him do it without me.

Leo came over and clapped Anton on the back. "We're out of here. You still going Upstate?"

Anton stood and gave Leo a hug. "Thanks for everything. I'll see you assholes in a week or so."

I rose as well and shook Leo's hand.

Leo lifted a finger before he left. "Oh, Samantha, I may have a job for you. We have this client. He needs someone who can help him keep his mouth shut and dig him out of the multiple lies he tells. Have Anton give you my number."

I nodded. "Gladly. I'm going up with him. Can it wait until we get back?"

"Probably not, but yeah. Take some time with this one. He needs a bit of R&R." Leo and Anton exchanged a long, silent look before Leo nodded.

Frankie joined us and shook my hand then glared at Anton. "No red meat."

Anton narrowed his eyes. "You secretly love me, Frankie. Don't try to deny it."

Frankie grumbled as he walked away, and Leo gave Anton a final tap on the back before following Frankie. He scooped up Fiona's little sister and kissed her on the cheek. They had a quiet conversation before both laughed and disappeared into the kitchen.

"You ready?" I asked when we were alone at the table.

"For a life without my mother? No. For a life with you? Maybe." Anton reached for my coat and held it out for me to thread my arms through. "You're not going to make me take shit slow and like woo you or some shit, are you?"

Once in my coat, I turned around and stepped in close. "Where's the fun in that?"

The playfulness in his eyes disappeared and his lids were slots. "What a fucking day. Thank you for being here. It helped."

"I'm sorry I wasn't there sooner."

"Yeah, but everything you did, you did for me. That's loyalty." Anton drew me closer and placed his chin on the top of my head.

"I'm pretty sure it's actually love."

Epilogue

Anton
One year later

A fire crackled in a massive stone chimney and the smell of burned wood lingered in the air. My former crew had officially traded in our black jeans and tanks for fucking monkey suits. We sat in two neat little rows to witness one of our own make the ultimate commitment. It was oddly fitting that, other than some random family members of Leo's, it was only us. I had briefly wondered if Leo would be nervous on his wedding day, but the twinkle in his dark eyes and the wide grin on his face as he watched Fiona walk down the aisle was far from fear.

Frankie whispered something in Leo's ear and he nodded—his gaze never leaving his bride. She'd chosen a simple white dress that, according to Samantha, had a sweep train, whatever the fuck that meant. But Fiona was stunning and her little sister could barely contain her excitement opposite Leo.

Samantha and I sat in front of Jackson and Lisa, with J.J. between them in a black vest and bowtie. The formal occasion hid all our tattoos and scars and gave the appearance we were just regular schmoes, supporting our friends on their wedding day.

But we were more than that. We were broken boys who had led broken lives, only to be put on the right track by strong women. My mother, Fiona, Samantha — even Lisa… It was like the crew hadn't known how to be proper men until they'd come along. Even that hacker shit M who had gotten me shot had been able to get Rafa out of Covington and make him not want to go back.

Every once and a while I would remember some stupid nickname we'd come up with for a junkie or a fight we'd picked and won and get a twinge of nostalgia, but I never wanted to go back to selling drugs. I'd even gotten to the point where I was thankful I'd been shot. It had changed my life.

Samantha gripped my hand tight. She'd better not fucking get all gooey and cry over this shit. That wasn't who we were. No, in the year since my mother had died, we'd officially become a 'power couple'. We were invited to stupid parties with obnoxious people, and as much as I hated it, I understood it would ultimately be useful.

I'd flipped three buildings from rat-infested, abandoned warehouses to luxury condos and it turned out I was pretty fucking good at it. And the blonde beauty to my left had begun managing the public relations of celebrities who had a tendency to get in trouble. She wasn't a fixer, per se, but she'd saved a lot of rich idiots from ruining their careers with their careless ways.

We'd worked through our trust issues, both agreed that we weren't interested in a family any time soon and had been living together in my mother's remodeled brownstone for three months. We had a normal fucking life. It was weird as shit, but I liked it.

The priest welcomed us. Leo had promised the ceremony would be short and not too sweet, just a happy formality to seal the bond with the woman who drove him insane. And after a little benediction, Leo started his vows. "Fiona. I promise to love, cherish and keep you and Violet safe, for the rest of my days..."

Never in all the back-alley dice games and courtyard brawls would I ever had imagined Leo Ricci to be such a fucking sap—or myself, for that matter. Because I had a big fucking rock waiting back at my A-frame with Samantha's name on it.

Fiona and Leo were going to their favorite camping spot for their honeymoon, so they'd booked a small lodge for the nuptials Upstate, only about a half an hour from my place.

I wasn't trying to upstage or copy Leo, but I'd known I was going to propose to Samantha at my cabin for a while. We'd just needed a weekend when one of us didn't have something in the city.

But as Fiona recited her simple lines back to Leo, I couldn't wait to do the same with Samantha. My mother, to no surprise, had been right. She was perfect for me. She challenged me but knew when to let me win. She motivated me to be better without nagging. But mostly, she'd accepted all things I'd done in the past without judgment. I was pretty sure her package was one of a kind and I was doing my best to not let it slip away. All those years I'd spent not wanting to be lonely and I'd filled with my crew, I never imagined someone like Samantha would be the ultimate answer to my prayers.

When the vows were over, Leo said something for Fiona's ears only and she mouthed something back. They really were a perfect fit. I could relate.

Thank fuck there wasn't any bubble blowing or rice throwing. My jaded brain would have had to draw the line or exploded. There was entirely too much nice going on in one day.

Once it got late and the kids started fading around the table, I congratulated my best friend and his new bride before Samantha and I set off in my mom's old Jag.

I merged onto the highway and she said, "I really appreciate how simple that all was. God, do you remember Eve's wedding last summer? It was like the decorator had bought every piece of gold she could find. *Blah.*"

Yeah, I remembered. I think I'd called it *"luxury vomit"*. "That night haunts my dreams."

Samantha kicked off her heels and tucked her legs under her ass. "Not exactly Mr. Modern and Sleek's cup of tea."

I shot her a side-eye. "Modern in the city. Rustic in the woods. We've been through this."

"Whatever." She shook her head to dismiss me but took my free hand. "Was it nice to see your friend so happy?"

"It's odd but yeah. I mean, we never wanted to be bad. We just couldn't figure out how to be good."

The rest of the way home we chatted about the funny moments at the reception and how while we thought J.J. and Violet were adorable, they may have been the greatest form of birth control we'd ever encountered. Neither one of us would have the patience for kids anytime soon. Samantha noted that Frankie seemed a bit sad and lonely, and I assured her that he was just pissed off that his little brother got married first then I recounted his latest dating flop. He seriously had the worst luck with women of anyone I'd ever met. He must have been a serious asshole. After one horrible date we'd sparred the next morning and I'd taunted him that he must suck in bed. I'd gone home with a black eye.

Driving down the tree-lined path to my Upstate house never got old. It represented privacy but so many memories with my crew. It had probably been the only thing that had kept us sane all those years, an escape from a life we all secretly didn't want.

It was late, but Samantha was a sucker for a fire, and I hadn't drank since I was driving.

"Night cap?" I asked as I headed to the chimney.

"Sure. But I don't think there's any more whiskey…unless you brought some."

"A glass of wine is great." I smiled over my shoulder.

"I'll have to open one. But we'll finish it tomorrow, right?" She dug in the drawer, the utensils clanking back and forth, then moved to another drawer where she also wouldn't find a corkscrew. I lit the kindling and blew on the fire then reached for the bottle opener I'd hidden behind a picture on the mantle with a ring wrapped around the spiral metal.

"This is hilarious, but I can't find the opener." She looked at me from across the room.

"Oh. It's here," I said with a shrug. "I used it earlier for a beer."

With my heart thudding loud, I walked over to the kitchen and handed her the curly metal and her face immediately fell.

She stared at the ring — it wasn't small — then slowly lifted her gaze. "What are you doing?" Her brown eyes were wider than I'd ever seen, and she pressed her lips together as her chest rose and fell.

"This last year — no lies, no drama, despite not having my mother — I've been happier than I thought possible. I never want that to go away, but I also wanted to say that your acceptance of my past, when I was a criminal, a liar, means more than you can possibly imagine. So, I'm going to go ahead and make this" — I rolled my eyes — "permanently exclusive." I took the corkscrew from her hand and dropped the ring into my palm. I got down on one knee to prove I was serious, and her hands flew to her face. "Samantha Powers, will you marry me, kick me in the ass when I need it and face everything the future holds head on with me as a team?"

She darted her gaze back and forth and her fingers fell until she made two fists under her chin. She fought a cheeky grin. "Depends... Can we elope?"

"Jesus Christ, I love you."

I held the ring between my index finger and thumb, waiting for her official answer.

"I would be proud to be your wife. So yes. *Yes.*" Her hand was shaking while I stood and slipped on the ring. Once in place, she leaped into my arms and I carried her over the fire where I got her naked and claimed her beautiful body for my own once more.

I stared into her eyes and took in all the love she sent back to me. I didn't think I deserved any of it after the crimes I'd committed, the addicts I'd preyed upon, the violence I'd gladly been a part of, but I did know I could lose it at any minute.

Samantha's betrayal had played long and hard on my ability to forgive and trust her again. But in the end, I was thankful for it. In a backhanded way, it had proved she was my equal, that she could hurt me as much as I could her. And ultimately, that was what I needed in my life — someone who stood by my side, not behind me.

I drew a fur blanket around us on the floor as the afterglow of making love was only highlighted by the dancing orange flames.

"I love you," Samantha whispered.

"I love you too, sunshine." I kissed her blonde head and held her tight. She was the most precious piece of my life — past, present and future.

Want to see more from this author? Here's a taster for you to enjoy!

The Covington Heights Crew: Force
Deana Birch

Excerpt

Frankie

I parked my baby blue Porsche in my brother Leo's cobblestone driveway. He'd bought one of those huge historic homes and made everything inside modern. I thought it was flashy and a bit of a way to gloat about how much money we were making, but he'd done it to make his girls happy. Besides, who was I to judge? My apartment overlooking the East River was just as over the top.

In truth, I loved that Fiona and Violet had given Leo the shove back to putting his family first. His friend Anton had taken too much of his loyalty over the years. I was glad it was focused back where it belonged. I rang the bell for Sunday dinner with my favorite bottle of Tignanello cradled in my arms like the treasure she was.

The door swung open, and Leo rolled his eyes. "Thank God you're here. Can you please explain to my very pregnant and very stubborn wife that she can't just hire a nanny after one Facetime because they 'bonded'." He air-quoted the last word, which was a mistake, because Fiona noticed it right away and stomped over. I had no idea how she moved so gracefully with her massive belly.

"I like her. She has a degree in early education. She'll be great for Vi and the twins. Plus, I'm the one who will be spending time with her. It's my opinion that matters."

I scanned the entryway for any signs of my aunt Chezzie, the dog or any damn neutral ally but found none.

Leo made way for me to enter then turned to his wife. "Fi, I'm just saying. Let me do a background check. It will take twenty-four hours." Calmer, and with a smile, he continued, "Then — if everything checks out — we can offer her the position."

I leaned over and gave Fiona a kiss on the cheek. "You look great. How you feeling?"

She narrowed her eyes. "Don't do that, Francis Ricci. Don't change the topic for his sake. But thank you, and I'm exhausted. Chezzie came early and took Violet to the beach, so I napped then hired a nanny." She grinned at Leo, whose nostrils flared as he reached for the bottle.

"Nice," he said as he read the label. Then, to his wife, "You gotta give me twenty-four hours. I can't let a stranger into our house — our life — without at least running her social security number. Come on." With his free hand he tucked a strand of her long brown hair behind her ear. "It's just to keep you safe. You know that."

Fiona frowned but Leo's soft tone had worked its charm. "Fine. But you have to promise not to be biased against something stupid like bad credit. That was me three years ago. There are people out there who just need a break." The little lift of her eyebrows and tilt of her head emphasized that she wouldn't budge on her final point. My sister-in-law was clear on many things. One, her house had to be immaculate at all times. It was how she respected the wealth she was experiencing. Two, Sunday dinners were mandatory. And three, she always remembered where she came from.

Leo cut his eyes over to me in a 'see what I'm dealing with here' glance. And I did — not that I would admit it in front of her. But we had to at least run a credit check on the new nanny.

I pointed my thumb to the door. "I have my laptop in the car. I can run her details while we eat then have a look after. You'll get your answer tonight like that."

Fiona smiled but Leo scrunched his face like he'd smelled something foul.

He shook his head down the hall to the kitchen and mumbled, "Always gotta be the hero."

It wasn't far from the truth. Since Leo and I had changed the direction of our lives, I'd gotten a lot of satisfaction from doing the right thing. But it was odd to let a talent go to waste. Not that I'd enjoyed killing people, but I was just so damn good at it. Our father had been an outstanding teacher. It was fucked up — *we* were fucked up — but there had been a perverse pride in a job well done, another unsolved murder. With our new roles as keeping people safe, the feeling wasn't the same. It was somehow status quo.

Fiona's mouthed a 'thank you' and reminded me that I had work to do then quietly clapped her hands to the kitchen where she kissed her husband. His annoyed stance from before melted like chocolate on a hot day. It was pretty fucking disgusting how happy they were, especially since I'd failed — yet again — to find a spark with the last woman I'd gone on a date with. Chezzie had told me I was 'emotionally unavailable'. To me, that sounded like a bullshit label to make a man feel guilty about not wanting to talk about stupid shit. Maybe my standards were too high. I'd seen what Leo had. I wasn't sure I deserved the same thing, but I wouldn't take any less.

I let myself out and grabbed my laptop from the small trunk then settled into Leo's study. Fiona bounced in with a sheet of paper and handed it to me. "Here's everything I know about her."

There was no date of birth or social security number, just a small photo, a list of odd jobs and her education. *Yeah, little brother, I see what you're dealing with.*

But there was contact information, a current employer and an address, so at least I had something.

I faked a smile to Fiona. "I'll get started. Call me when it's time to eat."

"You're the best. I appreciate this so much." She rubbed her belly over her white sundress and was gone in a whoosh.

Okay, Megan Walsh of small-town Iowa, let's find your secrets.

I started with social media. If she were a drunken party girl, there would be proof. But none of the Megan Walshes matched her photo or location. What twenty-something didn't want her face plastered everywhere so her friends could tell her how pretty she was?

Without a social security number, I couldn't run her credit, and finding her date of birth without some kind of hint from a public profile would require me guessing what county she'd been born in and hacking into their records — something I would have hired an expert to do. I did manage to find a picture of her apartment building, which was small and ugly. That only made her poor, but what person trying to be a nanny would be wealthy, anyway?

After about an hour, I didn't have much.

"Hey." Leo leaned into the study. "Please tell me she's a serial killer so I can be right just one damn time."

"She's not anything for the moment." I held up the piece of paper Fiona had given me and waved it. "There's not a lot here to go by."

Leo scrubbed his face. "What am I gonna do? I can't bring a stranger into our house. Shit. But dinner's ready. Let's eat."

I closed my laptop and followed him down the hall to where Chezzie and Violet were already at the table with Fiona. Leo had grilled some sausages and a massive steak. Three of Chezzie's best salads were in the middle of the table. I kissed my aunt and niece then sat opposite them.

"Uncle Frankie? Did you know that Nana's secret to making salad was to rub the bowl with garlic first?"

"I did." I winked and unfolded my napkin. I loved how Violet had blended perfectly into our family and made it her own. Chezzie had a way of highlighting all the positive sides of our past and keeping the dark secrets dead and buried where they belonged. I also appreciated the bond that my aunt had with Fiona's little sister. She'd never been able to have children, and my father had made her boyfriends uncomfortable, at best. No one had been good enough for his little sister. Leo and I hadn't been the only ones who'd suffered from his need to keep his family under his insistent thumb.

Fiona waited until everyone was served and we'd started eating before looking at me and saying, "So?"

"Sorry. Big nada for the moment. But the agency must have run a check on her, right?" I wiped my mouth and short beard with the cloth napkin.

"I think so." Fiona cringed a little and Leo pounced.

"Fi, seriously?"

"I know. I'm sorry. But I liked her so much. She's young and her dream is to live in New York." Fiona's whine was chipping away at my brother before our eyes. She continued, "And I need someone. Chezzie has a business to run. Those beautiful babies we made could come any day. I don't want a snooty old lady looking down on me for how I change a diaper or swear in front of Violet. I want Megan."

Leo closed his eyes and Chezzie shot me a glance to fix it, probably because she knew I could.

"I'll fly out tomorrow. Leo, you stay close to home, and Jackson can handle the security detail solo for forty-eight hours. I will check out this Megan Walsh and report back. Happy?" I turned to Fiona and offered a small smile.

"Yes. Thank you." Fiona beamed, Chezzie changed the subject and Leo discretely flipped me off while pretending to scratch his ear.

As soon as dinner was finished, I excused myself to go home to prepare. I booked my plane ticket for the next day. For some ridiculous reason known only to the airline gods and their intelligent fuckery of how to make air travel the least enjoyable experience possible, I had to fly south to Charlotte in order to fly west to Iowa. That meant that my entire day would be wasted. But what was I going to do? Fiona had probably the closest thing to kids in her belly that I would ever have and was doing a stellar job of raising the little girl who had captured all our hearts. That bit of family, those Sunday dinners, they were the only things keeping me affixed to happy and normal. They were my reminder that my life had changed and needed to stay on its current path. There was no way I would lose them.

* * * *

When I woke up early and took a car to the airport, I was sure I was a sucker. And yet, somehow, I was glad to do it. During my three-hour layover in Charlotte, a place that couldn't have been more random of a stop, I booked a cheap motel not far from Megan's apartment. I'd decided to be business casual, but as soon as I got off the plane in Iowa, I knew I was still too conspicuous. It was a different world.

Cargo shorts and sports T-shirts accosted my eyes. Jesus, I would never fit in. I'd blended into dozens of cities around the globe over the years, but the Midwest was an entirely different playing field. I called Leo to let him know I'd landed but mostly to complain and make him feel guilty. *What else are big brothers for?* At the one open kiosk in the airport, I bought a yellow and black baseball hat and promptly planted it on my previously well-groomed head.

I got my rental car—a four-door sedan in a shade of gold that I was sure didn't belong on an automobile—or anywhere, for that matter. I had about an hour drive north to Megan's town. The sides of the highway were peppered with massive water towers and occasional farms backlit by the setting sun. The little towns I passed through were just that—little and gone in a blink. It was a completely different world, and I'd never felt so out of place.

At the motel, a middle-aged woman greeted me with a massive smile from behind the counter. Right... People were genuinely friendly—also new and foreign.

I gave her my reservation number and she pulled it up on her screen as I got out my wallet.

"What brings you out to these parts, Mr. Ferris?" She glanced at my fake ID from Florida without suspicion.

"Work." I tucked the ID back into its spot then waited with a tight smile that begged her not to pry further.

After a good night's sleep with the occasional disturbance of an animal sound and not the restful hum of city traffic, I drove over to Megan's apartment complex and parked on the street. The address said she was number one, which meant she had the corner unit. I rolled down the windows of the sedan, and the oppressive Midwest humidity settled in like a swamp. I brought my phone to my ear and pretended to be making a call while a sheriff's cruiser pulled into the parking lot.

A petite brunette came out of the unit and locked her front door, checking the handle twice. That meant either OCD or nerves. *Noted.* She spun around and took a long blink when she spotted the cop. From inside his car, he pointed to his wristwatch and tapped twice before driving off.

What the hell?

The woman, who I was pretty sure was Megan, rushed to her car and climbed in. It made a horrible noise when she cranked the engine. I followed her to a mall, which was where she worked at a shoe store, and she rushed in.

It was exactly ten a.m. — interesting that she would wait until the last minute. I would have been fifteen minutes early. Then again, how many people are waiting to buy shoes first thing in the morning?

There was a huge department store attached to the mall and I went in to get a new wardrobe. In the public bathroom, I changed into khaki shorts, a plain cotton white V-neck and flip-flops. I stored my old clothes in the car and put on my new baseball hat for good measure.

I grabbed a soda from a pizza place—because I noticed everyone else was shopping with them—and headed to Burt's Shoe Showroom. Megan was at the register checking her phone, and her dark hair covered her face. I meandered by the running shoes, sipping on my drink and examining random models.

Megan whimpered then tucked her phone into her back pocket before heading in my direction. I kept my eyes forward on the display until she said, "Anything I can help you with?" Her voice was sweet. Lord, it was so genuine that it took me off guard.

I looked over and was met with two beautiful, green sparkling eyes. In the small picture, it was obvious that she was pretty but up close? She was fucking beautiful—light skin with a little powdering of freckles, zero makeup and high cheekbones. I didn't even know how to take her in. Her lips were the perfect shade of pink and had a slight pout. *Damn.*

"Sir?"

"I—" How was I at a loss for words? I was a grown man—a grown man staring at his brother's potential nanny. I blinked hard. It was apparently the only thing I could do.

"Are you a runner?" she tried.

I managed to find a story somewhere. "Thinking of taking it up. What about you? You run?"

She let out a nervous laugh then blinked. "Is that an East Coast accent?"

"Yeah. In town for work."

"Buying running shoes?" She lifted her eyebrows. *Fuck.*

Home of Erotic Romance

Sign up for our newsletter and find out about all our romance book releases, eBook sales and promotions, sneak peeks and FREE romance books!

About the Author

Deana Birch was named after her father's first love, who just so happened not to be her mother. Born and raised in the Midwest, she made stops in Los Angeles and New York before settling in Europe, where she lives with her own blue-eyed Happily Ever After. Her days are spent teaching yoga, playing tennis, ruining her children's French homework, cleaning up dog vomit, writing her next book or reading someone else's.

Deana loves to hear from readers. You can find her contact information, website details and author profile page at https://www.totallybound.com

www.ingramcontent.com/pod-product-compliance
Lightning Source LLC
Chambersburg PA
CBHW020559260626
47157CB00003B/771